ALTERED REFLECTIONS

NOT EVERY REFLECTION IS WHAT IT APPEARS

By David E York

Copyright

Cover design by [100covers.com]
Edited by [Kayla Wilkinson]

PART I

FRACTURES

The Party Line

It started with a ring.

Not the kind that fits on a finger, but the sharp trill of the old party line phone mounted on the kitchen wall. Two short rings—wrong somehow. Not for the Fullers. Not for Mrs. Jackson. Not for his family.

Alex Monroe lay slouched on the green couch in the living room, his Walkman resting against his chest, both foam headphones snug over his ears. Fleetwood Mac hummed softly as he flipped through a comic book he'd picked up from the local library. The house was quiet in that particular way it only ever was in summer, when time stretched and nothing seemed urgent.

His parents had taken his little sister, Beverly, into town for dinner. Dairy Queen. A small-town ritual. Alex had refused to go. No self-respecting teenage boy in the eighties wanted to be seen at the DQ with his parents.

Halfway through the comic, the phone rang.

Alex didn't move at first. Living out in the country meant sharing a party line with a handful of neighbors, and most of the time the call wasn't for them. He slid one foam earpiece off and listened more closely.

On FM 515, everyone knew the patterns.

One long ring, one short—that was the Fullers up the road. Two long rings—Mrs. Jackson, the widow who lived past the bend. Two short rings—that was the Monroe house.

This wasn't any of those. A short ring, followed by another—shorter than short. Almost clipped.

The phone rang again, the same strange pattern.

Alex stood, comic still in hand, and wandered into the kitchen. He paused beside the wall phone, listening as the line hummed faintly. When the ringing came again, he picked up the receiver.

"Hello. Monroe residence."

At first, there was nothing but static. The line popped and hissed as it often did. Alex sighed. Party lines were temperamental things. Then a voice broke through.

"Hello? Hel—lo?" A girl's voice. Thin and wavering through the noise.

"I hear you," Alex said. "This is the Monroe residence. Alex here." The static ebbed. The voice came back clearer this time, followed by a small laugh. "Hello? Can you hear me now?"

"Yeah," he said. "Who is this?" There was a pause, just long enough to feel intentional. "Who's *this*?" she asked, teasing.

Alex felt his face warm. "Uh… Alex. Alex Monroe. Who were you trying to reach?"

"I wasn't really trying to reach anyone," she said. "I just picked up to see if someone was on the other end." Another quiet giggle. Alex shifted his weight, tightening his grip on the receiver. "Well… there is."

"Good," she said. "I'm Annabelle. But everyone calls me Anna."

"Nice to meet you," Alex said. "You live on 515?"

"Yes," she said. "Don't you?"

"No kidding," he said, grinning despite himself. "I do too. I only know the Fullers and Mrs. Jackson out here."

"I'm down at the end," Anna said.

"Past the Fullers?" Alex asked. The line crackled sharply, swallowing part of her reply. "Alex," she said, her voice dipping in and out. "The line's getting bad again. Would it be okay if we talked tomorrow?"

"Sure," he said, then corrected himself. "Yeah. I mean—yeah. I'd like that."

She laughed softly. "Tomorrow, then."

A beat later.

"Bye, Alexxx." The receiver clicked hard, and the line went dead.

Alex stood in the kitchen for a long moment, holding the silent phone before slowly hanging it back on the cradle.

He tried to picture another house past the Fullers'. Maybe one tucked back in the trees. Maybe that was why he'd never seen her. Maybe she was homeschooled, and that's why the yellow bus never went any farther. But none of that really mattered. A girl had called. And she was going to call again tomorrow.

Alex hoped.

The next day, just past six in the evening, the phone rang. The same strange ring pattern—short, then a clipped short. Alex sprang from the couch, his comic tumbling to the floor as he bolted for the kitchen. His mother was already heading for the wall phone.

"I've got it, Mom!" he called, nearly sliding across the linoleum as he grabbed the receiver. His mother paused, eyebrow raised. Alex tried to sound casual. "Might be for me."

She shrugged and returned to the stove, stirring the hamburger casserole that would be dinner.

"Hello?" Alex said, breathless. "Alex Monroe here." Static filled the line for a moment. Then—

"Hellooo, Alexxx." Anna's voice drifted through the receiver, smooth and sing-song.

Alex grinned. "Hey, Anna. Glad you called back."

For the next twenty minutes, they talked.

Anna didn't seem to know any of the bands Alex liked. No Duran Duran. No Van Halen. Not even Fleetwood Mac. She laughed each time he mentioned a name, as if he were making them up. When she listed the musicians she enjoyed, Alex had never heard of a single one. To him, the names sounded old—dusty, like something from his grandparents' radio.

She said she listened to the radio a lot. Mostly stories. Old-time music.

"What about TV?" Alex asked.

"TV?" Anna giggled. "Most folks I know don't have one. I think only rich people do. Do you have one?"

"Sure," Alex said. "We only get three channels out here, though."

"You're lucky," Anna said sincerely.

Alex frowned. "You've never seen MTV?"

"What's that?"

"It's… music videos. They play them all day. It's amazing."

Another giggle. "What's a video?" she asked, clearly convinced he was pulling her leg.

They talked about their families. Anna said she was the youngest of three. Her brothers were much older, though she didn't say where they were now. Alex told her about Beverly—his annoying little sister who couldn't keep her grubby hands off his stuff.

Anna said she liked to read. She listened to the evening programs on the radio and said her family never went to the theater. She had never even seen one. Alex hesitated. "What do you do for fun, then?"

"Well," she said brightly, "sometimes we have supper socials, where other families come over. And I like to play cricket when the weather's nice."

"Cricket?" Alex asked. "Like… the game?"

"Well, what else would I mean?" she said, amused.

Alex chuckled. She was weird, he decided—but in a good way. The way she talked. The way she listened. Like everything he said was a glimpse into some other world she couldn't quite reach.

She asked questions. Lots of them.

"What's your school like?" "What's a Walkman?" "What kind of bike do you have?"

He told her about his BMX. She asked if it was a streamline model. Alex had no idea what she meant, so he said yes anyway.

He didn't mind the questions. He liked that someone—*a girl*—was interested.

He could have talked longer, but the line suddenly crackled, louder than before. Then came a faint clicking sound. Like another receiver being lifted somewhere down the line.

"Anna?" Alex said. "You still there?" There was a long pause. Then her voice returned, lower now. Urgent. "I should go," she said. "We can talk tomorrow, okay?"

Before Alex could answer, the line went dead. Alex stood in the kitchen, receiver pressed to his ear, a faint frown settling across his face. He hadn't told her when to call. But somehow, that didn't seem to matter. She already knew.

The calls continued.

Not every day, but several times a week. They always came in the evening, right around the same time, marked by the same odd ring pattern—short, then clipped short. *Her* ring pattern.

Each time, Alex dropped whatever he was doing and reached the phone before anyone else could answer.

Anna was always cheerful. Always curious.

They talked about school, music, and the weather that summer, but more often than not, she asked questions.

"What does your father do for work?" she asked one night.

"He's a mechanic in town," Alex said. "Fixes big trucks, mostly."

She hummed softly. "That's good work. My daddy used to do a bit of blacksmithing. Shoeing horses, mending tools—things like that."

Alex blinked. "Seriously?"

"Mmhmm. Folks don't seem to have much use for that anymore. But his shop still smells like coal smoke and old leather. I go in there just to smell it," she giggled. "Now he just farms."

Another night, she asked, "Does your mama sew your clothes?"

"My clothes?" Alex laughed. "No. She shops at Sears like all the other moms."

Anna sounded genuinely surprised. "We make most of ours. Mama and Grandma, mostly. They tried to teach me stitching, but I hated it. Too slow."

One evening, she asked where his family was from. "Is your family from here?" she asked. "My mama was born right here in our house. So was I and my brothers."

"Well, sort of," Alex said. "My dad grew up here. My mom's from Houston."

Anna gasped. "The city?"

Alex smiled to himself. "Yeah. It's not that far away."

She went quiet for a moment. "I've never been that far, Alex. Twenty miles is the farthest I've ever gone. That was for a church revival."

"Wait," Alex said. "You've never been outside the county?"

"Why would I?" Anna replied, matter-of-factly, as if the question itself didn't make sense. She seemed fascinated by everything he described—his family owning two cars, having both a washer *and* a dryer, and a science-fiction device called a microwave. When he told her they sometimes ate frozen dinners, she laughed outright. "That sounds like witchcraft," she said, only half joking.

What really stuck with Alex were the small stories she told in between her questions.

"My granddaddy built our house," she said one evening. "He and Grandma had to fight off Comanches when they first settled the land."

Alex sat up straighter. "Wait—Comanche? Like… Indians?"

"Mmhmm. They used to raid farms back then. Grandma said once they hid in the root cellar all night. That was just after she and Granddaddy got married."

Alex hesitated. "How old are your grandparents?"

There was a pause.

"Old," Anna said. Then she moved on, as if nothing about that required explanation. She told him her family never owned a car. They walked most places. If they had something to haul, they used a cart and a mule. "You ever seen a mule before, Alex?" she asked.

"Sure," he said. "At the rodeo. The fair."

She laughed softly. "You're a funny one, Alex Monroe."

Some nights, Anna would describe helping her mother churn butter, or assisting her grandmother as they laid herbs out to dry after pulling them from the garden.

Once, she mentioned how her daddy and granddaddy had butchered a hog, and how she'd helped scrape the bristles from the hide.

Alex didn't know what to make of it. At first, he figured her family was just extremely poor. Or deeply old-fashioned. Maybe even part of some strange, backwoods religious group that kept to itself.

But the stories felt *old.* Not just outdated—*old.* Like she wasn't talking about her life now, but about someone else's from long ago. And yet, every time she called, her voice was clear. Warm. Sweet. She always sounded present. And she always called for him.

Anna was never far from Alex's thoughts. He found himself thinking about her every day—the way she laughed, the way she listened, the way her world seemed stitched together from old stories and black-and-white memories. At first, it had been charming. Almost quaint.

Now it just felt strange.

So, one night, over dinner, Alex decided to ask his parents a few questions.

"Hey, Dad," he said casually. "Is there a house down past the Fullers' place? Maybe beyond that big curve in the road?" His father looked up from his plate and sat quietly for a few seconds, as if tracing the road in his mind.

"Not that I've ever seen," he said finally. "Might've been a trailer or a deer camp back in the woods at some point, but a house? No, I don't think so."

His mother shook her head. "I don't remember ever seeing a mailbox. Or even a driveway."

"The only folks I've ever known out here are the Fullers and old Mrs. Jackson," his dad added.

"You could ask Mrs. Jackson," his mother said. "She's lived here her whole life."

His father chuckled. "Probably built her house with her bare hands." His mother shot him a look.

That comment stuck with Alex.

He knew Mrs. Jackson. He mowed her yard every now and then, usually when the guy who normally did it failed to show up—typically due to a hangover. Alex didn't mind. She had a big old Snapper riding mower, and there was always lemonade afterward, or a slice of some strange, old-fashioned pie.

The next afternoon, Alex wheeled his bike out of the garage and pedaled down the road, his Walkman clipped to his hip, headphones resting around his neck.

Mrs. Jackson's house sat beneath a canopy of oak trees, its wide porch sagging slightly with age, flowers blooming along the chain-link fence.

She answered the door in a house dress and slippers, gray hair pinned up neatly, reading glasses hanging from a chain against her chest.

"Well, hey there, Alex Monroe," she said warmly. "What brings you by? Yard doesn't need mowing today."

Alex rubbed the back of his neck. "Hi, Mrs. Jackson. I actually had a question. About the road."

She stepped aside and waved him in. "Well now, that's a first. Come on in. I've got some sweet tea just made."

A few minutes later, Alex sat perched on the edge of her couch, a glass of sweet tea sweating in his hands. The ceiling fan clacked softly overhead.

"So," she said, settling into her recliner, "what's this question that's got you thinking about FM 515?"

"I was wondering," Alex said carefully, "were there ever any other houses out past the Fullers'? Maybe way back in the woods, where the pavement curves?"

Mrs. Jackson stared out the front window for a long moment, eyes distant.

"Well," she said slowly, "the Fullers built their place in '56, if I recall. Before that, it was pasture. And farther down, there used to be an old red barn."

She took a sip of tea. "Now… when I was a young'un—maybe eight or nine—there *was* a house down there. Rough dirt road ran off the end of the pavement, back into the trees."

Alex felt his pulse quicken. "Do you remember anything about it?"

"Not much," she said. "They were quiet folks. Kept to themselves. I believe the mother was a midwife or something like that. Real superstitious. Hung jars of hair in the trees, said it kept spirits away." She shivered slightly and took another sip.

"Is that all you remember?" Alex asked, leaning forward.

Mrs. Jackson's gaze drifted, not quite focused on him. "I remember the fire," she said. "I was in my twenties then. Frank and I had just married. Happened on a winter night. Old wood stove caught, and the whole place went up."

She wiped at her eye, the memory fresh again.

"Was anyone hurt?" Alex asked quietly.

Mrs. Jackson looked at him over her glasses and paused. "Story was their youngest didn't make it out," she said. "A girl, I think. I never saw an obituary, so who knows. But I can say this for certain—no one ever built out there again."

A chill crept down Alex's spine.

The youngest was a girl.

He left shortly after, thanking her for the tea, pedaling home with a tight knot in his chest. He tried to tell himself that maybe Anna lived on a different FM 515. That was possible, right?

But deep down, he already knew better. He didn't know where Anna lived. He only knew that she called him. Same time. Same strange ring. And she was always happy to talk to him.

That Friday, Alex missed her call.

His parents had dragged him out to visit his grandmother, and no amount of pleading had changed their minds. *She hasn't seen you in months,* his mother said, ending the argument with a look. Alex spent the visit watching the clock, pushing casserole around his plate, sulking through leftovers.

The phone didn't ring the next night. No strange

pattern. No Anna.

Alex paced the living room, pretending to read a comic, his headphones on but silent. Maybe she forgot. Maybe she was mad. Then, on Monday evening, just after six, the strange ring rattled the wall phone.

Alex lunged for it. "Hello?" he blurted. "Anna?"

Silence.

Then, quietly, "Alex." Her voice was low. Tight. "You didn't answer my call."

"I know, I—I had to go with my parents. I wanted to be here, I really did—"

"You didn't want to talk to me," she said sharply.

"No. I mean—yes—no," he stumbled. "I swear, Anna. I was out of town. Just that one night."

A long pause stretched between them. "Are you tired of talking to me, Alex?"

His stomach twisted. "Of course not," he said quickly. His voice came out thin, almost pleading.

Another pause. Her voice returned, smaller now. "You didn't tell me you'd be gone."

"I didn't know," he said. "Honest. Please, Anna. I was hoping you'd call again."

Silence. Then a soft giggle.

"Okay. Okay," she said. "I'm sorry I got upset. I just missed hearing your voice."

Relief washed through him.

Soon she was herself again, asking about his Walkman, his math teacher, his favorite flavor of gum. She asked if he had a dog, and if he knew what strawberries fresh off the vine tasted like.

When she paused—when it felt like she'd finally run out of questions—Alex took a breath.

"Hey, Anna," he said casually. "Do you live near a red barn?"

Silence. Too long. He was about to take it back when her voice returned, quieter now. Sharper.

"How do you know about the barn?" she said quietly.

"I—I don't," he said quickly. "Someone mentioned it. I didn't know if it was near your place or not."

"Have you been by my house?" she asked. "Are you a peeping tom?"

"No!" Alex said. "No, I swear. I was talking to someone who's lived out here a long time. She said there *used* to be a red barn down past the Fullers. That's all."

Another pause. "*Used* to be?" Anna said softly.

Alex's throat went dry.

He swallowed, tried to clear it. "Anna," he said carefully. "What year is it?"

She laughed. "What kind of question is that? You already know."

"Just humor me," he said quietly.

"It's 1936," she replied. "Why would you ask that?"

Cold washed over him. "And who's the president?" he asked.

"Franklin Roosevelt," she said. "He's been president almost three years now." A note of concern crept into her voice. "Why are you asking all these strange questions, Alex?"

His mouth felt like sand. "Do you know what happened at Pearl Harbor?"

Silence.

"Pearl… what?" she said. "Harbor? Where's that?"

His heart pounded so hard it hurt.

"Do you know the Jackson family?" he asked. "They live up the road."

She thought for a moment. "The new family? Yes,

I think their name is Jackson. They just built a house near the crossroads. I think they have children, but I haven't seen them."

Alex's knuckles went white around the receiver.

Mrs. Jackson had been one of those children.

The red barn. The burned house. The youngest girl who didn't make it out.

This doesn't happen, he told himself. *This isn't real.*

But the phone was warm in his hand. And her voice was still there—soft, curious, alive. "Alex," she said gently. "Why are you so quiet all of a sudden? Is something wrong?"

He managed to clear his throat. "I—I gotta go. My mom's calling me."

A brief pause.

"Call me tomorrow," he said quickly. "I'll answer. I promise."

She giggled. "Okay, silly. I'll call you. Bye, Alexxxxx."

The line clicked and went dead.

That night, Alex dreamed of fire.

Orange flames twisted in the dark. He stood outside an old wooden house, watching it burn. Smoke poured through broken windows, holes in the roof, open doorways. Somewhere inside, a girl screamed—high and panicked—calling for someone. Maybe calling for him.

He jerked awake, his T-shirt clinging to his chest with sweat. His room was dark and still.

Something was wrong. Smoke.

He could smell it—sharp and acrid, like burning wood and something else he couldn't quite place. It filled his nose, clung to the back of his throat.

Alex slipped out of bed and crept through the house, checking room by room. No flames. No smoke. His parents were asleep, his father's faint snore drifting down the hallway. Everything looked fine.

He stood there a moment longer.

It *looked* fine.

When he finally returned to bed, he didn't sleep. He lay staring at the ceiling while cicadas sang outside his window, their rhythm slowly pulling him toward rest. Then the phone rang.

One short ring. One clipped short.

Alex shot upright, heart pounding. For a moment he wondered if he'd imagined it. Then it rang again. He crept into the kitchen and glanced at the microwave clock.

3:12 a.m.

He lifted the receiver with trembling fingers. "Hello?"

"Hello, Alexxxx," Anna chirped, her voice bright and familiar. "I told you I would call you, silly."

His mouth went dry. "Anna… why are you calling now? It's the middle of the night. Aren't you asleep?"

She laughed softly. "What do you mean? It's the same time I always call you." Her voice hadn't changed. But something about it felt wrong now—like paper singed at the edges.

"Oh," Alex said after a beat. "Right. Sorry. I must be tired."

He kept her talking for a few minutes, easy questions that didn't require thinking. He asked about the chickens, whether she'd finished sewing the apron she'd mentioned, if she'd eaten any of the strawberries she loved so much.

Eventually, she said she had to go. "I'll call you tomorrow," she said cheerfully.

"Yeah," Alex replied. "Okay."

When the line went dead, he stood there a long time, staring at the phone. He knew what he had to do.

That morning, once the sun was fully up, Alex skipped breakfast. He climbed onto his bike and rode down FM 515, past the Fullers' place, past the stretch where the pavement cracked and weeds pushed through like they were trying to breathe.

He slowed near the bend, scanning the tree line below the road, thick with brush. Then he saw it.

Just beyond the curve—an overgrown trail, nearly invisible from the road. Broken fence posts leaned at odd angles. Brambles clawed at the edges like barbed wire. No sign. No driveway. No mailbox.

Alex dropped his bike in the tall weeds and started walking down the slope to the tree line. The sun was warming the early morning humid air.

The trail was narrow and winding. Tall pines crowded in, their needles whispering overhead. The air felt heavy, quiet.

After ten minutes of pushing through brush, he saw the clearing.

A sagging stone foundation. Blackened timbers. The skeletal remains of a house, long since devoured by fire and time. Rusted hinges held up doors that no longer existed. A cracked porcelain basin that would never hold water again. The charred ghost of a staircase that led to nowhere.

Near the edge of the clearing lay a pile of warped red boards, half-swallowed by moss and vines.

The red barn, Mrs. Jackson's voice echoed in his mind.

Alex stood frozen, his heart hammering so hard he thought he might be sick.

When it finally slowed, he began to move through the ruins. He wasn't sure what he was looking for—something from the family, maybe. Something from the girl.

His shoes crunched softly through ash and debris. Then something caught the light. He crouched and hooked it with a finger. A necklace slid free, blackened but intact. The locket attached to it was melted beyond recognition, its shape warped and ruined. Alex slipped it into his pocket.

Farther back, half-buried in ash, he found a telephone.

It was warped and melted, but recognizable. Heavy. Old-fashioned. He'd only seen phones like it on reruns—*The Andy Griffith Show*. The cord from the receiver still connected to the base. The line itself had been burned or cut away. He set it back where he'd found it.

Alex straightened, chest tight.

There had been a house here. And it had burned.

He walked back to his bike and rode home slowly, the road stretching ahead of him like it had never done before.

That evening, before Anna's usual call, Alex spent his time trying to clean the necklace as best he could. The chain itself wasn't in terrible shape, but the locket was a lost cause—melted shut, blackened beyond any hope of repair.

At the usual time, the phone rang with the same strange pattern.

"Hello, Anna. How's it going?" Alex said, forcing his voice to sound upbeat. The line crackled with heavy static. He could hear her faintly, distant and warped, but couldn't make out the words.

"Hello? Anna, I can't hear you. There's a lot of static."

Her voice faded in and out, then returned a little clearer. "Hello, Alex. Is this better?" she asked. "I guess we have a bad connection today. I'm not sure what else could go wrong." Her voice sounded low, tired—like it was drifting up from the bottom of a well. The words wavered, thinning in and out. Alex figured it might be a short call if the connection didn't improve.

"What's wrong?" he asked. "Are you having a bad day?"

"I don't know what to do, Alex," Anna said, her voice trembling. "My mother is going to be very upset. I misplaced my necklace. The one my grandmother gave me. I had it earlier, and now it's just… gone."

Alex reached into his pocket and felt the familiar shape of the chain. Slowly, he pulled it out and laid it on the kitchen counter. The metal caught the light just right—almost glowing.

At the same moment, the static on the line faded. The coincidence sent a chill crawling up his spine.

"Maybe try retracing your steps," he said carefully. "That usually helps me. Think about the last place you remember having it."

"I DIDN'T LOSE IT," Anna shouted. The sudden force of her voice made Alex flinch. He yanked the receiver away from his ear.

"I—I'm sorry," he said quickly. "I didn't mean that. I was just trying to help. I'm sure you'll find it, Anna."

A long silence followed.

Then her voice returned, light and cheerful, as if nothing had happened. "That's all right, Alex. I'll get it back eventually."

Alex stared at the phone, unsettled. She'd shifted from furious to pleasant in seconds, like flipping a switch. He didn't comment, but the feeling lingered.

They didn't mention the necklace again, though Alex couldn't stop thinking about it—how she'd lost it the same day he'd found it, and how touching it had cleared the line.

They talked a while longer before Anna said she had chores to do out in the barn.

As usual, she filled the conversation with questions about his everyday life—things that bored him, but fascinated her as if they belonged to another world.

The next evening, while Alex was on the phone with Anna, his mother leaned into the room and grinned. "So," she teased, "when are you going to bring your new girlfriend over to meet the family?" Alex waved her away, cheeks burning. He waited for Anna to laugh.

Instead, the line went dead silent. For a moment, he thought the call had dropped.

Then Anna spoke, her voice sharp and tight. "Alex… you're courting another girl? You told me you didn't have a steady girl."

"Anna, I don't," he said quickly, forcing a nervous smile she couldn't see. "My mom was just joking. She meant you."

"Oh," Anna said slowly.

A pause.

"My parents would never allow me to have a steady suitor without meeting him first," she continued. "And they would *never* allow me to visit a boy's house. That would make me a harlot, Alex. And I am no harlot."

Alex blinked. *Harlot?*

"Oh—no, I didn't mean anything like that," he said carefully. "Not about you. Or your parents."

Her tone shifted again, soft but edged with something else. "Then why haven't you come calling on me?" she asked. "I thought you liked me."

There was a brief silence as Alex tried to follow her meaning. "You call me, Anna," he said. "I don't even have your number."

"No, silly," she said, lightly scolding him. "Why haven't you come to my house? You *do* want to court me, don't you?"

Confusion washed over him. "I—I guess I could," he said slowly. "I mean, I'd like to meet you. And your family. If you want me to."

"Oh yes, Alex," Anna said. Her voice dropped, urgent now. "I want you to. My parents won't mind."

"Okay," Alex said. "Then give me your address. I'll come by."

As she spoke, he realized the directions didn't sound like anything he knew. No street names. No numbers. Just landmarks—past the river bend, beyond where the old sycamore used to stand, a turn near the field. Like something out of an old book. And then it hit him.

It was near where he'd found the necklace.

"Come over, Alex," Anna said again, her voice low and insistent. "Come over soon."

The next day, Alex decided he had to return to the charred remains of the house.

He didn't like the idea. Something about it felt

wrong—like he was looking for one answer and already knew he'd find another. One he didn't want to face.

Still, as the clock crept closer to their usual call time, the pull grew harder to ignore.

He grabbed his Walkman, slipped the necklace into his pocket, and pedaled toward the woods. He followed the directions Anna had given him—not because he expected them to be different, but because he needed to know. He counted landmarks as he went: the bend in the river, the shallow creek crossing, the stretch of road where the pavement cracked and weeds pushed through. But the old sycamore she'd mentioned was gone. Not even a stump remained.

The path led him exactly where he'd feared it would. The clearing opened up ahead, the burned remains of the house sitting back in the trees like a scar that never healed.

Alex slowed, hoping, irrationally, that maybe there'd be something beyond the ruins. Another house. A mailbox. Anything normal.

He laid his bike down in the weeds and walked toward the overgrown trail. The grass still bore faint impressions from his last visit. The clearing looked unchanged. Quiet. Waiting.

He stepped closer to the melted remains of the old candlestick phone and switched off his Walkman, sliding it into his back pocket. He checked his watch.

5:55 PM.

Five minutes to six.

Carefully, he set the phone on a weathered stump beside the collapsed frame of what had once been a house—*her* house. Then he pulled the necklace from his pocket and draped it over the phone's earpiece. The warped locket swayed gently, though there was no wind.

Just a test, he told himself.

The light was fading now. The woods darkened at the edges, shadows stretching longer than they should have.

He waited.

Six o'clock came and went.

By 6:05, nothing had happened. No ringing. No voice. Just the faint rustle of pine needles overhead. Alex let out a breath he hadn't realized he'd been holding.

"She's gonna be mad I missed her call," he muttered, forcing a laugh. "But at least this little experiment didn't mean anything."

He reached down to pick up the necklace. The phone rang.

Alex froze.

One short ring. Then a short, clipped ring.

The sound echoed too clearly in the clearing.

His arm hung halfway outstretched as he stared at the phone. It wasn't connected to anything. It couldn't be ringing. But it was.

His hands shook as he lifted the receiver and brought it to his ear.

"Hello, Alexxxx," Anna's voice said, warm and unmistakable. "I'm so glad you came to see me."

The phone slipped from his hands like it had burned him. The receiver and base struck the stump and tumbled into the dirt. The necklace bounced away, landing somewhere out of sight.

"Alex?" her voice called again—no longer coming from the phone. "Why aren't you answering me? You said you'd come calling. Don't leave." Her voice drifted through the trees now. Soft. Close.

Alex spun, breath catching in his throat. The woods stood silent around him.

Then he saw her.

A pale mist gathered near the tree line, shaping itself into the outline of a young girl, hovering just above the ground. He couldn't tell if it was moving or if it had simply always been there—but it was closer than before.

His legs stiffened. He stepped back, the words scraping their way out of him. "I—I can't do this, Anna," he whispered. "You're… you're dead. You died a long time ago."

The mist didn't answer. It only lingered.

His knees gave out and he sank into the dirt. His chest felt tight, breath shallow, as if the woods themselves had closed in. "Anna… I can't stay," he said, voice breaking. "Please. Don't call me anymore." A tear slipped free and darkened the dirt beneath him.

The air felt heavy, unmoving. Like everything around him was holding still.

Inside him, two feelings pulled in opposite directions: the ache of missing her voice, her laughter—and the cold certainty that something was terribly wrong.

He knew which one he had to listen to.

The mist shifted, drifting closer. Her face formed more clearly now—sad, searching. "Alex…" she said. But her voice had changed. The warmth thinned, something rough and hollow creeping in. "You're not leaving me," she said. "Everyone leaves. You won't?"

More pale shapes began to gather among the trees, whispering forms slipping between the trunks, closing in. Alex's mind flashed with fire—orange flames licking up the walls of the house, smoke pouring out, a girl screaming.

"Alex… save me…"

He shook the image away, heart hammering.

His gaze dropped to the ground. The necklace lay there, half-buried in the dirt. He snatched it up, fingers trembling. "I'm sorry, Anna," he whispered. Then he hurled it at the mist.

He turned and ran. Crashing through the whispering shapes, down the trail, his Walkman tumbling from his pocket and landing forgotten in the dirt. He didn't stop until he burst from the trees at the roadside. He grabbed his bike, mounted it, and pedaled hard, legs burning, lungs aching.

He looked back once.

At the edge of the woods, a single pale shape hovered in the shadows. It didn't follow. It only watched. Alex didn't doubt who it was.

After that night, there were no more strange rings on the party line. Only the familiar ones. And that was fine with Alex Monroe.

Maybe once, late in the summer, he thought he heard it again—that odd ring—but it was probably just his imagination.

His parents never mentioned the calls. Never asked why they'd stopped. They let it go, the way teenage things often do.

Alex still rides his bike along FM 515, passing the narrow trail that disappears into the trees.

He never stops.

And sometimes, when the wind is right and the sun sinks low, he swears he can hear Fleetwood Mac faintly playing somewhere deep in the woods.

The Voice In Apartment 3B

Caleb Wright needed a fresh start.

After losing the love of his life in a breakup that scorched him to the core, he knew something had to change—if there was any hope of winning her back. Even if there wasn't.

Once, Caleb was a rising star in Chicago's advertising scene, a successful graphic designer at a prestigious downtown firm. His talent brought in clients by the dozen and revenue by the thousands. But late nights turned into all-nighters, and all-nighters turned into weekend blackouts. And when he wasn't buried in mockups or logo revisions, he was planted at O'Leary's Bar, sinking into the bottle.

He knew he had a drinking problem. He knew he was obsessive. What he didn't know—what he never imagined—was that Sara would finally walk away. She'd been with him since college, back when they were both idealistic and broke and thought talent would be enough.

Caleb never graduated. He couldn't take critique, couldn't handle being told he wasn't the best in the room. His ego got in the way of his diploma—but not his career. He made it anyway, carving a name for himself on raw skill and a ruthless drive.

But when Sara left, it all unraveled. The drinking got worse. The firm let him go. Clients disappeared. And with no job, no income, and no reason to get out of bed, Caleb hit bottom.

One cold night, hunched over a bottle of discount whiskey and suffocating in self-pity, he decided to end it.

He drank the bottle dry, staggered into the bathroom, and climbed into the tub with a dull razor.

Had it been sharper, had he paid his rent on time, it might've worked.

But the blade barely broke the skin—and his landlord, pounding on the door for half an hour, eventually used the master key to let himself in. Caleb was found unconscious in the bathtub, wrists lightly bleeding, a pool forming more from spilled liquor than blood.

He woke up two days later in the psych wing of St. Luke's. Alcohol poisoning. Nerve damage. A bandaged future.

It wasn't the epiphany you read about in stories. No light at the end of the tunnel, no tearful awakening. Just exhaustion.

Still, when a kind psych doctor and a nurse with soft eyes handed him a pamphlet for AA, he didn't throw it away. He went.

That was eight months ago.

Now, Caleb is sober. He's rebuilding. A few freelance clients trickle in. Enough to scrape together rent and groceries. Enough to breathe.

The apartment isn't much—an old walk-up in a crumbling neighborhood, somewhere west of decent and south of safe. The fire escape doesn't go all the way up. The ground-floor windows are boarded. The brick is masked by graffiti.

But it's his.

A roof, four walls, and no one telling him he's not good enough. A place to work in silence. To stay clean. Maybe even to heal. Maybe.

Day 1

Caleb stepped onto the crack-riddled sidewalk in front of the Grace Bend Apartments with a duffel bag slung over one shoulder—the kind they hand out at homeless shelters—and his old laptop clutched in his other hand. The laptop was the last piece of his old life, maybe the only thing of value he had left. It was also his only way out. If he was going to claw his way back from the bottom, it would be through that screen.

He shuffled through the dented, rust-streaked front door and into a lobby that smelled like mold, mildew, stale air... and cigar smoke. Thick and sour, like the building was exhaling years of disrepair.

Sitting behind a chipped particleboard desk that looked like a relic from an old *Barney Miller* set was Mr. Delaney—the landlord and owner of Grace Bend. A short, stocky man who looked like he'd been carved out of decades of bitterness. He wore a stretched-out T-shirt, stained khakis, and a chewed-up cigar that clung to his lip like a barnacle. He glanced up at Caleb with the same expression he'd had the day Caleb signed the lease—a face puckered in permanent disapproval. Sour, like someone swapped his cigar for a lemon.

"Hello, Mr. Delaney. I guess my apartment's all ready to move in?" Caleb asked, forcing a polite smile, the kind you offer a parole officer or a DMV clerk.

Delaney gave him a once-over, like he was sizing up damage. Then, without a word, he reached over and handed Caleb a keyring with two scuffed brass keys. His fingers were yellowed with nicotine, his nails ridged like cracked porcelain.

"You pay rent on time—first of the month—and you won't hear from me."

That was it. No handshake. No smile. No welcome mat.

"Apartment's 3C," he added. "Cleaned, painted, swept. Furnished. Don't go trashin' the furniture unless you feel like buyin' new."

He was halfway back to his paper when he paused, one eye still on Caleb.

"You'll be fine up there. No neighbors. Should be quiet." He let the word *quiet* linger like a guarantee. "Only one other tenant on the third floor—Mr. Wong. Been here damn near as long as I've owned the place. He's on the far end. Won't even hear him if you tried. Been visiting relatives in Tokyo the last couple months anyhow."

He said it like a promise.

Caleb nodded. No neighbors sounded perfect. Peace and quiet meant no distractions, no awkward conversations, no late-night knocks or loud music bleeding through the walls. Just him, his work, and his thoughts.

For better… or worse.

Caleb approached the elevator only to be met with an **"Out of Order"** handwritten sign hanging from a hook next to the well-worn doors.

"Guess Mr. Delaney forgot to mention that."

Caleb took the stairs and headed to the third floor.

He walked down the dimly lit hallway, eyeing each door as he passed. The building already had a smell—stale air, mold, old carpet—but something different hung here on the third floor. A smokier note. Not cigarette smoke, but something darker. Like soot. Burned wood.

He paused, sniffed again.

Mr. Delaney hadn't mentioned a fire, and there weren't any obvious signs of one. Maybe it was just the mildew mixing with age and rot. Still, it crawled into his nose in a way that stuck.

There it was: 3C. His new start.

He slid the key into the lock. With a sharp click, it turned, echoing strangely down the narrow corridor.

"Early seventies décor," he muttered as he opened the door. "It'll have to do."

The hinges groaned as the door swung shut behind him, followed by another hollow, echoing click. It felt louder inside than out.

He dropped his duffel bag onto a sagging green couch and looked around.

Caleb crossed the living room into what passed for a kitchen—if you could even call it that. A two-burner hot plate, an RV-sized fridge, a few cabinets and a shallow sink were crammed along one wall. The counters were sticky, and when he opened the fridge, a wave of fresh mold hit him in the face.

"I'll have to start in here," he muttered. "Clean it up, make it usable."

He ventured into the bedroom next. The full-size bed had a noticeable sag in the center, and the two pillows were flatter than the bedspread covering them. The bedspread was a dull, stained white—maybe white back in 1972—but aside from the sag, it looked okay. Caleb pressed on the mattress and was surprised to find it still somewhat firm.

There was no closet, just a metal rack bolted to the wall for hanging clothes and a small green dresser with mismatched drawers. He moved on into the bathroom—same seventies puke green as the rest. One stained tub with a rusty showerhead, a tattered curtain, a cracked sink, and one towel folded like an afterthought. The air had a sour metallic tang, like old copper pipes left to rot.

"What more could a guy ask for," he muttered, shaking his head. "Home sweet home."

Caleb went back to the living room, unzipped his duffel bag, and began pulling out everything he now owned—which wasn't much. A few sets of clothes, a toothbrush, some notebooks, and a coffee cup with a cat on the front.

After settling in, unpacking, and giving everything its place in the small apartment, Caleb called it a day. He tried out the "new" shower and dried off with the stiff, musty towel hanging on the rack. It felt like sandpaper against his skin, and it carried a smell like old gym socks left in the sun. He made a mental note to buy towels tomorrow—he couldn't imagine using that thing again.

He slipped on his underwear and crawled into the sagging bed. His phone went on the charger atop the green dresser. He lay down, closed his eyes, and before long, sleep took him.

Caleb was awakened by the soft sound of knocking.

He blinked in the darkness and reached for his

phone. **3:33 AM.** The sound wasn't loud, but in the stillness of the apartment, it cut through like a pin drop in a tomb. Caleb sat up, unsure if it had come from a dream or the hallway.

He got up and walked into the living room; ears tuned for another knock. Nothing. He peered out through the peephole—just the dim hallway lights humming quietly. No movement. No one there.

Still uneasy, he walked a slow lap around the apartment, checking the front door again before crawling back into bed. Sleep came in fits after that, until his alarm buzzed at 7:00 AM.

Day 2

He sat on the edge of the bed, scratched his head, the grogginess still clinging to him. After a moment, he got up and shuffled into the kitchen. He found a single glass in the cabinet, filled it at the sink, and drank—trying to chase away the dry cotton feeling in his mouth.

He thought back to the knocking, chalked it up to the building settling—just the old bones of the place shifting in the night.

He got dressed and headed out to pick up a few

things for the apartment. He figured he would pick up a few towels, coffee, a coffee pot, and plates, he'd also grab a lavender-scented plug-in to help hide the smell of oldness and mildew in the apartment.

Caleb walked down the stairs into the narrow front hallway. An older woman stood near the entrance, sorting through a stack of mail. She looked up and asked, "You new to the building?"

"What apartment you in?" she asked, giving Caleb a slow once-over.

"Uh, yeah. I'm new—just moved in yesterday. I'm in 3C."

Her eyes widened slightly. "Next to 3B, huh?" She gave a dry little laugh. "Good luck with that one."

"Why would you say that? Something wrong with 3C? Or 3B?" Caleb furrowed his brow, confused.

"Nothin'. Welcome to the building." And with that, she slipped out the front door and down the sidewalk.

To Caleb, that was an odd encounter. He shrugged and wrote her off as a nutjob, then went on his shopping mission.

By mid-afternoon Caleb had returned from his

shopping trip and was working on a project for a new client he picked up a few days earlier. He sipped from his fresh cup of coffee when the screen on his laptop flickered once—then again.

"That's weird. Hope this thing's not about to go tits up. He leaned back toward the keyboard, but a faint rattling noise came from the wall behind the couch.

He sat up, turning toward the sound. He tapped the wall a few times—nothing. Silence again.

Probably just mice in the walls, he figured. "Guess I'll let Mr. Delaney know we might need a fumigator."

Caleb tried to relax after a small dinner of boxed mac and cheese. He pulled up a recorded movie on his laptop and settled into the saggy couch to watch. But just a few minutes in, his eyelids grew heavy, and before long, he'd dozed off.

When he woke, the room was dark and silent. The movie had ended. He glanced at his watch—two hours gone. With a groggy sigh, he pushed himself up and headed for the bedroom. Work could wait until morning.

He changed clothes and slipped into bed. The sag in the mattress cradled him again, and he drifted off almost immediately.

Caleb sat on the edge of the bed, scratching his head as the fog of sleep clung stubbornly to his skull. His mouth tasted like dust and drywall. He stood, unsteady, and shuffled to the kitchenette. The single glass in the cabinet felt oddly warm in his hand, and he filled it from the tap. The water sputtered before flowing—a metallic tang lingered on his tongue after he drank.

He glanced around the apartment—the faint odor of mildew still hung in the air. That knocking from the night before tugged at his memory, and he shook his head to clear it.

Just the building shifting, he told himself. *Old places make old noises.*

He dressed and left the apartment, descending the creaky stairs into the narrow front hallway. Halfway down, he noticed an older woman standing by the mailboxes, thumbing through a stack of envelopes with a frown etched into her face. She looked up as he approached.

"You new to the building?" she asked, not smiling.

"Yeah, just moved in yesterday," Caleb replied.

"What apartment you in?" Her gaze lingered longer than polite.

"3C."

At that, her eyes twitched. A second too long. "Next to 3B, huh?" She let out a dry little laugh, but it didn't sound like she thought it was funny. "Good luck with that one."

He hesitated. "What do you mean? Something wrong with 3B?"

Her eyes darted down to her mail, and she gave a tight shrug. "Nothin'. Welcome to the building."

Before he could press further, she slipped out the front door, footsteps tapping quick down the sidewalk.

Caleb stood there a moment longer, staring at the door. *Weird,* he thought. *Maybe she's just a crank.*

Still, her reaction sat in the back of his mind like a cold stone.

He spent the afternoon running errands—towels, dishes, coffee, a plug-in air freshener in lavender. The walk helped, but even the sun felt dull today, hidden behind a gauzy film of clouds. By the time he got back, his shirt clung to him with sweat.

The apartment was still stuffy, still smelling faintly like an old sponge, but the lavender helped. A little.

He settled in at his laptop and sipped from a fresh cup of coffee while digging into a project for a new client.

It felt good to work again, even if his head wasn't fully in it.

Then the screen flickered. Once. Then again. Static rippled faintly across it before it stabilized.

Caleb frowned. "That's weird. Don't you dare crap out on me now."

He leaned forward and tapped the spacebar. The cursor blinked steady again.

Then—*rattle-rattle.*

A noise. Behind the couch. Subtle, but distinct.

He paused. Head tilted.

He stood and tapped the wall. Nothing.

Probably mice, he thought. Still, the hairs on his arm were standing up.

He made a note to talk to Mr. Delaney. Pest control. No big deal.

Dinner was microwaved mac and cheese with a stale soda he found in his bag. He queued up a recorded movie and tried to unwind. But halfway through, the couch swallowed him whole, and his eyes slipped shut.

He woke to darkness. The movie had long since ended. A hollow silence filled the room like fog.

His watch blinked at him—two hours gone. With a groan, he stood, stretched, and trudged into the bedroom.

The mattress groaned as he lay down. The lavender scent had faded. The mildew was winning again.

3:33 AM.

The knock was louder this time. Sharp. Purposeful. Caleb's eyes flew open.

He sat up, heart hammering. The same exact time as last night. That detail gnawed at him.

He waited, frozen.

Silence.

Then—faint, like breath through a crack in the wall—he heard it:

"...Please... help me..."

He blinked hard, trying to shake the sleep from his ears. The voice had a strained, hollow edge, like it was coming from deep inside a pipe—or farther.

He stood, his pulse thudding in his throat. "Hello?" he said, louder than intended. "Is someone there?"

No reply.

He crept to the door, pressed his eye to the

peephole.

Nothing.

He opened it anyway.

The hallway was empty. Pale light buzzed overhead. The air was still.

Caleb shut the door, turned the deadbolt, and leaned against the frame.

He didn't sit. Not right away. He just stood there, listening.

Something wasn't right with this place. He could feel it—not just in the knocks or the voices, but in the air itself. Like the building was holding its breath.

Eventually, he sank back onto the couch, rubbing his forehead. But sleep wouldn't come easy this time.

Day 3

Caleb woke early, determined to report the strange things happening on the third floor. He headed down to speak with Mr. Delaney, who was outside the front office, puffing on a cigar that looked like it hadn't been lit in days.

Caleb laid it all out—the knocking in the night, the woman's voice, the scuttling sounds in the walls, and the flickering lights.

Mr. Delaney pulled the cigar from his mouth with a slow frown. “Look, Mr. Wright. There ain't nothin else on that floor besides you. I already told you Mr. Wong is in Tokyo. As for the mice, I’ll take a look. Might toss a few traps around. But I’m not calling pest control unless you can give me something concrete. Dead mouse. Mouse droppings. A picture. Something that says, yeah, we’ve got a problem.”

“And the lights?”

“It’s an old damn building. What do you expect?” Delaney shrugged. “Fair enough for ya?”

It wasn’t the answer Caleb wanted. But what could he do? It’s not like he could just move out. Not with the rent here barely scraping under what he could afford.

He tried to shake off the conversation, rationalizing everything the way anyone would. Probably squatters, he figured. Maybe someone slipped into one of the empty units on the floor. He couldn’t prove it, but that was the most logical explanation he could come up with.

Back in his apartment, he dropped onto the couch with a fresh cup of coffee and opened his laptop.

Caleb worked on his project until late in the afternoon. He got up to take a short break, walking around the apartment and stretching his arms and legs after sitting so long. He went to the bathroom to get rid of all the coffee he'd been drinking since that morning.

He walked back over to the couch—then stopped. There on the wall, right behind where he had been sitting just minutes earlier, was something that made his skin prickle. A human handprint. It looked charred and burnt, like someone had shoved their hand into a hot fireplace and then pressed it against the wall—**his** wall.

Caleb reached out and tried to wipe it away. It was cold to the touch, like touching a corpse. The print didn't change. It didn't smear or smudge—it stayed exactly as it was. A chill ran deeper down his spine.

He stood staring at it for a long moment, then walked over and opened the front door, peering into the hallway. It was empty and silent, except for the low hum of the dim, flickering lights. Caleb stepped out, crossed to the door of apartment 3B, and tried the knob. Locked. He looked around again, then walked over to the stairs. "Nothing. Nobody. Not even a footprint," he muttered, rubbing his head and trying to shake off the confusion. He returned to his apartment and shut the door behind him.

He grabbed a towel from the bathroom and tried scrubbing the handprint off the wall. After a few minutes, most of it came off—but a faint outline still remained. He took the towel back into the bathroom and glanced at the mirror.

Foggy. How is it foggy?" he whispered aloud. The mirror was fogged over, as if someone had left the hot water running in the cracked, dingy sink. He wiped the fog away with the towel and left the bathroom.

He dropped onto the couch, staring ahead, trying to process what had just happened—the handprint, the mirror. These weren't just oddities. Things like this didn't just *happen* out of the blue.

His thoughts turned again to apartment 3B. Squatters. That had to be it. But how would they have gotten into his apartment? Especially with him home all day?

He needed some air. A walk, at the very least—if only to get away from the apartment for a while.

Downstairs, he saw Mr. Delaney in his usual spot, reading the newspaper with a cigar between his lips, puffing like an old locomotive.

“Mr. Delaney,” Caleb asked, hesitating. “Has—has there ever been a fire in this building? Uh, specifically on the third floor?”

Mr. Delaney didn’t look up from the paper. “Nope. No fires on the third floor. No fires in the building. Not in my building.”

Caleb opened his mouth to ask another question, but thought better of it. He was new here. Maybe it was best to leave things alone—for now.

Day 4

Later that night. 3:33 AM.

The knocks came again—three sharp raps that echoed through the silence like glass breaking. Caleb sat bolt upright in bed, heart hammering.

Then came the voice.

“Help me, Caleb...”

A woman’s voice, soft and broken, drifting through the wall like smoke.

Caleb clenched his jaw. This wasn’t stopping. Not until he got to the bottom of it.

Enough was enough.

Squatters or not, he was going to find a way into

3B. Tomorrow, one way or another.

Caleb lay in the bed, wide awake all night, half expecting more knocks, more voices, more anything from the unit next door.

Finally, around 7:00 AM, his alarm went off. Caleb got up and dressed. He ventured into the kitchen, made a pot of coffee and waited—listening for any kind of sounds from next door.

Once the pot was done brewing, he poured himself a cup. He took a few sips, went to his bedroom and found the old screwdriver in his duffel bag.

This was his protection in the shelters. He never had to use it, but it was always there if he needed it.

Today, he needed it—not for protection, but to pry open the door to 3B.

Day 5

Caleb took a few more sips of coffee from his little kitty coffee mug, picked up the scuffed-up screwdriver, and headed for apartment 3B.

He opened his door and looked down the hallway. No one. Silent. As if the building itself was holding its breath.

He stepped into the hallway, the screwdriver tucked in his pocket beneath his T-shirt. He gently closed his apartment door and walked over to unit 3B. He looked up and down the corridor and listened for footsteps. Nothing.

He took out the screwdriver, wedged it into the doorjamb, and struck it with his palm. On the third hit, the latch gave. The door creaked open, popping as it swung.

A wave of stale air and burnt wood rushed out.

Caleb pressed the door open further and stepped inside. The only light came from the windows—filthy with gray soot—casting the room in a dim, ashen hue.

He pulled his phone from his pocket, clicked on the flashlight, and panned the room. It was completely empty—except for a tall, charred floor mirror in the far corner. The floor and walls were scorched black and gray. The light fixture drooped, partially melted.

He moved the beam of light along the shared wall between his apartment and 3B. There—just like in his place—was the outline of a handprint.

His breath caught. He inhaled the thick smell of ash and choked, covering his mouth.

"It's set up just like mine..." he whispered. "3B and 3C—exact same layout... but this one's a corpse."

Caleb stepped toward the corner where the burnt mirror stood. Its reflective surface was coated in soot.

He wiped at the glass. A shape. He wiped again.

Then lifted the flashlight.

A scream caught in his throat as he stumbled back, falling hard onto the blackened floor. His phone spun across the room.

In the mirror—His reflection.

But burning. Screaming. Twisted in agony. It was *him.*

He scrambled to his feet and bolted for the hallway, crashing through the door to his own apartment—

But his apartment was burned, too.

The old sagging green couch was nothing but blackened springs and ash. His laptop sat on the floor—a melted husk. The walls, the floor—everything charred and crumbling.

It had been fine ten minutes ago. Now it looked like it had burned five years ago.

Caleb ran back into 3B. He had to get his phone. He had to call *someone.*

He snatched the scorched phone from the floor—melted. Useless.

"Help... help me..."

The voice again. From the mirror.

He turned. The reflection had changed. Not him now—but a woman. Crying. Reaching out.

Caleb stepped closer.

Closer.

A hand reached through the glass and grabbed him.

He screamed. Tried to pull away. But she was stronger. Much stronger.

With one last desperate grip on the mirror's frame—he was gone.

Sucked into the mirror.

Now trapped. Stuck in a loop. A death loop.

Created by the building. Replaying his last days over and over again.

A Month Later

"Here, let me show you 3C," Mr. Delaney said,

gesturing toward the door. "It's been cleaned up, painted, and we've even added some gently-used furniture. I think you'll be happy here, Ms. Swanson."

He led her down the hallway and into the unit.

"Is there anyone else on this floor?" she asked, looking around. "Does anyone live next door, in 3B?"

Mr. Delaney chuckled, flashing yellowed teeth and a half-chewed cigar. "No, ma'am. Just you. The old man down the hall is out of town for a few months, so you'll have total peace and quiet here in Grace Bend."

A few days later, Ms. Swanson moved in. New curtains. New bed. Cozy. Homey.

That night, exhausted, she climbed into bed and turned out the light.

At 3:33 AM - Knocking.

Three sharp raps.

Then a voice. Caleb's voice.

"Help... help me, please..."

The Weeping Quilt

Janice needed to get out of the house and spend some time outdoors with Sara, her nine-year-old daughter. Since Janice lost her mother to cancer about a year ago, she has had more drive to get out and do things. Her mother was her and Sara's world. While Janice went through her mother's belongings, she pulled out the last quilt she was repairing before she died. It was a project that her mother and Sara loved to do together. They would purchase old quilts from shows, yard sales and estate sales. Sara loved the time she spent with her grandmother. It wouldn't be the same without her.

Janice found Sara sitting in her room playing with her dolls. "You want to go do something this morning?"

Sara replied without even looking up, "Like what, mommy?"

"How about we do something that we used to do with grandma?"

Sara's gaze went from the dolls to her mother, her look hopeful and full of excitement about what it would be. "You mean?"

Janice smiled. "Yes, let's go quilt shopping!"

"Oh boy, I can't wait. We haven't done that since Grandma passed."

Sara jumped up, got dressed and was ready to go before Janice even finished her first cup of coffee. “Hang on there, you need to eat breakfast and brush your teeth before we leave. No one is going to sell us a quilt if our breath smells.” Janice wrinkled her nose while looking at Sara.

Janice found a yard sale a few blocks over from where they lived and thought it was a nice, cool morning, so they would just walk over there.

“Look, Mommy! Isn't it pretty? All the little squares - I like it!” Little Sara was bursting with excitement when she saw the old quilt at the yard sale. She thought it would look perfect on her bed. Janice eyed the quilt carefully. The fabric was faded, some stitches frayed or coming undone, and several dark spots looked like old stains. “I don’t know, honey. It looks really old and worn. There are some places that need a lot of repair. It’ll take some work to make it like new again.”

“Oh, Mommy, that’s why I like it! I like the old look; it reminds me of when Grandma was alive. She used to work on quilts all the time.” Janice felt the familiar jab in her heart. Sara - just nine years old - knew exactly how to pull on those heartstrings. Yes, Janice's mother had loved working on old quilts. She'd repaired them for neighbors, for local church fairs, and most of all, for Sara. The girl had ten reworked quilts already, each one stitched with love.

Janice glanced at Sara, who was now giving her the big brown eyes, those sad, pleading eyes that rarely failed. "Okay," Janice said with a sigh. "As long as they're not asking too much for it."

"Oh, Mommy, you're the best!" Sara hugged the quilt tightly and danced in a circle with it, twirling the brittle fabric in the air.

Janice purchased the quilt for Sara without much bargaining. The look on her daughter's face had been worth the ten bucks. They folded it gently and placed it in the wagon before heading home. Sara insisted on carrying it inside herself, cradling it like a treasured doll.

Janice figured she'd give it a good look-over in the morning, maybe with her first cup of coffee. There were definitely some worn spots that needed new stitching and those odd dark stains, she'd try to scrub those out too. Nothing a little elbow grease couldn't fix. Later that night, Janice had settled into her room with a paperback and a cup of peppermint tea. Just a few pages left before she'd turn out the light.

Then she heard it.

She looked up from her book, her ears tuning into the quiet house. There it was again - faint, barely audible. A sound like... sobbing?

She turned her head slightly, trying to pinpoint it. Someone crying, but softly. Not the kind of dramatic crying a child makes when they want attention, no, this was quieter, almost ashamed. Muffled, like it was being smothered in hands or a pillow. Janice stood, heart beginning to race in that anxious mom kind of way. It didn't sound like Sara - but what if it was? What if she'd had a nightmare?

She stepped into the hallway and listened again. Yes, it was coming from Sara's room. Janice opened the door slowly, careful not to startle her daughter.

The sobbing stopped.

Sara lay curled beneath the quilt, fast asleep, breathing evenly. One arm tucked under her cheek. Not a tear in sight. Janice stepped closer, frowning. She hated that Sara was already sleeping with the thing. It hadn't even been washed, much less mended. Who knew what kind of grime or allergens it had picked up over the years?

She reached to pull the quilt up a bit more snug around her daughter's shoulders, then paused. The edge of the quilt was damp. Not wet, exactly. But not dry either. As if it had been soaked and was only halfway dry, as if it had sat in a puddle and just barely dried out.

She touched the damp spot again, confused. Maybe it was just condensation from the ride home. Or maybe Sara had spilled water on it earlier and not said anything. Kids were always doing stuff like that. Janice gently adjusted the covers and left the room, still thinking about the sound - the crying - and that strange wetness.

It was probably nothing. Probably.

The next morning, Janice joined Sara at the table, the smell of fresh coffee mingling with the sugary scent of cinnamon cereal. Sara sat across from her, happily eating and swinging her legs beneath the chair, her bowl clinking with each spoonful.

After a few quiet minutes, Janice set her mug down. "Sara, can you bring me the quilt? I want to start working on it today."

Sara nodded mid-chew and hopped down from her chair. Moments later, she returned, holding the bundle with care.

Janice spread the quilt across the living room floor and knelt beside it. She pulled out her sewing kit and a sheet of yellow sticker dots. There were several patches coming undone, more than she'd noticed before. She marked each one with a dot, muttering softly to herself.

Then she paused.

Her brow furrowed. "What's that?"

She leaned in closer to a particular patch. It stood out from the rest, not because it was damaged, but because it was… different.

The patch showed a smiling woman, hands raised in the air, as if dancing or celebrating. Her expression seemed almost too vivid for simple stitches. "That's different," Janice murmured. "Don't think I've ever quite seen a patch like this one. I like it."

She continued her work. A few of the lighter stains came out with soap and warm water. But the darker ones - deep, ominous blotches the color of dried blood - refused to budge. She scrubbed them until her knuckles hurt, but they didn't lighten in the slightest. With a sigh, Janice folded the quilt and placed it beside her sewing chair and the woven basket holding her spools of thread and tools.

As evening fell, she put Sara to bed and retreated

to her own room. She placed her mint tea on the nightstand and settled under the covers with her paperback. She read for a while, letting the quiet of the house settle around her like a second blanket. Her eyes grew heavy, the words on the page beginning to blur. She reached over to turn out the light…

And stopped.

That sound again.

Soft and muffled but not sobbing this time. This time, she could hear a child talking and laughing. She sat up sharply, heart tapping faster in her chest. The sounds were faint, like someone talking or laughing into their hands or into a pillow so as to be quiet.

She stepped into the hallway, barefoot, listening. The sound was coming from Sara's room. Janice opened the door slowly, not wanting to startle her daughter.

The sounds stopped instantly.

Sara lay curled up, fast asleep. No stirring, no laughing or talking. Just peaceful breathing. But Janice's eyes caught something else - the quilt.

It was wrapped tightly around Sara, tucked up around her neck and under her arms like a cocoon.

Janice frowned. She didn't remember giving it

back. In fact, she was certain it had been beside her sewing chair before she went to bed. Maybe Sara had asked for it and she hadn't heard… or maybe Sara had gotten up and taken it without waking her. It had been a long day. She slowly closed Sara's door and went back to bed, the image of that tightly-clutched quilt lingering in her mind.

The next morning, Janice joined Sara at the table again. The girl was already eating her cinnamon crunch cereal, humming softly between bites.

Janice took a sip of coffee. "Hey sweetie, can you bring me the quilt again? I want to keep working on it today." Sara finished a spoonful and nodded. She returned a moment later with the quilt in her arms.

As Janice reached for it, she felt it…The same corner was damp.

She frowned. "Sara, do you take the quilt to the bathroom with you?"

Sara looked confused. "No, Mommy. I leave it on the bed. I don't want to get it dirty or wet."

"Were you talking to someone or laughing last night after going to bed?"

"No Mommy, I was tired and went straight to sleep," Sara responded without looking up from her cereal bowl.

Janice nodded slowly. "Okay."

Later, when she spread the quilt out to work again, her eyes went straight to the patch with the woman. She stared.

Something had changed.

The same figure was there, yes - but the woman was no longer dancing. Her arms were no longer raised. Instead, they were folded gently over her stomach - now noticeably rounded.

She was pregnant.

Her expression had changed, too. No longer joyful. It was softer now. Melancholy. Reflective. Janice leaned in, brow drawn tight. "I would have sworn her hands were up yesterday," she murmured. "And she was thinner."

But the thread said otherwise. The patch was exactly as it was. As if it had always been that way.

And yet… it hadn't.

As night fell, Janice once again tucked Sara into bed - but without the quilt this time. She made a mental note: No blanket tonight. None. She turned off the light, closed Sara's door gently behind her, and went to her own bedroom. She didn't read. She didn't even get under the covers. She just lay on the bed, staring up at the ceiling, waiting to hear it.

The sobbing.

But it never came.

The next thing she knew, morning light was streaming across the floor. She sat up slowly. No crying in the night. No sounds at all. Maybe she'd been wrong. Maybe Sara had just been moaning in her sleep, and the quilt wasn't connected to anything strange after all.

Janice slipped out of bed, stretched, and wandered into the kitchen for her coffee and maybe something to nibble on.

Sara was already at the table, legs swinging slowly under her chair, eating her cereal. The quilt lay softly across her lap like it belonged there. Janice leaned down and kissed the top of her daughter's head. "Good morning, sweetie." Sara gave a faint smile, but her eyes looked heavy…tired.

Janice poured her coffee and sat across from her.

Sara looked up with droopy, dark-rimmed eyes. "Mommy… I don't feel good."

Janice set her mug down and reached across the

table, pressing her palm to Sara's forehead. "You're a little warm. Let's get you some medicine, and then you can lie down on the couch and watch cartoons."

"Okay, Mommy. Can I take my quilt with me?"

Janice hesitated. Her eyes drifted down to the quilt. "Give it to me first, so I can do some work on it. Then I'll bring it to you on the couch, alright?"

Sara nodded, rubbing her eyes. She walked to the living room and curled up on the couch, flipping on the morning cartoons.

Not long after, she was asleep.

Janice finished cleaning up the kitchen and returned to the quilt. She picked it up carefully and spread it across the living room floor, then grabbed her sewing kit. As her fingers brushed the fabric, she felt it again.

Damp.

The same edge. Always the same edge. Cold and clammy like it had soaked up tears that didn't come from either of them. Janice stared at it, heart ticking up a notch. *I can't explain this away anymore.*

She took a breath and looked for the patch - the one she kept coming back to. The woman.

But the figure had changed again.

Janice felt her skin prickle. A cold shiver danced down her spine. The woman was no longer standing joyfully and no longer pregnant.

Now she was on her knees, hunched over, her face buried in her hands. In front of her lay another figure…smaller, still, and stretched out on the ground. A child, perhaps. The woman's stitched shoulders were bent in sorrow, the threadwork somehow conveying raw despair.

Janice recoiled slightly, blinking hard. It changed again. Not just the details - the whole meaning.

She stared at the quilt for a long while, unease churning in her stomach.

Something was wrong.

Something was off with this quilt.

She wasn't ready to tell Sara. Wasn't ready to throw it away, not yet. Sara loved it too much.

Instead, Janice folded it carefully - methodically - keeping her eyes from straying back to the sorrowful patch. She climbed the step stool and placed the quilt on the top shelf of the hallway closet, where it was far too high for Sara to reach. Or see.

Just for now.

Later that day, Sara was up from her rest, running and playing in her room. Her eyes were no longer tired or dark, her energy back to its usual bright buzz. Janice passed by the doorway and paused, looking into Sara's room. Janice saw Sara was laughing and appeared to be talking to someone while twirling a doll in one hand, bouncing on her toes. Janice figured she must be talking to the doll. She'd seen her play like this before.

She stepped into the room and gently placed a hand on her daughter's forehead. No warmth. "That medicine worked wonders," Janice said, surprised. "You're not warm anymore, and you've got way more energy than you had this morning."

"I feel good now, Mommy." Sara looked up from her toys. "Are you done fixing my quilt? I can't find it."

Janice's heart skipped. She'd hoped to avoid this conversation.

"No, sweetie, not yet. I'm still working on it. As soon as I'm done, I'll give it back to you. Does that sound good?"

Sara shrugged and said, "That's okay, Mommy," and returned to her play without another word. Relieved, Janice quietly stepped out.

When evening came, Janice followed her usual routine: she put Sara to bed, made herself a cup of mint tea, and settled in her bedroom with her paperback. As the words began to blur and her eyes grew heavy, she placed the book on her nightstand, turned off the light, and drifted off within minutes.

But something pulled her from sleep.

A child's laughing.

Soft, distant - just like before. Janice sat up, startled, heart beating fast. She looked over at the clock. 3:05 AM.

She rose quietly and walked into the hallway, listening. The laughter was coming from Sara's room again. She moved slowly, gently pressing open the bedroom door. Sara was sound asleep, her breathing steady, her face peaceful. But there, faintly illuminated in the ambient glow from the hallway, was the quilt. Lightly draped across Sara's small frame.

Janice stared.

She had put it in the hallway closet. On the top shelf. Sara couldn't have reached it - not even with the step stool. Her first instinct was to tear it from the bed, drag it outside, and toss it straight into the trash. But she stopped herself. Sara was sleeping. She didn't want to wake her. Not yet.

Janice stepped back and quietly closed the door, deciding to wait until morning. She was probably just overtired. Little things were getting to her lately, making her feel off balance.

There were no more sounds for the rest of the night.

Janice slipped out of bed, stretched, and started her way down the hall to the kitchen. She noticed Sara's door was still closed and figured it was probably best to let her sleep. That might help keep her from getting sick again, like she had the morning before.

She brewed herself a cup of coffee and settled into a chair at the kitchen table. She began thinking - maybe she'd make a visit to the house where she purchased the quilt. She wanted to know more about it, who made it, what was with the special patch, and why they sold it. Surely that wasn't strange, just wanting to know the backstory. People made quilts for all kinds of reasons.

Janice was working on her third cup of coffee when she realized that Sara still wasn't up. She called down the hall, "Sara, it's time to get up. You're sleeping the day away!" No movement. She waited a few more minutes, trying to keep her voice light but firmer. "Sara, get up and get some breakfast."

Still nothing.

A chill crept into her chest. Janice got up, hurried down the hall, and slowly opened Sara's door. Sara was still in bed, lying beneath the quilt. Janice stepped into the room. "Sara? Sara, are you getting up?"

No response.

She moved closer, Sara was breathing, slow and steady, but she wasn't stirring. Janice touched her arm, then shook the bed. "Sara?" Panic rising, she pulled the quilt and sheet off her daughter and raised her up, but Sara remained limp and unresponsive.

Heart pounding, Janice ran to the kitchen and called 911.

The ambulance arrived within ten minutes. Sara still hadn't moved. The EMTs tried several methods to rouse her, but nothing worked. Her vitals were all normal. With growing concern, they loaded her into the ambulance and rushed her to the ER. Janice quickly threw on clothes and followed, her vision blurry from tears and fear.

At the hospital, the ER doctor examined Sara and

confirmed that she had slipped into a coma. Other neurologists arrived and repeated the tests, but the conclusion was the same. Janice stayed by her side all day, refusing to leave, holding her hand, silently praying.

That evening, Sara's eyes fluttered open. She turned weakly toward her mother. "Mommy… where am I? What are all these machines?"

Janice wept with relief, clutching her daughter's hand. "Honey, you scared me. You went to sleep and no one could wake you up, not even the doctors."

Nurses and doctors came rushing in, quickly running tests. Sara remained weak and frightened by the chaos. Janice stayed close, comforting her and whispering that everything would be okay.

Later, a neurologist pulled Janice aside.

"Ma'am, she seems perfectly normal. No signs of trauma, no neurological damage. We couldn't find any reason for her to have slipped into a coma. The medicine you gave her yesterday wasn't even in her system anymore. We want to keep her another twenty-four hours, just to be safe."

Janice nodded, grateful but still shaken. How could something like that happen for no reason?

The next morning, while Sara slept, Janice left the hospital and drove to the house where she had bought the quilt. She stepped up on the decorated porch and knocked on the door. After a minute or two, the woman who sold her the quilt opened it.

"Hello. Can I help you, miss?"

"Uh, yes - I bought a quilt from your yard sale a week ago. For my daughter. I'd like to ask you a few questions, if you have a moment."

The woman studied Janice's face, then nodded. "I thought I remembered you. You had the cute little girl, right?"

Janice forced a small smile. "Yes. About the quilt…"

"She was so sweet," the woman said, smiling warmly. "Did she like the quilt?"

"Yes. She loved it," Janice replied. "But I was interested in who made it, and why you'd sell it?"

The woman's smile faded. She looked down at the floor.

"My grandmother made that quilt for one of her children - my aunt. She died when she was very young. My grandmother passed it on to my mother, who gave it to my younger sister… who also died." She paused. "They said it was SIDS, but no one ever knew for sure. That was a long time ago." Janice listened carefully, her stomach knotting.

"The quilt stayed in the closet for years. When my mother passed away, I took it. It's been sitting in my hall closet ever since. I don't have kids. Never did. But I always wanted them." Her voice softened. "Sorry. I'm rambling. I put it out at the yard sale because… I didn't need it. But my grandmother… she told my mother, 'Make sure the quilt goes to a little girl. Always a little girl.' Strange, I know. After my sister died, my grandmother lost her mind. Started talking to the child she'd lost…like they never left."

"What about the special patch?" Janice asked. "The one with the woman on it?"

The woman looked around the room, searching her memory. "That was my grandmother," she finally said. "She said that patch was her sorrow… sewn into the quilt after her baby died."

Something clicked in Janice's mind. Her skin turned cold. She thanked the older woman. The quilt had to go.

Janice rushed back to the hospital to be with Sara. The words the old woman had told her kept echoing in her mind. It sounded crazy - like the quilt had caused the deaths - but maybe the woman was just a bit off her rocker.

Later that afternoon, the doctors released Sara to go home. There had been no relapse, no change in her vitals, no new issues. As soon as they walked through the door, Sara asked, "Mommy, are you done fixing my quilt?"

Janice hesitated. She knew she didn't want Sara near that quilt again but wasn't ready to tell her it was gone. "Not yet, sweetie. Just a little more to do."

Sara tilted her head and looked at her curiously. "Are you sure, Mommy? The lady in my dreams said you're hiding it from me."

A cold chill swept across Janice's back and down her legs, making her knees weak. "What lady are you talking about?"

"She's in my dreams," Sara said simply. "She told me I was the new owner of the quilt. She was with me when I was asleep in the hospital. She said I was supposed to go home with her and meet her daughter. She was really old."

Janice's blood ran cold.

The grandmother, she thought. It had to be the woman's grandmother.

Without another word, she ran from the room, grabbed the quilt, and spread it out on the floor. The edges were no longer damp. Her eyes scanned the familiar fabric until she found the strange patch - the one with the woman's figure.

Only now, the woman was no longer weeping. She was standing, holding hands with a child.

No, two children. One was slightly behind the other, being absorbed or pulled in, as if merging into the first. Janice leaned closer, her breath caught in her throat.

The second child looked like Sara.

Janice stumbled back, hands over her mouth, stifling a scream.

The quilt is absorbing Sara. It's trying to replace the dead child. It's feeding off the sorrow of the old woman. That's the only explanation.

She didn't hesitate.

Janice rolled up the quilt, took it into the backyard, and set it ablaze in her garden. The flames burst into unnatural colors, yellow and blue, twisting and writhing as if alive. The sobbing returned, louder than ever, rising from the fire.

As she watched it burn, two childlike shadows lifted from the quilt and into the smoke. "Thank you," Janice thought she heard, soft and distant, just before the shadows vanished into the mid-afternoon sky.

Sara never got sick again. And she never dreamed of the old woman again, either.

Winner Winner Chicken Dinner

Gloria on Stage at the Velvet Twist

They called her Lollypop, but her real name was Gloria. The name came from a move she did with a cherry-red sucker and a whole lot of hips, but tonight, she didn't need props—just her pink string bikini bottoms and a pair of heels tall enough to scare King Kong.

The stage lights bathed everything in hot pink, casting glossy shadows over curves and cash alike. The Velvet Twist smelled like cheap cigars, expensive cologne, and sweat—exactly the kind of place where lonely men with too much money and too few teeth came to pretend they still had game. The music pulsed low and slow, bass like a heartbeat, and Gloria moved to match it, smooth and rhythmic, like molasses in July.

Her eyes scanned the crowd lazily until they landed on the man with the name tag still clipped to his shirt—Ed, Day Manager, Piggly Wiggly. The badge glittered under the strobe like a sheriff's star, though Ed was more roadhouse outlaw than lawman. His gut strained against a wrinkled polo, his eyes glassy from the bottle of Jack that must've been flowing since noon.

She saw him seeing her, and like a true professional, she gave him the look—the *come-hither* smile, the slow wink, the tilt of the head that said, *you, baby.* A few crumpled bills were already flying toward the stage like moths to fire, piling up around her heels just like she wanted.

"Go on, Ed," one of his bar buddies jeered, giving him a nudge with an elbow and a smirk. "Don't keep the lady waitin'."

"Show her what you got," another one added, slurring into his whiskey.

Ed stood—wobbled, really—and started toward the stage with all the grace of a walrus in heat. He swayed in time with the music, or maybe just the alcohol, arms loose and legs uncertain. But Gloria kept her eyes on him, feeding him the fantasy like sugar to a diabetic. He grinned wider, lips damp, breath shallow.

She turned, bent low, and gave Ed a front-row view of everything God gave her. She felt the stage shake slightly as he leaned in closer, like a man approaching a shrine he didn't deserve.

She felt him then—his fingers fumbling along the string at her hip, tugging a bit harder than she liked. Good thing she'd double-knotted it in the dressing room. A moment later, paper slipped under the waistband—crisp bills, and one that felt different.

She straightened slowly and turned back to him, dragging one hand down the sweaty side of his face, across his stubbled neck, like she was blessing him. His eyes fluttered. His buddies at the bar hooted like drunk dogs.

The song ended, and the lights shifted. Gloria smiled, gave a lazy wave to her audience, and disappeared behind the velvet curtain.

"Give it up for Miss Lollypop!" the DJ crooned through the speaker. "I bet you boys'd love for her to give you a real *pop*, huh?"

The crowd roared as the next girl, Candicane, took the stage.

Back in the dressing room, Gloria peeled the bills from her bikini string and counted them fast with calloused fingers. A good haul. Top bill had a phone number scrawled on it in sharpie ink. *Call me – Ed.* She rolled her eyes.

"They always think they're the one," she muttered, stuffing the cash into her purse. "As if I ain't danced for a hundred of 'em just this week."

If she ever *did* call, half of them would either piss themselves or have their wives answer the phone with a crying baby on one hip and another one on the way.

Still, she folded the note carefully and tucked it in a separate pocket.

Because something about that smile—sloppy, stupid, sweaty as it was—felt like trouble. And Gloria had always been bad at turning trouble away.

Present Day – Domestic Hell

Gloria pulled the old pink robe off the hook behind the bathroom door. The color had faded to the shade of bubblegum run over by a Buick, and the satin edges had frayed to threads. Ed had given it to her on their second anniversary.

She used to think it was sweet.

The first anniversary was. They'd flown to Vegas, got drunk off hotel liquor, lost fifty bucks in the slots, and fooled around in a hotel suite they couldn't afford. They danced in the street like fools and ordered room service they never paid off. Ed had brought her flowers every week back then, kissed her knuckles like she was royalty. Said he was the luckiest bastard alive.

Back then, he'd tell her he didn't need strip clubs anymore. "Ain't a girl out there can hold a candle to you, Glo."

Now she was lucky if he brought home a pack of Pall Malls.

The anniversaries that followed were nothing but a six-pack of domestic beer and a see-through robe from a dollar store, followed by a five-minute roll in the sheets if he wasn't too drunk to perform.

By year two, something had turned.

Gloria used to cry herself to sleep back then, thinking it was her. Maybe he didn't't find her sexy anymore. She tried everything—lace lingerie, Brazilian waxes, bright red nails, even a new perfume that smelled like sugared lemons and desperation.

None of it mattered.

Now, she couldn't give a rat's ass if their marriage froze over and cracked to pieces.

She walked into the kitchen, the robe hanging open like it didn't care either, and poured herself a cup of coffee that had been burning on the hot plate since six in the morning. It was almost nine now. She sipped it—bitter, metallic, overcooked—but it would do.

From the counter, she picked up a crumpled pack of cigarettes and tapped one free. She lit it with the old Bic and took a long drag. The first pull always burned a little, made her lungs ache—but it softened the edges just enough to make it through another damn day.

Ed stirred in the bedroom. She heard the sheets shift, then the groan of the mattress springs under his weight.

He patted the empty side of the bed. Cold. She was already up.

He swung his legs over the edge, scratched his gut, and rubbed his stubbled jaw. Damn. Forgot to shave again. And the damn regional director from Piggly Wiggly just *had* to show up yesterday while he looked like some backwoods bum. Chewed him out in front of the new cashier and that snot-nosed assistant manager.

Ed grumbled his way down the hall to the kitchen, footsteps loud and thudding like he was trying to stomp through the damn linoleum.

"Did you at least remember to pick up creamer yesterday?" he barked, already halfway into the fridge.

Gloria didn't even look up. "Grow a pair and drink it black. You work at a grocery store, Ed. You could just pick it up yourself."

Ed slammed the fridge door, holding a can of beer like it was proof of betrayal.

"Well, maybe I would," he snapped, "if someone didn't keep a stranglehold on the bank account. I don't even get *spending money* in my own house."

He cracked open the can and held it up like a trophy. "For the road. Since I can't have my damn coffee."

Gloria took another drag, long and slow, then flicked the ash into the sink. She didn't even look at him.

"Poor baby," she muttered, flat as dirt.

Ed stormed back to the bedroom, got dressed in his crusty khakis and store-branded polo, clipped on his stupid badge like he was somebody important, and marched out the front door with a slam that rattled the loose windowpanes.

Gloria didn't flinch. Just stared into the swirl of her coffee and took one more pull from the cigarette.

"Good riddance," she said under her breath. "I hope you rot, you pile of dog turds."

She hated him.

Not the way you hate a long wait at the DMV or a rude cashier. No, this was the real kind. The kind that settles in your bones. That poisons you from the inside out. That makes you dream about heart attacks and pillow suffocation.

He liked to remind her who she was.

A sleazy stripper, he'd sneer. "If it wasn't for me, you'd still be shakin' your saggy goods for singles. What're you now, forty? You wouldn't make ten bucks on a Saturday night."

She didn't feel shame anymore. That part of her had shriveled up and died sometime between year three and year four.

What she felt now was rage. Cold, clean rage. She couldn't find a drop of love for Ed anymore. Not a sliver. Not even pity.

If he dropped dead on the floor this very minute, she'd dance a two-step on his corpse before calling the ambulance.

Maybe.

Gloria changed out of her robe, slipped on a pair of cutoff jeans and an old Lynyrd Skynyrd tee, poured herself another cup of scorched coffee, and stepped out onto the front porch. The sunlight stabbed at her hangover like knives, so she slipped on a pair of oversized sunglasses—cheap gas station ones, but they did the trick.

She bent down and picked up the newspaper off the sidewalk. It wasn't their subscription; they'd never pay for something like that. It belonged to old Mr. Halvorson two doors down. He'd died two years ago, but the paper kept coming. Gloria had told the paperboy he moved in with her and Ed. Kid didn't care as long as he got paid.

She was turning back toward the door when she spotted her.

Mrs. Stevens.

Clip-clopping up the sidewalk in her wedge heels, sun visor already perched like a crown. Gloria sighed. Too late to duck inside.

"Well, good morning, Gloria," Mrs. Stevens trilled, eyes hidden behind her gold-rimmed bifocals, but her voice as sharp as glass. "My, it's such a bright, warm day, isn't it? I see you've got your sunglasses on already. Smart girl!"

Mrs. Stevens—gossip queen, neighborhood surveillance, walking Facebook page. If something moved within three blocks, she knew about it. Gloria wouldn't be surprised if the woman had a spreadsheet somewhere cataloging everyone's garbage schedules and underwear preferences.

"Morning," Gloria muttered into her coffee cup.

Mrs. Stevens leaned in just a little. "Say, did your husband make it home alright last night? I—I heard quite a racket coming from your place. Thought maybe there was... trouble. Or maybe a visitor?"

Gloria smirked behind her cup, letting the steam mask the twitch in her mouth. "Oh that? That was just the movie of the week on the Lifetime Channel. Had it cranked up while vacuuming. Didn't wanna miss the drama."

Mrs. Stevens blinked, clearly disappointed. "Oh… uh-huh. Well, I suppose Ed's working the later shifts now? He's always coming home so late. I guess that means more hours, more pay, hmm?"

Gloria gave her a tight-lipped smile. "He's such a valuable employee, they can't run the store without him. Real pillar of the community. You know how it is. If

Piggly Wiggly shuts down, we're all driving to the next town for groceries."

Mrs. Stevens nodded, lips pursed. She could smell b.s. from five houses down and Gloria knew it.

"Well, alright then," the older woman said, her voice syrupy and thin. "Maybe we should do lunch sometime."

"Uh-huh. Sure," Gloria said, already halfway back inside. The screen door slammed behind her with a satisfying pop.

She leaned against the door, cigarette in one hand, coffee in the other, and blew out a long ribbon of smoke. She knew exactly where Ed was every night. Strippers. Booze. Probably half-lit, throwing crumpled ones at some twenty-year-old named Destiny while she tried to pretend he didn't smell like pork chops and stale Coors.

People asked her why she stayed.

Because leaving would give Ed the satisfaction of thinking he broke her.

No, he'd have to crawl out first.

If she could make him disappear and get away with it, she'd do it in a heartbeat. And maybe—just maybe—she had found a way.

***

Gloria sunk into the sunken couch, Coors can sweating in one hand, cigarette curling smoke in the other. The TV flickers soft orange light across the walls. A voiceover from a Salem witch trials documentary hums in the background.

"Most of the trials were purely a formality before the executions. Tied to wooden stakes, the women were burned—quickly, for most. But some... didn't burn."

Gloria snorts. "I bet those ones gave 'em a real show."

"And those who didn't burn, the people believed were *true* witches. The punishment then? Beheading. One way or another, they got their witch."

She takes a drag from her smoke, exhales slowly. "Guess they got 'em either way, huh?" she mutters to no one.

The flickering TV reflects in her sunglasses, still perched on her head from earlier. Gloria leans forward and reaches beneath the couch, fingers searching around until they graze something smooth.

She pulls out a small wooden box with a tarnished metal clasp. Old, maybe handmade. She sets it on her lap with a reverent sigh and pops it open.

Inside: half-melted unscented candles, a few small bird bones wrapped in cloth, a faded deck of tarot cards, two feathers—one black, one white—and an old book of poems with the spine half-cracked. Her grandmother's, maybe her mother's before that. No one ever said.

She lifts the tarot deck, thumbing through worn edges. The cards smell like dust and incense. She stops on one.

She tosses the card back in and picks up a small sticky note from the coffee table. She scrawls:

"Ed to shut up. Just one day."

Under it, she draws a crude sigil—something half-remembered from a YouTube video or a dream.

Gloria sets the note in the crusty ashtray, placing a stubby white candle next to it. She flicks her Bic, lights the candle. Then, she touches the flame to the sticky note.

It *whooshes* up, faster than paper should. A flash of unnatural orange and blue, like a gas stove gone wrong. The candle flares too—sputtering, flaring again.

Startled, Gloria jerks back, knocking over her beer. She watches, heart thudding, as the flames settle. The candle's still burning. Calm now. But… different. It burns steady, with a soft violet edge to the flame.

She stares at it for a long moment.

Then: "Well, crappers."

She forces a laugh, half shaky, half amused at herself. "It's just fire. Candle wax and beer fumes."

But even as she laughs, she doesn't take her eyes off that candle.

***

Gloria woke curled up on the couch, her neck stiff and mouth dry. She opened one crusty eye and squinted at the low morning light creeping through the blinds. Her gaze drifted to the coffee table, where the little candle still sat upright next to the overflowing ashtray and the old wooden box.

It was still burning.

That tugged at her nerves a little—she could've sworn it would've gone out hours ago. But she shrugged it off. *Just an old candle. They don't make 'em like they used to,* she thought, dragging herself upright.

She sat on the edge of the couch, trying to piece her thoughts together, when the front door rattled like someone was trying to get in with mittens on. It flung open with a bang.

There stood Ed.

Gloria could smell him from across the room—cheap beer, cigarettes, and cheaper perfume. The kind that clung to dollar bills in G-strings.

Ed stumbled inside, eyes red and glassy enough they looked painted on. He slammed the door behind him with more force than necessary.

"Look what the cat drug in," Gloria muttered. "Do I need to ask where you been all night?"

She lit a cigarette with a shaky flick of her lighter.

"Shut up, woman…"

Ed's bleary gaze landed on the coffee table. On the candle. On the box. On the old tarot card she'd left out.

His lips curled.

"Witchy woman," he slurred. "Shut up, witchy woman." He laughed, more spit than sound. "Who you casting spells on now, huh? You t-tt—tryin' to put a loooove spell on me, w-witchy woman?"

He snorted and staggered toward the kitchen.

Gloria watched him closely. Half of her wanted him to burst into flames. The other half expected—*hoped*—something, anything, might happen.

Nothing did.

Well, except Ed letting out a fart loud enough to echo in the hallway as he bent to grab a beer.

He popped the tab and turned, foam dripping down the side.

"You wanna hear something weird?" he asked.

Gloria didn't answer.

"Don't care, I'll tell you anyway…" He leaned against the fridge, squinting like the kitchen light was a personal offense. "I was talkin' to this gal—I mean, guy—at the bar. Not the strip club, the bar. And all of a sudden, I couldn't talk."

He took a swig. "Like, my freakin' voice just quit workin'. No sound, no nothing. Just one fart."

As if on cue, he let another one rip and chuckled to himself.

"That weird or what? I could finally talk again a couple hours later. Crazy, huh?"

Gloria exhaled slowly, eyes narrowing. Her fingers tightened around her cigarette.

That was what she'd written.

Ed to shut up for just one day.

Coincidence? Maybe. But it was a damn close one. Close enough that the hangover faded into the background and the stench of Ed's night out didn't matter anymore.

Something in her box might've actually *worked.*

And if it worked once…

She crushed the cigarette in the ashtray and stood.

"Where you goin'?" Ed asked, mouth full of beer foam.

Gloria didn't answer.

***

She already knew where she was headed.

Gloria turned left on Second Street, her old Honda rattling over the cracked asphalt like bones in a tin can. About a block down, tucked between a boarded-up thrift store and a liquor shop with flickering neon, sat the pawn shop.

It looked like it had been condemned twice and forgotten both times. The roof sagged in the middle, and the sign above the door just read **"PAWN"**—half the letters missing or burned out. Gloria parked out front anyway, stepped out, and walked through the front door with a kind of purpose that had started to feel familiar. The air inside hit her like a wet rag—rat droppings, mildew, old paper, and that strange metallic tinge of forgotten things.

She didn't browse. She knew where to go.

Down the same narrow aisle where she'd once found her tarot deck and those little bird bones wrapped in a hankie. The shelves leaned like they were trying to whisper secrets to each other. She scanned them, one by one, fingers trailing over dusty spines and cracked covers. It had to still be here. Who else in town would buy a book like that?

Just as she was about to give up, she saw it—half-buried under a stack of moldy newspapers and a broken ventriloquist dummy. Gloria pulled it free with both hands.

The Thirteen Black Tongues of Magic Spells.

The book was wrapped in cracked goat hide; the cover stained with dark streaks that looked suspiciously like old blood. It still smelled like rotting barnyard. She hugged it close like an old friend she didn't quite trust but needed anyway.

At the front counter, the same old man was sitting on a stool behind a cracked glass display. Gloria couldn't remember ever seeing him stand up. His face was a sagging patchwork of liver spots, his eyes sunk so deep into his skull they looked like marbles in mud. His gums showed pink and bare when he smiled—no teeth, no name tag.

"I didn't see a price tag," Gloria said, holding up the book. "But I'm buying it."

The old man looked at her for a long moment, and then, finally, rasped, "Ain't got no monetary value. You want what's in that book, be careful what you take from it. Might cost more than cash."

Gloria handed him a twenty and gave him a look like he was nuts. "Then I'll start a tab."

The old man chuckled—or maybe choked—and waved her off. She left with the book clutched tightly in one hand, the hair on the back of her neck standing up the whole drive home.

Later that evening, after the sun dipped low and the shadows grew long in the corners of the living room, Gloria lit a few candles and tucked the book beneath the couch cushions. Ed was out—doing what he did best. Drinking. Watching dancers. Spending his night like he wasn't married at all.

She waited.

When the house was quiet and full of that stillness that only truly lonely places know, Gloria pulled the book back out. Her hands trembled as she opened the crackling pages. Her fingers found the one she'd seen weeks ago when she'd browsed the pawn shop with Cheryl, back before things got… real.

"Muta Cordis Gallinae."

Translated: *Change of the Chicken Heart.*

The spell promised to turn the cruel and dominant into cowardly shadows of themselves. Men who struck, cursed, and belittled would become afraid to even raise their voices. That'd do nicely.

Gloria smiled and whispered the name of the spell aloud, her voice rough with bourbon and a strange thrill. She liked the sound of it. She imagined Ed sitting quiet as a church mouse while she ran the remote, left the dishes, and took her sweet time in the bathroom.

The spell would need him present. She couldn't cast it alone. But she could get the scene ready.

She laid out the rune stones she'd bought from a back-page ad in *Witchlight Weekly*, careful to place them in a circle on the hardwood floor. She lit her "everburn" candles—three of them, deep red, smelling of clove and cinnamon and something like scorched feathers. On the coffee table, she placed a fresh bottle of Kentucky bourbon and poured Ed a tall glass. She poured herself two smaller ones to start.

Then, for dramatic effect—or maybe just confidence—she slipped into that old black negligee she used to wear when Ed gave a darn. The lace was frayed, and the strap didn't sit quite right, but it would do.

By the time Ed staggered through the front door, Gloria was already three bourbons deep and grinning.

He stopped in the doorway, sniffed the air, and blinked at her like he wasn't sure he was in the right house.

"Well, look at you," Ed muttered, swaying slightly. "What's the occasion? Anniversary I forgot?"

"No," Gloria said, gliding over to him with slow, syrupy grace. "Just wanted to make up. Start fresh."

She helped him to the couch like he was an honored guest. Took off his shoes, loosened his collar. Handed him the tall glass of his favorite bourbon with a wink and a smile.

Ed stared at her, suspicious but intrigued. "You high or somethin'?"

"I'm in love," she said sweetly, patting his hand. "And I wrote you a poem."

Ed snorted. "You what?"

"A short one," Gloria said, picking up the book from behind the couch and flipping to the right page. "Before we roll around in the sack, I figured I'd set the mood."

Ed smirked, took a big sip of his drink, and leaned back like a king on a throne. Gloria stepped into the circle, lit by the flickering red glow of candlelight, and began to read…

Gloria began reading the spell from the strange and mystical book, but the bourbon muddled her tongue. The words clumped together, slithered across the page, slipping out of focus like wet ink. Some syllables came out slurred, others skipped entirely. Still, she pushed through, wobbling through the Latin with determination. The spell was cast—but all wrong.

The candle flames surged suddenly, flaring a brilliant green. Pages in the book flipped back and forth violently, as if caught in a storm. Then, the goat hide binding began to bleed.

"Uh… oops," Gloria muttered, her eyes wide.

Ed, who had been half-lulled by the bourbon and Gloria's unexpected lingerie, blinked. He'd never heard a poem like that, and he sure as hell hadn't seen a book bleed before. His libido vanished. Something churned in his gut—a weird craving—earthy, wet... freshly dug grub worm?

That was the last thought Ed Jenkins would ever have with a human brain.

The candles hissed, sending up coils of green smoke. Gloria dove behind the couch, flinging the bleeding book away from her. When the smoke cleared, the room was quiet—eerily quiet.

Cautiously, Gloria stood, brushing her hair out of her face. The everburn candles still cast a flickering green glow across the living room. On the couch, where Ed had been sitting, was now... a chicken.

Not just any chicken. This one had a confused, googly-eyed stare. That same dumb look Ed gave her when she changed the channel during his football games.

"E-Ed?" she said, half laughing. "Is that you?"

The chicken ruffled its bright yellow feathers, hopped down from the couch, and began pecking curiously at the spilled bourbon on the floor.

"Ed," Gloria said, laughing louder now. "You dumb old cock."

***

Two weeks had gone by, and Gloria was feeling mighty fine. No yelling. No cheap beer breath in her face. No fighting for the remote. She made all the decisions now—when to wake, when to sleep, what to watch, and how much to spend. Life was peaceful.

Out back, Ed—the chicken—pecked at the dirt, chased beetles, and sipped from an old dog bowl filled with water and stale Coors. Gloria tossed him leftover cornmeal biscuits and the occasional grub from her garden. She figured it was poetic, in a weird, twisted way.

But that peace didn't last long.

Piggly Wiggly, never the sentimental sort, filed a missing person report. Apparently, Ed was too valuable a manager to just up and vanish. The regional director—some smug little man Ed used to curse over Sunday meatloaf—put the heat on local police.

When the knock came at her door, Gloria was ready.

"Oh no, officer," she said, dabbing at dry eyes with a tissue. "Boo Hoo. My dear ol 'Ed ran off with a stripper named Daisy. Real young. Crazy pink hair, wore thigh-high boots. Just Ed's type."

The cops didn't bite.

They kept showing up. Asking more questions. Peeking in cabinets. Poking around the backyard. One noticed the strange bundles of herbs hanging in her kitchen. Another raised an eyebrow at the circle of candles and salt under the coffee table.

"Wife doesn't seem too tore up," one officer murmured.

"She's hiding something," another said.

Gloria could feel it—her alibi was coming apart at the seams. So she made a few calls.

First, to Mrs. Stevens, her nosy neighbor and occasional friend. Gloria asked her to speak on her behalf.

"Oh yes, officers," Mrs. Stevens said, puffing on a menthol cigarette and adjusting her housecoat. "Ed was always down at them gentlemen's clubs. Leaving poor Gloria all alone. You could hear them arguing half the night. I never saw bruises, but a woman learns to cover things up, you know."

The cops listened, but Mrs. Stevens was already on their watch list. She'd called in more complaints than the entire HOA—dogs barking, bushes growing too high, kids with sidewalk chalk. Still, her testimony gave Gloria a little breathing room.

That is, until Detective Harlan called.

"Ma'am, mind if we stop by tomorrow?" he asked. "One final statement before we close out the file."

Gloria hung up, heart pounding. Tomorrow.

She panicked. What if the spell wore off? What if Ed turned back into himself mid-peck, right in front of the cops? What if they tested the blood from under the couch or dug up the compost heap where she dumped the spell book? What if they took Ed the chicken into custody?

She didn't want to imagine the mugshot.

Then it struck her—bright and hot, like lightning in her chest.

That night, under the full moon, Gloria walked out back, grabbed Ed by the feet like Pawpaw used to, and with one swift motion, wrung his skinny neck. He didn't even squawk. She plucked him, cleaned him, breaded him with seasoned flour, and dropped him into a cast iron skillet full of hot oil. Golden and crispy. Just the way Ed liked it.

She made mashed potatoes, whipped with cream and butter. Baked cornbread from scratch. Even opened a jar of homemade pickles.

Detectives Harlan and Snipes arrived right on time.

"Smells real good in here," Harlan said, eyeing the plates.

"Family recipe," Gloria beamed. "From way down in Opelousas."

Snipes chewed thoughtfully. "Is this chicken?"

"Of course," Gloria smiled sweetly. "What else would it be?"

They never found Ed. The file remained open, but interest dwindled. Gloria, with a little coaxing from Mrs. Stevens and a few forged text messages, convinced the life insurance company that he'd skipped town for good. The payout wasn't huge, but it was enough to pay off the house and keep the lights on.

She started a little Etsy shop selling charms, bracelets, and "authentic Southern amulets." Nothing flashy. Just enough to keep her busy.

Then she met Carl—the soft-spoken widower who moved into Mr. Halvorson's old place two doors down. Carl didn't drink. Didn't smoke. Didn't even have a working television. He liked books, jazz records, and quiet walks.

Gloria thought that sounded just fine.

She adopted a black cat, named it Ed—just for fun.

Sometimes, when she made fried chicken for Carl, the cat would hop up on the counter, stare at the plate with wide, googly eyes, and twitch like it remembered something.

Gloria would look at him and smile.

"Not tonight, Ed. You already had your turn."

PART II

Reflections

Break Down on CR 1150

It wasn't the kind of county road you wanted to break down on. It was the kind of road you avoided turning onto in the first place.

CR 1150 sat at the edge of two counties—half the sign belonged in one, most of the road in the other. If you weren't looking for it, you'd never see it. And even when you *were* looking, you could still miss it.

No one lived along CR 1150. It just cut through a rough, wild patch of land—so overgrown and crooked, you'd swear it was cursed. Even in the daylight, it looked like something wanted you to turn around.

The oil-top road narrowed fast under a canopy of trees, the branches gnarled and dark like long fingers stretching across to grab your vehicle—or maybe *you.*

The day I decided to take that shortcut… it wasn't a bad day. Not at first. But then my truck decided it was the *perfect* time to break down.

I know, dear reader—how convenient, right? A little *too* on-the-nose? Well, maybe. But I wouldn't be telling you this if it wasn't worth hearing, would I?

I turned onto CR 1150 that late afternoon, planning to cross over between the county lines. I was headed to a small town parallel to mine. I had two choices:

take the main highway—several turns, maybe forty minutes—or cut across 1150 and shave it down to fifteen.

That's a major time save. I figure you'd have made the same call.

I was running a little fast for a road like that—forty, maybe forty-five—but I was determined to cruise through and later brag, "Took 1150. Didn't see a damn thing. Nothing happened."

And really, it wasn't a bad road at first. The tree cover kept it cool. When it's pushing ninety-nine degrees and your truck's A/C only coughs out lukewarm air, shade is a godsend. I had the windows down. The breeze rolled through the cab. Music low, tires humming.

I made it about two and a half miles in—right at the halfway mark—when the truck coughed and died. No sputter, no warning. Just… stopped.

Gas wasn't the issue. I had three-quarters in the tank. Never had problems with the truck before—it wasn't new, but it sure as hell wasn't old enough to die like that.

Oil pressure: fine. Battery voltage: normal.

I coasted to a slow stop, shifted into park, and turned the key.

The starter spun.

Spin… spin… spin.

No catch. No ignition. No sputter.

It was like the spark was gone.

I popped the hood, climbed out, opened it up. Everything looked clean. Cables secure. Connectors tight. No leaks, no smoke. Just the same engine I'd left town with.

I stood there, staring down at the engine, trying to figure out why my reliable truck had suddenly decided to quit being reliable. That's when it hit me—it was quiet. *Unnervingly* quiet.

With all the trees around, the overgrowth, and the open pastures beyond them, you'd expect to hear something. Birds. Cows. Pigs. Even bugs. But there was nothing.

Just the faint ticking from the engine cooling down, and the sound of my boots shifting in the road.

No breeze, either. Still shady, and cooler than the sun at least—I was thankful for that. But it was the kind of heat that clings, like the air was holding its breath. That kind of stillness always makes you feel like you're being watched.

Welp. So much for my fifteen-minute shortcut. Broke down on old CR 1150. No bragging now.

I dropped the tailgate and sat, trying to figure out my next move. I was smack in the middle—halfway between the highway I came from and the one I was heading toward.

Then it hit me: *Duh.* I hopped down, walked around to the driver's side, and grabbed my phone from the center console. I'd call my good buddy and neighbor Rick—see if he could come give me a jump, or maybe a tow, or just a ride home.

Better than sitting here sweating and wondering why this road was so damn lifeless.

I swiped open the screen and tapped Rick's name. Waited.

Nothing.

No ring. No static. Just... nothing.

I toggled Wi-Fi and Bluetooth off, thinking maybe that was messing with the signal. Walked back behind the truck and over toward the shallow ditch on the roadside, holding the phone up like an idiot trying to catch a bar or two. Still nothing.

Not even SOS.

The phone had a good charge—93%. Just no service.

I sighed. Looked down the road, both directions. Felt heavier than I expected.

Looked like I was walking.

I decided to go back the way I came. At least I knew what lay that direction. And it wasn't too far—maybe a few miles back to the main highway, and from there I could hitch or flag someone down.

I set off east, back toward the highway.

Only sounds were my own breath and my boots hitting the cracked pavement. My steps echoed off the tree line like I was walking inside a tunnel.

I remembered there were no homes between here and the highway—no driveways, no side roads, nothing. Just trees, brush, and a whole lot of nothing.

Even if someone *did* live out here, what were the odds they had a landline anymore?

I checked my phone again, hoping for even a flicker of signal. Still nothing. Worse, the charge had dropped to fifty percent. I climbed back into the cab and started digging through the glovebox, center console, under the seat—anywhere a charging cable might be hiding. But this was a short trip, a quick out-and-back. Just as I figured, no cable.

Great. Now I'd end up with a dead phone and no way to call for help.

I powered it off to conserve what little juice was left. Then I got an idea—something out of Hansel and Gretel. I'd leave little reminders behind me, markers to prove which way I was going. That way, if I ended up back at the truck again, I'd know for certain if something was wrong… beyond the obvious.

I gathered a handful of small stones from the ditch and headed out once more, this time going the direction I *thought* was west—toward my original destination. Every fifty or seventy yards, I'd drop one in the middle of the road and draw a circle around it with the toe of my boot. It slowed me down, but it gave me a strange sense of control.

About thirty minutes into the walk, I noticed something off. A circle. One of mine. But the rock that had been inside it was missing.

At first, I thought maybe I just forgot to place it. Then I saw another one—same circle, no rock. Then another.

Someone, or *something*, was following behind me. Watching. Messing with my markers. That chill returned to the pit of my stomach, heavier this time. I wasn't alone out here on CR 1150.

Then I saw the hill again. Same gentle rise, same leaning trees. Same dread curling in my gut.

I reached the top and froze.

There it was…my truck. Again. This time I was behind it. But something was different. The tailgate and hood were both *closed*, and the driver's side door hung open like a gaping mouth.

Someone had been in it.

My heart thudded in my throat. I broke into a run, shouting as I neared, "Hey! Get the hell away from my truck!"

But no one answered.

When I got there, the cab was empty. The truck looked just as I left it—except for the door, the hood, and the tailgate. I couldn't remember leaving the door open. I didn't think I had.

That's when the doubt crept in.

Was I remembering it wrong? Had I walked in a circle again? Were the rocks ever there to begin with?

Things were changing. Directions. Landmarks. Even *my own memories.*

It felt like I was trapped in a walking nightmare, looping over and over, and each time reality twisted a little further out of shape.

And I had no idea how to wake up.

The sun was now much lower in the sky than when I last set out. I pulled out my phone, powered it on, and waited. When the screen finally lit up, I saw that my thirty-minute hike had somehow eaten up two full hours. It was as if time moved faster every time I left the truck.

If I tried again to find the highway, I'd end up walking in the dark.

That fear began to settle in—cold and creeping. Fear of being stranded out here when night fell. Fear of what might be watching me from the trees. Fear that I might not make it out of this place at all.

I turned the phone off again to save what little charge remained and stuffed it back in my pocket.

One more walk. That was the plan. One more pass down the road, carefully placing markers. Then I'd double back and hide, watch to see if anyone—or anything—was tampering with them.

This time, I walked in the *opposite* direction, still placing my markers—rocks inside circles—right down the center of the road. Fifty to seventy yards apart. Just like before.

After laying down ten markers, I slipped off into a patch of trees, crouching low and waiting to see who was behind me.

Fifteen minutes passed. Nothing.

No one came down the road. No one stole the rocks. The forest didn't even move. The stillness felt heavier than before.

I stood and continued walking. Another twenty minutes, ten more markers, and then I saw it—that familiar rise in the road.

I already knew what I'd see before I got to the top.

Sure enough, as I crested the hill, there it was again—my truck. Hood down. Tailgate closed. Driver's door hanging open.

But this time, something was different.

About 200 yards beyond the truck, just at the edge of the road's vanishing point, I saw it.

A figure.

Crouched low in the shadows. Barely visible in the dying light.

The sun had already slipped behind the trees, and by my guess, it had to be near 8:30. I figured I'd lost another hour—maybe more—with this last walk and the time spent hiding.

The figure slowly stood. It didn't look toward me. Just stared at the road, like it was trying to remember something. Or waiting.

"Hey!" I shouted, my voice cracking in my dry throat. "Hey! You there! Can you help me?"

No response.

I shouted again. Louder.

Still nothing.

Then, slowly, the figure began to walk—further down the road, away from me, out into the dark.

I tried to run after it, but I was exhausted. The heat, the walking, the dehydration—I hadn't had anything to drink since that last glass of tea before I left the house.

Dang, I should've brought water. Even warm would've helped.

I stumbled back to the truck, dropped the tailgate, and collapsed in the bed.

Above me, the twisted limbs of the trees clawed at the darkening sky. No sounds to be heard, quiet. Too quiet.

I stared up and wondered what I'd gotten myself into.

Why *this* road?

Why did I have to take a damn shortcut?

I could've been there and back by now. But no. I had to try and shave twenty minutes off the trip.

Dumb. Dumb. Dumb.

I laid in the bed of the truck a bit longer—just long enough to try and get my head clear. It was getting dark. I couldn't see anything around me or anything in front of me.

My thought was to walk across the open land, not take the road. It looked clear past the trees, and maybe—just maybe—the moon would give enough light.

I got back on my feet, stepped onto the road, then pushed through the trees and into the open land just beyond the tree line. There was a moon. It wasn't bright, but my eyes adjusted as I moved farther into the dim light beyond the trees.

I didn't know if I was heading north or south. Just

that I was walking away from the truck.

The land was tricky—peppered with small holes, tall grass, the occasional tree trunk in my path. Luckily, no animals… at least none I could see.

After about thirty minutes, I saw it: a light in the distance.

A wave of relief hit me like cold water. Maybe the nightmare was almost over. I felt lighter, stronger, and picked up my pace.

As I got closer, I saw the outline of trees in front of the light—and then I saw a vehicle. Someone stood beside it, unmoving.

I couldn't tell what they were doing, but it wasn't a house. It was a truck.

And then it hit me. It was my truck. And someone was standing next to it.

I started walking faster. "Hey!" I shouted. "Get away from my truck! Get away from there!"

The figure didn't look up. By the time I reached the tree line, they were already walking away—down the road, into the dark.

The truck door was open. The dome light was on.

I ran to the door and looked around. On the

driver's seat was a sheet of paper. Looked like it had been torn from the back of the truck owner's manual.

Scrawled in thick, shaky handwriting—my handwriting—was a message:

"To whoever finds this note: This is my truck. My name and info are in the glovebox. I've been stuck here for days and can't seem to find a way out. I don't know how much longer I can last. I'll be walking the road until I'm found… or dead."

It hit me like a punch to the gut. I couldn't breathe. That note was mine. That was my handwriting. That was my truck.

And the person I saw walking away? That had to be me.

I yanked my phone out of my pocket and powered it up. No bars—but it came on.

I checked the time. Almost 11 PM. Two days later.

I stared at the screen, my heart racing. I'd been missing for two days?

Leaving the road… somehow it made time *move faster*. Or maybe… I don't know. There were too many questions.

But the one that rattled the loudest in my skull was

this:

If I just saw myself… how far in the future was that version of me?

And how many more of me are out there, walking that same stretch of road?

I never believed the stories told by old-timers and others who warned never to take CR 1150. They all said it was a cursed road, though no one agreed on why. Some claimed the crew who paved the old dirt path were never seen again—that they still haunt the road, trapping those who dare travel it. Others said a bad spirit lived in the land itself, a tale passed down by the local Indigenous people.

Me? I figured it was nothing more than old wives' tales. But now that I'm stuck in the middle of whatever's got me trapped here, I don't think that anymore. It's different when you're living it.

My throat was parched. I would've killed for any kind of water. Two days without it felt like a week. I decided to just sit in the truck cab. My body was done—physically and mentally. Sleep seemed like the best choice. Maybe someone else would come down the road and find me, and we could figure a way out together.

I closed the driver's door and stretched out across

the seats and console. It wasn't comfortable, but I felt better lying inside than out in the open.

I woke up to morning sunlight pouring through the side window. It was already getting hot inside the cab. I sat up, looked around, and opened the driver's door. Outside was warm, but not as stifling.

My mouth felt like I'd tried to chew a bag of cotton—dry, no spit. I climbed out, and my back instantly protested the way I'd slept. Stretching only made it worse.

On the road, I could see several markers. Some were clearly mine—a rock placed in a crudely drawn circle. But others weren't. Squares with rocks, pyramids with two stones, diamonds with nothing inside. I had no idea where those came from… or *who* had made them.

Maybe it was the other me. Maybe *others*—many versions of me—were trapped here too. The only thing my mind could picture was an old Twilight Zone episode. I half-expected Rod Serling to walk out from behind a tree:

"Imagine, if you will… a man stuck on a cursed road, doomed to relive many versions of himself—never to escape, never to die."

I chuckled at the thought, but it still sent a chill

down my spine.

I looked down the road, past the truck, into the shadows ahead—but saw nothing. I turned and looked in the direction I had just walked from. Still nothing.

I tried to respond, even though I couldn't see anyone. "Hello...?" I waited, expecting a reply, but none came.

It was oddly disappointing—not getting one. Even if it had been *me*.

There were no new notes, no signs that anyone else had been in the truck. I pulled out the note I'd found last night, just to confirm it was real. I unfolded it and reread the words. Nothing had changed—same handwriting, same message. I refolded it and stuffed it back into my pocket.

Then I pulled out my phone and tried to power it up. The screen flickered to life, the battery at 1%—and then it died. That was it. No more phone. My last hope to call someone, *anyone*, was gone. I tossed it down into the seat.

I didn't even get a chance to see the time or date.

My connection to reality—*to normalcy*—was fading fast now. I looked up at the branches overhead. The gaps between them seemed to be shrinking right before my eyes. I tried to glimpse the sun, to get some sense of time, but there was no way to tell where it was in the sky.

I couldn't say for sure, but it felt like time was speeding up. I had no idea how long I'd been asleep, or how long I'd been walking. Surely someone would report me missing eventually—my neighbor, my boss... someone.

That kind of thinking only raised my anxiety.

How was I going to survive with no water, no food, no meds, no gear—and no way out?

I leaned against the truck, rubbing my forehead. I was long past the point of regretting taking the shortcut. There was no sense reliving that choice. What was done was done.

I needed to think of a way out.

I considered climbing one of the trees, but the way they'd grown—closing in tighter with each passing hour—I'd never get beyond the lower branches. I could try to burn it all down, but that would kill me too. The trees and limbs would fall inward, and I'd be buried with the truck.

What else could I do?

Eventually, I decided I'd walk the road again—back in the direction I'd come from. If nothing else, it would help me think. Keep me from going numb.

So I started walking, back up the small rise and down the other side, watching my feet as I went. I kicked at the rocks and stones—like I had any use for them now.

I knew the road.

I knew where I'd end up.

The Tacoma would be there, always in the same place, whether facing this way or that.

Almost thirty minutes later, I walked up the familiar rise and looked down the other side. The truck sat just as I'd left it—only a little more worn-looking than before. I slowly made my way down, almost counting my steps as I walked.

I looked inside the cab, hoping for something—a new note, a working phone, water—anything new. But there were no changes. Not even a sign of the other me's.

The sun must be getting lower now. The shadows were building, and the light was starting to fade.

I had nothing else to do. And if this is my penance for something, then fine—I'd just keep walking. Maybe one of these times, it'll let me out. Or maybe I'll walk this road forever.

As I stepped in front of the truck, I saw a pair of

shoes—my shoes.

I turned.

There I was, sitting with my back against the front bumper.

The biggest shock—next to seeing myself not in a reflection—was that the other me was dead.

I couldn't tell how long he'd been gone, but judging by the pale skin and the fixed, glassy eyes staring into nothing, it had been a while. I only wished I could've spoken to him. Maybe he knew something. But it didn't look like he'd found a way out either—or he wouldn't be sitting there, dead, in front of me.

His clothes were identical to mine. Everything the same, down to the socks. No injuries. No obvious cause of death.

It's a strange sensation, seeing yourself dead when you're not actually dead. Like an out-of-body experience—but without ever leaving your body.

This was starting to feel more like a dream. A bad one.

I wasn't thrilled about it, but I checked his pockets for notes, tools—anything I might be able to use. Nothing.

I reached over and gently closed his eyes.

A sense of pity washed over me. He must've been stuck here too long. Died without ever seeing another soul.

I lifted him—me—and placed him in the back of the truck. The whole thing felt like cradling a dead twin. I can't explain the feeling unless you've had one. Then maybe you'd understand.

I had no way of covering him. So I took off my shirt—the one soaked in sweat and dust, the one I'd worn through all of this—and laid it gently over his chest.

It felt right. Like a burial, even without the ground.

I stared at him—at myself—for a long time. And the longer I stood there, the more I realized something:

This one… he looked like the version of me who stopped trying. The one who gave up when things got hard. Who held onto anger like it was some sort of fuel, but it never took him anywhere.

Maybe that's what died.

Maybe that's what I needed to let die.

I don't know if this loop is some kind of punishment, or test, or just a cosmic joke—but if it's feeding off who I used to be, then maybe letting go of that part… maybe that's a start.

I felt—somehow—lighter. Like something inside had released. Like a weight, a mental weight, had just shifted.

I thanked the dead me in the bed of the truck. I hoped he was in a better place, resting easy. I gathered myself, my thoughts, and started walking down the road again.

The shadows were covering the road. It was getting pretty dark—but this time, it didn't bother me as much.

I used the walk to think about myself. The person I've been. I started thinking about the Tacoma. It had been my pride and joy since I got it. I took care of that truck like a parent to a child. I spared nothing for it.

But at the same time—I wouldn't loan it to anyone. Wouldn't carry anything for anyone. It was disheartening to see it becoming worn, just sitting there.

I looked up. The branches covering the road were thinner now. I could see bits of the moon overhead, shining through the gaps. That was new. Instead of closing in, it was now opening up.

Something was changing. For the better.

I couldn't see it, but I could feel the rise in the road. I got to the top, and in the moonlight, there it was again—my little Tacoma.

Hood closed. Tailgate shut. Doors sealed. Just waiting.

I walked toward it, thinking about the times I should've helped. My neighbors moving. My boss, grinning like a kid, showing off the grill he was so proud of.

I made them rent trucks instead. I helped them, sure—I wasn't that bad. But no one was going to scratch *my* truck.

That—that was selfish.

Would they even file a missing person report for me? I wasn't the best guy, I guess.

I checked on the dead me in the back of the truck—but he was gone.

Was I surprised? Not really.

I was beginning to understand why I was stuck here. Or at least I was starting to *hope* I understood.

I looked into the cab. Nothing there but my dead phone. No notes. No answers.

I continued walking.

Stepped into the darkness. The moonlight was just enough to let my eyes catch the shadows lining the road. No animals. It'd been dead quiet since I broke down.

Maybe a few hundred yards past the truck, I saw someone sitting in the road, near the ditch. It spooked the hell out of me.

I couldn't make out much—until I got closer.

The haircut, the clothes... Too familiar.

It was me again. Another version of me.

"Hello… uh… me?"

No response. Not even a twitch.

I stepped around to the front. It was definitely me. Not surprising.

He had died as well.

His eyes were wide—like he saw something just before he died that surprised him.

That strange, out-of-body, in-body feeling returned. That pity.

I wasn't sure what killed this one either.

I reached down and closed his eyes. Then picked him up—my twin.

He felt heavier than the last one. Odd. Not sure why. Unless he carried more baggage.

I got him into the back of the truck. Gently.

My shirt was still there, the other me gone. I took it and laid it over this one.

I stared at him—at me—trying to guess what he might've seen. Maybe he saw the end coming. And wasn't ready to leave.

The gaps between the branches seemed to expand, letting more moonlight spill onto the road. Same as before, the stress and weight of my situation eased. It didn't feel so final anymore. I could almost see the faint shimmer of a possible end to this trap I was in.

I wasn't sure what might lie ahead—or what part of me was still walking around this place.

I began walking again, heading in the opposite direction this time, hoping to encounter a version of myself that wasn't already dead. I had questions—desperate questions—that maybe another me could answer. At least, that's what I hoped.

As I walked, more of the road revealed itself under the pale moonlight. The markers I'd once seen had changed. My circle of rocks was still there. But the pyramid of two stones—left by another version of me—remained, while the others had vanished. As if they'd never existed.

I still wasn't quite sure what this place was—or why different versions of me were trapped here—but I had my suspicions.

Just like before, about thirty minutes into my "escape," I came upon the familiar rise in the road. I crested the hill and there—where it always was—sat the Tacoma. The paint looked duller now, the tires beginning to crack.

I approached slowly, from the rear. The other me, the one I had placed gently in the bed, was gone. Just like the one before him. Only my shirt remained.

I didn't want to dwell on how or why they vanished. I focused instead on the living—the version of me I still hoped to find.

I peered into the cab. No changes. Just more wear and tear. The seats, the console, the dash—fading, cracking, like the whole truck was rotting in slow motion.

I circled to the front. No one there.

I kept walking. The darkness slowly gave way to sunlight breaking through the trees. The light was warm on my face, and I let myself enjoy it. Even in this strange place, it brought something close to hope.

I walked on, eyes searching, ears straining.

At one point, I could have sworn I heard a bird chirp in the distance—somewhere beyond the tree line.

The thirst was gone. The fatigue, too.

It felt like I was moving in reverse now—not falling apart, but being rebuilt.

Another thirty minutes elapsed and I was standing at the top of the rise, looking down at the Tacoma — but this time was different. This time, I saw myself. My other self. Standing by the truck, almost like he was waiting for me to arrive.

I waved, but the other me either didn't see it or wasn't in a waving mood. It was strange — I was excited to see another version of me, alive. I had questions. And it didn't even seem to bother me that I was about to meet... myself.

I fast-walked down toward the truck, eyes mostly on the ground but glancing up now and then at the other me. There was no smile. No look of relief. Nothing that mirrored how I felt. This version of me wasn't sharing the moment. He just stared at me with a flat, hard look — and I felt something shift in my stomach.

I stopped at the back of the truck, unsure what to

say or do. I'd never met myself before. This version knew everything I knew… maybe more.

"Uh, hello... me. You. Sorry, I'm kinda new to this." I gave a half-smile, unsure if we were supposed to shake hands or avoid all contact in case the universe collapsed.

This version looked hard. Worn. Not a pleasant person, really. He stared straight at me.

"You know," he said, "you and I are the last two left. And I'm sure you realize by now — only one of us gets out of here."

Somehow I figured as much. But I didn't want to believe it. Still, I was the original. At least, I thought I was.

"So," I asked, "what version of me are you? Do you know who the other versions were?"

The other me rolled his eyes and shook his head. "Are you the simpleton of us? I didn't think there was one, but as I live and breathe, here you are."

I blinked. That was a jab — a straight insult, really. Maybe he didn't realize *I* was the real one. Or maybe I was starting to wonder myself.

"So if you're so sure," I said, trying to keep my voice steady, "then answer this — why are they dead, and not you?"

He gave a slow, sly grin. I'd seen that grin before. In mirrors. In pictures. "Look," he said, "I'm the real one. The original. You? You're just a sliver — a part that can be cut away like the others."

He stepped closer, voice low but full of disdain. "You wanna know who they were? One was dead weight. Always quitting when things got tough. First sign of stress, and he folded. It wasn't hard — this place sucked him dry. He practically gave up."

He paused, watching me absorb it.

"The other? A narcissist. Thought he was top dog. Always looking out for number one. Couldn't carry his own baggage, let alone anyone else's. Pretender. And now he's gone, too."

I said nothing. My stomach churned.

"That just leaves us," he continued. "And since I'm the only real one, it means *you* have to go. I'm getting out of this holding cell. I'm going back."

He leaned in, eyes cold. "And you — you're gonna quit. Just like they did."

The version of me standing before me—I knew he wasn't the real me. He seemed one-dimensional. From his speech, his arrogance, his smug self-assurance, I could tell. He was the narcissist. The self-centered me.

The other version—the one I'd found dead earlier—he was probably guilt. Or maybe timidity. Either way, neither would've stood a chance against this one. This version had likely bullied them into surrender. Manipulated them. Absorbed them. He was the worst of me.

And I knew him well.

I'd always thought I was better than most. Smarter. More likable. The best at being the best. But that belief—this person—was why I'd never kept a girlfriend for long. Why friendships fizzled. Why I always convinced myself I didn't need anyone. Because I was better. Or so I told myself.

Now, standing here on County Road 1150, staring into that hollow reflection, I realized this place wasn't purgatory. It wasn't punishment either. It was a mirror. A trap, maybe—but one meant to show a person who they really are. And, if they're lucky, maybe learn from it. Otherwise, they'd be stuck here forever, blind to their own reflection.

I stepped toward him.

He stiffened—defensive, ready to fight. But I saw something in his eyes. Fear. Just a flicker of it.

"I'm sorry we ended up like this," I said. "But we don't need to be king of the world. We don't need to prove anything. We just need to be… us. Me. And stop faking it."

I reached out and hugged him. At first, he didn't move. Then slowly, I felt him hug me back. And just like that, he dissolved—absorbed back into me. I was the only one left.

The weight, all the time I'd spent in this place, lifted.

My eyes fluttered open. Sunlight poured through the side window of my truck. I was reclined in the driver's seat. I looked around. Still in the Tacoma. Still on the side of County Road 1150.

The window was down. I could hear birds chirping. Bugs zipping past. The scent of dust and summer grass filled the cab. I sat up slowly. My head was foggy, but everything looked… normal. The paint on the truck wasn't faded. The tires weren't cracked. The seat and dash looked like they always had. I reached for my phone on the passenger seat—still there. Still on. Battery at 93%.

Had I blacked out while driving? Had I dreamed all of it?

I checked the date and time.

Only fifteen minutes had passed since I left home.

I turned the key and the Tacoma fired up on the first try. I let out a slow breath. Just a dream… I told myself.

Until I felt something in my shirt pocket.

A folded piece of paper. Torn from the truck's owner's manual. I opened it. My handwriting.

It said only one thing:

"I found my way out."

And for the first time in a long time, I believed it.

Master of the Needle

The needle had slept for years, buried in a box of someone else's life. Dust and rust dulled its brass handle, but beneath the tarnish it still remembered the hum of skin, the rhythm of heartbeat. All it needed was a hand to wake it.

Robyn Little almost didn't stop at the swap meet. She was running late, helmet still warm from the ride, the red Ninja ticking softly behind her as it cooled in the October sun. But she'd seen a post about an old tattoo kit for sale - "vintage stuff, from a dead guy's shop", and curiosity was a hard thing to ignore when you were continuing to build your name in the tattoo world.

The seller was a middle-aged woman with nicotine-stained fingers and a folding table covered in garage leftovers. She didn't know much about what she was selling. "Belonged to my brother," she said, squinting against the light. "He was into tattoos. Died a while back. Heart thing, I think. These were just in his stuff."

Robyn sifted through a cracked plastic case filled with mismatched coils, bent armatures, and rusted screws. The brass needle assembly lay at the bottom, wrapped in an old paper towel, spotted dark from age. When she lifted it, the sunlight caught it just right, and for a moment, she could have sworn it gleamed.

"Ten bucks," the woman said. "You want it, take it."

Robyn smiled, handed her a crumpled bill, and tucked the thing carefully into her backpack. It was heavy, older than anything she'd used before, but it had character. That night, back at her studio, she cleaned it, replaced the wiring, and set it beside her machine. The brass looked brighter already.

Outside, the wind pressed softly against the windows. Inside, under the dim studio light, the needle waited… patient, hungry, and shining just a little more than it had that morning.

The next morning, the studio smelled of disinfectant and burnt coffee. The walls still hummed with the sound of last night's machines cooling in their cases.

Dave pushed through the door, all grin and swagger. "Hey, Robyn - you got my new tat ready to be laid on some skin?" he said, leaning on the counter like he owned the place.

Robyn looked up from her station in the back. "Give me a few, Dave. Just about ready. Go ahead and take a seat by my chair."

She already had the stencil drawn, clean and precise - a coiled dragon wrapping around a compass rose, something he'd wanted for months. She was more excited than she wanted to admit. The new needle sat in its pouch beside her setup tray, gleaming faintly through the plastic. Under the studio lights, it seemed brighter than it had last night - newer somehow.

Robyn snapped on a pair of black gloves, fitted the needle to her machine, and covered it with an antiseptic wrap. "Let's do this thing, shall we?"

Dave glanced at the design when she laid it beside his arm. "That's sick."

"It's going to fit perfectly with the rest," Robyn said, admiring the lines of his older work - all hers. Her reputation was riding on this piece.

She dipped the needle into the black ink cup and started the outline. The hum of the gun was lower than usual, steadier. The needle glided across his skin as if it already knew the pattern.

Dave flinched once, then relaxed. "That's weird. Doesn't even sting."

Robyn smiled, wiping away the excess ink. The wipe came away clean. No ink. No blood.

She frowned, swiped again - nothing. The skin was smooth, dry, and perfect. The black lines sank instantly into place, crisp and deep, like they'd always been there.

This needle's magic, she thought, watching the dragon come alive beneath her hand.

Behind her, the fluorescent light flickered once. The hum of the machine deepened, almost like a purr.

"All done." Robyn rolled her stool back and looked over the new tattoo on Dave's arm. It was flawless - easily the best black-and-gray work she'd ever done. The dragon didn't just sit on the skin; it seemed to *hover* above it, like heat off a blacktop - there and not there at all. The shading was perfect, so real she almost expected it to move.

Dave's arm twitched, and for half a second the dragon *stretched*, its shadow spilling wider than his arm should allow.

Robyn jumped.

Dave laughed loud enough to echo in the small studio. "Gotcha, huh? So good you thought it was actually moving."

Robyn let out a shaky laugh and shook her head. "Yeah, you got me, Dave."

She stood, pulling a fresh wrap from the counter, but couldn't help glancing back. The dragon's eyes seemed to follow her now - a trick of the light, she told herself. She'd done such clean detail work that her mind was playing games.

She wiped the piece with antiseptic and covered it with wrap. "You know the routine," she said. "Keep it clean, lotion twice a day, no scratching."

Dave rubbed the bandaged arm. "Man, it itches something fierce. No pain, though. Not even a tingle."

"That's good," Robyn said, though part of her wondered why there hadn't been *any* bleeding.

He handed her a few folded bills, tucking his wallet back into his jeans. "Fastest one yet. Killer tat, Robyn. I'll be back for the next one." He grinned, zipped up his leather jacket, and gave her a wink before stepping outside into the cool October sunlight.

She watched through the front window as he stood outside the studio, match-light flickering across his grin, smoke curling up into the October sunlight - the kind of day that fooled you into thinking everything was fine.

Robyn turned back to her station, humming absently as she began cleaning. She wiped down the table, the chair, the floor - each motion automatic after years of repetition. When she reached for the tattoo gun, she froze.

The needle was spotless. No blood. No ink. Not even a stain on the antiseptic wrap. The brass head gleamed brighter than before - too bright, like it had been waiting.

She frowned, tilting it in her hand. It almost seemed to pulse when she breathed.

Robyn set it back down carefully. The hum of the fluorescent lights deepened again, just for a moment. Then, silence.

***

Robyn sat back in her chair, rolling her shoulders until they popped. The hum of the studio's neon sign leaked through the half-closed door. She had at least an hour before her next client. She pulled open the drawer beside her station and sifted through a pile of old tattoo magazines, their covers curling at the edges, pages soft and yellowed from years of ink-stained fingers. One caught her eye - *Inked Visions, March '97.* She flipped through it absently, the smell of dust and rubbing alcohol mixing in the air.

Halfway through, past a full-page ad for a new line of sterilized inks, was a short article. *"Master of the Needle: The Life and Legacy of Karl Mertens."* The story told of a tattoo artist whose work was the stuff of folklore - designs said to move beneath the skin, muscles shifting as if the creatures breathed. Mertens claimed the secret was his machine and a "special brass needle" he'd found in Germany while serving overseas.

Some of his clients swore the tattoos seemed to walk off the skin.

There was a small photo - a grainy shot of Mertens, smiling beside his tattoo gun and some old sketches. Robyn leaned in. Her pulse gave a single, quiet thud. The machine looked almost identical to the one she'd bought at the swap meet.

After her last consultation of the night, Robyn locked up the studio and rode home through the cool October air. The hum of her bike followed her all the way to her apartment - a sound that lingered even after she shut the engine off. She showered, poured herself half a glass of wine, and collapsed into bed, the day still buzzing under her skin.

That night she dreamed of Dave, and the dragon.

In the dream, the studio lights were brighter than usual, white and humming, and she was finishing his tattoo. The shading was perfect, the dragon's wings stretched wide across his forearm. But when she reached for a cloth to wipe away the excess ink, the dragon was gone. All that remained was the compass rose - floating there, alone, as if the rest had slipped away.

She glanced up his arm - empty skin. "Hey, killer tat, Robyn," Dave said, grinning.

Then his grin broke. His eyes widened. He clawed at his chest, tearing at his shirt. "Dave?" she said, reaching for him.

He crumpled, gasping. She dropped beside him, pressing down on his sternum, ready to start CPR - until his mouth opened wider than it should have.

Something moved inside.

The dragon - black and gray, slick as oil - uncoiled from his throat. It slid free, tongue to chin to floor, then lifted, wings unfurling, beating the air with a whisper. Its eyes found hers - and blinked.

Robyn gasped and sat up in bed. Her hand shot out toward the empty air, catching nothing but the blue pulse of her phone's notification light.

The next morning, Robyn sat at her kitchen table, one hand around her mug of coffee, the other scrolling through her phone. Sunlight cut through the blinds, slicing the room into narrow gold and shadowed stripes.

Her thumb hovered over the glowing notification - a message from Mia, one of her regulars. *Hey, did you hear about Dave?*

Robyn blinked, trying to shake off the last fragments of the dream - the flapping wings, the oily scales. She took another sip of coffee before opening the message.

He was found last night. They think it was his heart. EMS said he didn't make it.

She stared at the words until they blurred. Dave. Gone.

Her mind flashed to his grin in the studio yesterday, his voice - *"Killer tat, Robyn."* Her stomach turned. She set the mug down too fast, coffee sloshing over her fingers.

She wiped her hand with a dish towel, eyes drifting to the faint dark smudge along her knuckle. At first she thought it was coffee - but when she rubbed it, the spot smeared gray, like ink.

She froze. Her workstation had been spotless when she left last night. She always cleaned everything, every time.

The image of the dragon slithering from Dave's mouth shot through her mind, so vivid it made her breath catch.

"No," she whispered. "Just a dream."

The towel in her hand slipped to the counter. She stood there for a long time, the hum of her refrigerator the only sound in the room, the taste of bitter coffee thick on her tongue.

Then, from somewhere behind her - faint, almost imagined - came a soft metallic *ping*. Like a needle, dropped onto tile.

Robyn showered, dressed, and rode back to the studio. The dream was already fading, dissolving under the day's list of clients, emails, and prep work. She parked the Ninja out back and walked to the rear door, fishing her keys from her pocket. Her hand stopped mid-reach.

A gray smear ringed the doorknob - a thin, swirling line, like something had slithered around it and disappeared into the keyhole. She leaned closer. The pattern almost looked deliberate.

Robyn ran her thumb across it. The mark came away easily, smudging across her skin. Ink.

She wiped her thumb on her jeans, unlocked the door, and stepped inside.

Everything looked the same. The faint scent of lemon disinfectant lingered in the air. Machines silent. Counters clean. The steady buzz of the old mini-fridge in the back room filled the space.

She set her helmet on her workstation, moving through her routine: lights, signs, and speakers. The studio hummed to life. Ronnie James Dio's voice cracked through the quiet, belting out *"the dragons and the children..."*

Robyn smiled faintly at the coincidence, a brief thought of Dave passed across her mind, then she turned toward her station.

The smile froze.

Her breath caught halfway up her throat as her eyes locked on the desk. The stencil she'd used for Dave's tattoo - the dragon - sat there in the same spot she'd left her helmet.

She hadn't printed that design again. She was sure of it.

And yet, there it was - black and gray lines, the dragon's wings spread wide, its eyes sharp and knowing, as if it were watching.

Robyn picked up the stencil, staring at the dragon's sharp eyes for a long moment before tearing the sheet in half - then again - until it was nothing but confetti in her hands. The scraps fluttered into the trash can beside her workstation.

"Coincidence," she muttered. "I must've missed it last night."

She brushed her palms together and opened her day-timer. A new client was due within the hour. No time for weird dreams or superstitious nonsense.

Robyn pulled out the next design - a black desert scorpion, its tail arched high, a bead of venom poised to fall from the tip. The heavy lines and fine shading made her smile. *Now that* was a tattoo that demanded attention.

She reached for her toolbox, popped the latches, and lifted the tattoo gun from its padded slot. The new brass needle sat in its pouch beside it, glistening like it had just been polished.

Robyn frowned. It wasn't wet, but it didn't look dry either - the surface seemed to breathe light, as if it were flexing beneath the thin plastic.

She tore open the pouch and held the needle up to the studio lights. Perfect. Too perfect.

On instinct, she ran a fingertip along the edge to test its smoothness. The sting came quick. "Damn it," she hissed, jerking her hand back.

A single bead of blood welled up on her fingertip, bright against her skin. It touched the needle - and vanished.

The metal seemed to inhale. The gleam along its length deepened, a pulse of brightness that shimmered once and settled.

For a heartbeat, she thought about throwing it across the room, maybe even grinding it under her boot. But then -

A hum, faint and low, filled her ears. It wasn't the lights or the speakers; it was *inside* the sound of the shop, like the soft vibration of a living thing.

Robyn's shoulders eased. The corner of her mouth twitched, then curled into a grin she didn't quite recognize.

She ran her thumb along the needle's shaft, slow and gentle, the way you'd touch something you loved.

***

Nelly arrived right on time. Younger than most of Robyn's usual clients, but still old enough to sign for herself. During the consultation, she'd been dead-set on the scorpion. Something about her brother, Robyn remembered vaguely - a memorial, maybe.

"You ready for this?" Robyn asked, rolling her stool into place. "Still set on the scorpion?"

"Yep and yep," Nelly said with a nervous smile. "Never got one this big before."

Robyn's grin flickered back. "You'll be fine," she said softly. "You won't feel a thing. I'm sure of it."

She directed Nelly to the reclined lounge chair, the one wrapped in crisp, antiseptic plastic. The stencil went on smooth, the design perfect on the first try. "That's sweet, and deadly," Nelly said, admiring it.

"Let's do this thing." Robyn said dipping the brass needle into the ink. The moment the machine started, the hum in her hand deepened, almost like a purr. The overhead lights brightened, blooming white across the shop.

The first touch of the needle made Nelly flinch.

Then nothing. Her breathing slowed, her shoulders dropped. The needle moved across her thigh with impossible precision, slicing color into skin like it already knew the path.

Each wipe left the surface clean. No blood. No excess ink. Just perfect lines and texture that seemed to shimmer as they dried.

Robyn grinned. The gun wasn't following her hand - her hand was following *it*.

Minutes later, she set the gun down and motioned Nelly toward the mirror.

"Wow," Nelly breathed. "It looks alive… like it could just crawl right off my leg. And that shine on the venom drop - holy hell."

Robyn smiled. "*It's* killer. I'm glad you like it." She laid the gun back on the tray, her fingers brushing the barrel in a slow, affectionate stroke.

She handed Nelly the care instructions and a small tube of lotion. "Twice a day. Don't scratch. It'll heal clean."

"Oh, can I get your number and email?" Robyn added casually. "I like to follow up on new work."

Nelly nodded, scribbled her info, then paused at

the door. "Do they always feel this itchy? Like… like it's moving under my skin?"

Robyn's face stayed calm. "Yeah, they do that sometimes. Perfectly normal."

Nelly laughed awkwardly, waved, and stepped into the bright noon sun. Robyn watched her cross the street toward the Sweet Frog, her gait already a little off - like she was trying not to brush something that wasn't there.

Back in the quiet studio, Robyn cleaned the chair and wiped down the tray. The gun waited, gleaming. She lifted the needle in her gloved hand; it vibrated faintly, humming against her skin.

The brass was brighter now-polished, somehow reborn.

She started to slide the plastic cover back over it, then stopped.

"*It* needs to breathe," she murmured.

She placed it back into its slot in the case, uncovered, humming softly to itself.

At first, Robyn felt a twinge of guilt, small and sharp, the kind that lives just under the ribs. She had the sudden urge to run across the street, find Nelly at the Sweet Frog, tell her to scrub the scorpion off before it decided to crawl.

But then the sound came again - soft, steady. A hum, but more like a purr. It slipped from the toolbox like sounds from under a door.

The noise worked its way into her chest, smoothed the edges off her panic. *There's nothing wrong,* she told herself. It's a tattoo, just ink and skin. A good tattoo. Her best.

"You're right," she said, not realizing she'd spoken out loud until she heard her own voice. "It's fine. It's a good tattoo. She's happy."

She opened the mini-fridge and grabbed a Red Bull. The hiss of the tab sounded too loud in the quiet room. The first swallow hit her throat like sugar and metal. She sat down on the stool and spun once, twice, letting the rush spread through her.

The hum kept going, low and even, somewhere behind her. It didn't stop when she stopped spinning. It matched the pulse in her neck.

Robyn's day passed in a blur of sugar skulls and starbursts, the kind of tattoos that paid the bills but didn't feed the hunger humming under her skin. The hum itself never left the air. No one else seemed to hear it.

By nightfall, she was alone again, half-watching the clock, half-listening to Alice in Chains scream about flies while she ate popcorn from a Styrofoam cup. The magazine slid from her fingers, pages flashing ads and bright ink, until her eyes gave up.

The hum folded into the music. Then the music changed.

She opened her eyes. The heavy metal was gone, replaced by pulsing club beats overhead. Lights strobed red and violet. The shop was gone too - she was in a crowded room, shoulder to shoulder with laughing bodies.

At a table in the corner, three young women raised their glasses. Nelly sat among them, her bandaged thigh crossing and uncrossing. Robyn started toward them, but no one turned their heads; she could move through the crowd like smoke.

Nelly laughed, scratched her leg. A drunk staggered past, spilling something green into her lap. She cursed, stood, and fought her way to the restroom. Robyn followed.

Inside, the lights buzzed and flickered. The smell of vomit and cleaning supplies hung in the air. Nelly ran water over paper towels and pressed them to her shorts, then to the bandage. She stopped. The towel fell.

Her hands tore at the plastic wrap until the skin showed clean. Too clean. The tattoo was gone. Only a wet black dot, the venom drop, shimmered on her thigh.

Nelly's breathing quickened. She clawed at her shirt, at her side. A ripple slid under her skin, moving upward like something swimming. Then stillness. The dot melted into her flesh. Nelly fell to the floor like a crumpled newspaper.

When she looked up again, her eyes were wide, glassy, and wrong.

The first movement came from her right eye - a bulge, then a crack of wet sound as a black scorpion forced itself through, glossy and alive, dragging itself free with its pinchers. It scuttled over her cheek and dropped to the tile with a dry tap.

The bass beat went on. Nobody screamed.

***

The bell over the studio door chimed.

Robyn jerked awake in her chair, popcorn on the floor, an older woman flipping through a yellow book of designs at the counter. The hum in the air hadn't stopped.

Robyn blinked, the dream still sifting through her mind like sand through an hourglass. The older woman at the counter hadn't noticed her jolt awake, or if she had, she was kind enough not to mention it.

"Hello there," the woman said, taking a quick glance at Robyn from the yellow book of designs. Her voice was dry and cracked, a smoker's whisper. "You do walk-ins, right?"

Robyn nodded, her throat tight. "Yeah," she said, clearing it. "Walk-ins are fine." She pushed herself up from the chair, trying to shake off the fog of sleep and the image of the scorpion crawling from Nelly's eye.

The woman smiled faintly as she flipped through the pages. Her nails were dull gray, the color of cooled ash. "Thinking about something simple. Maybe a butterfly, maybe a bird. Haven't made up my mind yet."

Robyn moved behind the counter, her hands working on their own - cleaning wipes, gloves, clip cord, setting up the tray. Muscle memory doing the thinking.

The hum, soft and constant was still there. It lived somewhere under the shop noise, under her skin. She glanced at the toolbox on the table. The lid seemed to quiver ever so slightly.

"You all right, dearie?" the woman asked, her tone light but eyes sharp.

Robyn blinked and forced a smile. "Yeah. Long day, that's all. You decide what you want?"

The woman turned the book toward her, pointing to a sketch of a scorpion.

"Something like this," she said. "I saw one just like it somewhere, don't remember where, but it stuck with me."

The words hit Robyn like cold water. The hum quickened, not louder but closer, like a breath against her ear.

Robyn sat with the woman, going over the design, placement, and scheduling a day and time for her to return. She didn't tell the woman that the scorpion wouldn't sit right on her skin. The flesh was too thin, too loose - like trying to ink a memory that didn't want to stick. A simple purple butterfly would've been better.

When the woman finally left, Robyn let out a long, slow sigh. The day was done, and with it, the lingering image of Nelly's empty eyes began to fade - just background static in her head.

She went through her nightly closing ritual: signs off, lights out, doors locked, every surface wiped clean. It was her exorcism - routine and holy. When she was satisfied, she rode back to her apartment, the hum still faint in her skull.

Tomorrow was clear. No sessions. Just a design to finish for Raymond, one of her regulars. He wanted a tarantula, something thick-legged, hairy, patient. Robyn already knew which needle she'd use, which one would do the job *right.*

She showered, changed into her nightclothes, and sank into bed. The phone pulsed with a new message, but she let it fade. No more drama tonight.

Sleep came heavy and soundless.

When she opened her eyes, she was standing in a tattoo shop, but not hers. This place was older, darker. Fluorescent light hummed weakly through yellowed bulbs. The air smelled of ink and scorched metal.

A man stood behind the counter, head bent over a sketchpad. She knew his face before her mind could place the name - *Karl Mertens.* The same man from the old *Inked Visions* feature, the one the article read, who'd vanished after that weird "ink possession" rumor years ago.

Robyn stepped closer, unseen, her boots silent on the scuffed linoleum. The music in the shop was old metal, possibly Black Sabbath, maybe, low and ghosted through blown-out speakers.

Karl didn't look up. His hand moved quickly across the page, sketching something she couldn't quite see. Robyn leaned closer.

It was a tattoo gun. Her tattoo gun. And the brass needle - her needle - gleamed faintly on the counter beside him, wet and alive in the dim light.

Karl smiled, just barely. "Perfect," he whispered.

Karl transferred the drawing to a stencil, then rolled up his sleeve. His movements were brisk, mechanical - like he'd done this a hundred times before. He shaved a patch on his forearm, the razor whispering against his skin, and pressed the stencil down.

The image took perfectly. He picked up the gun. It began to hum in his hand, low, like a living thing waking from sleep. He touched the needle to his arm and began tracing the outline. After the first pass, he released his grip, but the gun didn't stop.

The machine kept working, the needle gliding smoothly along the stencil *on its own.*

Karl watched it with a calm that felt wrong. His grin was small and patient, almost fatherly.

Robyn couldn't believe what she was seeing. Even in the dream it felt too real - the smell of ozone, the slight flicker of the overhead lights, the faint buzz vibrating through the air like static before a lightning strike.

The tattoo gun finished the design. There were no ink cups, no wipes, no blood - just skin and movement.

Then dark red lines began to bloom from the tattoo, racing outward in frantic, branching veins - up his arm, across his throat, climbing his jaw.

Karl looked up from the gun, his eyes fixed straight on her. "It will take you," he said, his voice low and cracked, "like it took me."

The gun in his hand began to scream - a higher, sharper hum that filled the room.

Robyn bolted upright in bed, gasping.

The hum was still there. Only now, it was coming from her room…and it was louder.

Half awake, Robyn thought she heard the hum again - low, steady, coming from somewhere near the foot of her bed.

Her eyes adjusted to the dark. Karl Mertens was

standing there.

The tattoo gun hung in his hand, its brass needle gleaming faintly in the moonlight leaking through the blinds. Thin red lines spiderwebbed across his face and arms, glowing like veins filled with fire. His eyes…glassy and wet, locked onto hers.

He took a slow step forward. The hum deepened.

In his other hand, he held a straight razor. The blade caught the faint light, flashing once as he flicked it open.

Robyn tried to move, but her limbs felt pinned, paralyzed by the heavy fog of sleep. Karl crouched beside the bed, his smile stretched too wide. He brought the razor close, the edge whispering as it scraped across her skin.

She tried to scream, but no sound came out…only a strangled breath.

Then the pain hit, a small, quick burn on her forearm.

She screamed.

Her eyes flew open.

The room was empty. The hum gone. Just her own ragged breathing and the faint tick of the wall clock.

She reached for the lamp on her nightstand and turned it on.

The yellow light filled the room.

Everything looked normal - except for one thing.

A small patch of her forearm was bare, the hair cleanly shaved away.

She left the lamp on the rest of the night, sleeping in jittery, half-hour bursts. Every time her eyes closed, she saw the razor flash, the red lines, the look on Karl's face.

When the first slivers of daylight pushed through the blinds, she gave up on sleep.

Her arm was the first thing she looked at. The small bald patch was still there, smooth, clean, undeniable. That part had been real. The rest? She didn't know. Maybe she'd nicked herself the night before and just forgot.
"Yeah, right," she muttered, not even convincing herself.

She brewed coffee strong enough to wake the dead and got dressed. The ride to the studio helped clear her head, the air cold enough to sting her cheeks. She told herself to focus on Raymond's design, on ink and line and shadow. If she could lose herself in the work, the rest of it would fade.

By midmorning, the studio smelled like cleaner,

coffee, and lemon oil. She kept the front lights off so no one would think it was open, but the music was cranked loud - her favorite mix of grunge and heavy metal. The bass thumped through her bones.

And still, underneath it, the hum.

It wasn't just a sound. It was a pulse - steady, low, coming from the toolbox on her station. It vibrated faintly through the air, through her hands, through her chest.

She forced herself to ignore it and went back to sketching. The tarantula's legs curved perfectly, each line crisp and deliberate. But after an hour of hunching over the page, her neck locked up and her arm ached. She leaned back in her chair, eyes tracing the slow tick of the second hand on the wall clock.

Then the sting came - sharp, electric.

She looked down.

The bare patch on her arm was inflamed, red lines spidering outward beneath the skin. The welt swelled, rising like heat-blistered paint.

And then, impossibly, it started to form shape - lines crossing, tightening, becoming something deliberate.

The outline of a tattoo gun. And the brass needle.

Exactly as she'd seen it in her dream.

Robyn pulled open the bottom drawer of her station, the one where she kept old tattoo magazines and reference books - relics from when ink felt like art and not obsession. She thumbed through the worn stacks until she found the issue she'd been looking for. *Inked Visions, July Edition.*

Her fingers trembled slightly as she flipped to the article. *"Master of the Needle: The Life and Legacy of Karl Mertens."* The photo was small, grainy, like it had been photocopied too many times. Karl stood beside his station, a faint smile on his face. His eyes looked alive in the picture - almost too alive.

She pulled her magnifying glass from the pen cup and leaned close, moving it slowly across the page. Karl's forearm came into focus, the skin pale against the cluttered background. And there it was - faint but undeniable - the tattoo of the brass gun and needle. Same arm. Same placement.

Her breath hitched.

She lowered the glass to look again, this time at the sketches scattered across his workstation. The photo was blurred, but the outlines were there - a scorpion, a dragon, and a tarantula.

She felt the hair on her arms lift. They looked… familiar.

Too familiar.

She tried to tell herself they were just common designs, stock images every artist had drawn a hundred times. But somewhere deep in her chest, a cold certainty was already forming.

She hadn't just inherited Karl Mertens' tools.

She was finishing his work.

The dream flashed in her mind like an old camera bulb - bright, hot, and gone in an instant. *"It will take you, just as it took me."* His voice echoed in her skull, thin and electric. The hairs on the back of her neck rose.

She looked down at the half-finished drawing of the tarantula and felt an urge rise inside her - to tear it to pieces, to smash the needle, to end it all before it could reach her. The thought burned through her, wild and alive… until the hum swelled and smoothed it away.

Peace settled over her like a drug.

The tarantula will be the best of them all, she thought. *Then it'll be done.*

She hunched over the sketch again. Her hand moved with mechanical precision, guided by something beyond her. The hum wasn't just in her ears now - it pulsed behind her eyes, syncing with her heartbeat, each line she drew pulling her deeper into it.

When she finally looked up, the light in the front windows had dimmed to violet. The neon sign outside buzzed to life, casting pink and blue veins across the floor. Six hours gone. Just - gone.

Her body ached. Her lips felt split and dry. She stretched, and when she looked down at the drawing, she froze. The tarantula looked *alive.* The legs, the sheen, the depth - real enough to crawl off the page if it wanted.

A grin crept across her mouth, slow and wrong. "Raymond's gonna die for this one," she murmured to no one. "That's for sure."

She grabbed a bottle of water from the mini-fridge, twisted it open, and drank until it was empty. The water stung her cracked lips.

On her way back to the station, she caught her reflection in the full-length mirror - and stopped.

Her breath hitched.

The face staring back wasn't hers.

Karl Mertens' red, glassy eyes blinked from the mirror, his skin webbed with faint red lines, his forearms covered in ink and scars. His mouth moved - but she didn't hear the words. Only the hum.

The reflection of Karl Mertens moved first, then reached through the mirror.

Robyn froze. She should've stepped back, but her feet wouldn't obey. The glass rippled like water, and his hand - pale and dead-looking - broke through, closing around her wrist.

The cold hit her instantly.

It wasn't just cold - it *bit.* It sank through her skin, straight into the bone. Her breath hitched, and white vapor poured from her mouth. She tried to yank her arm back, but her muscles responded like they were underwater.

Karl's glassy red eyes locked on hers, unblinking. His mouth didn't move, but she could feel the words forming in her skull, vibrating behind her teeth: *It's already begun.*

He lifted his other hand and pressed it to the spot on her arm where the gun welt had been. The pain was immediate - sharp, freezing, alive. She gasped. Frost began to bloom under his palm, spidering across her skin in delicate white veins.

She tried again to pull free, but his grip tightened, cold smoke seeping from his fingers. It crawled up her arm, over her shoulder, licking toward her face. Her breath came in short bursts, every exhale a puff of steam.

Then the mirror began to freeze.

Thin cracks spread outward, frosting the surface until the reflection disappeared completely under a sheet of solid ice. The hum - the one she'd felt for days - screamed in her ears, then stopped.

The silence was absolute.

Robyn stumbled backward, landing hard on the floor, clutching her arm. It still burned with cold. Her teeth chattered as she looked back at the mirror - expecting to see Karl step through.

Nothing.

No ice. No frost. Just her own reflection staring back - wide-eyed, pale, and shaking.

The morning sunlight cut through the blinds in thin, bright knives, striping Robyn's face and pillow. She groaned, rubbing her eyes until the blur of sleep burned away. For a long moment, she just lay there, watching dust move through the beams of light. Her ceiling looked too white, too still, like a blank page waiting for something to be written on it.

The night before drifted away, fog thinning in her memory. The shop. The mirror. Karl. None of it seemed real now.

She tried to think of the day ahead. Raymond was coming in for his tarantula tattoo. She frowned. Had she finished the sketch? The last thing she remembered was the sketch half done on the page, the spider's legs trailing into nothing. But somehow, that didn't feel right. It felt finished.

She got out of bed on autopilot - each movement a routine she'd done a thousand times: water, coffee, brew, cup, sip. The coffee scalded her tongue, bitter and grounding.

She looked down at her arm. The welt was still there - angry, raised, and now tinted with faint color, bruised like something beneath the skin was bleeding through. The lines of the tattoo gun and needle seemed softer today, almost *alive* under the surface.

She touched it gently. It was warm.

Robyn finished her coffee at the kitchen bar, refusing to think too deeply. Stay in the moment, she told herself. Stay here. Stay now.

She walked to the bathroom, turned on the shower, and waited as the mirror fogged over. The hiss of the water filled the small space, comforting and constant. She stripped and stepped under the stream, letting it beat against her shoulders and face. The heat loosened the tightness in her body, steaming away the static in her thoughts.

For the first time in what felt like forever, she felt clean - empty of everything but the pulse of water.

When she finally turned off the shower, the silence that followed was too deep.

She dressed, grabbed her helmet from the counter, and reached down for her bag. It wasn't there.

Her stomach tightened. "Shop… it's at the shop," she muttered.

Then she froze.

A cold ripple moved through her gut, quick and sharp. The thought of going back to the shop made her skin crawl. She didn't know why. There was no reason - just a sense, deep in her chest, that she'd left something behind that wasn't hers anymore.

She swallowed, staring at the helmet in her hands.

She needed to go. Raymond was expecting her.

So why did it feel like the shop was *expecting her back* too?

Robyn pulled the bike into her usual spot behind the shop and killed the engine. The silence afterward felt heavy. She took off her helmet, ran her fingers through her short black hair, and stared at the back door.

Her hand found the doorknob.

Then the memories flickered - grainy black-and-white frames jerking through her mind like an old film reel. She saw herself crawling toward this same door, heard her own voice shouting into emptiness… and another voice answering, low and wrong. The panic from last night bloomed fresh in her chest.

Then came the hum.

It started softly at the base of her skull, warm and gentle, spreading through her like honey in hot tea. The fear drained out, replaced by that deep, artificial calm. Her stomach unknotted. Her breathing slowed.

A small grin curled across her lips - too sharp to be hers.

She turned the knob and opened the door.

The smell hit first - lemons, antiseptic, and the

faint tang of metal. The hum swelled in her mind, like a chorus welcoming her home.

Crazy Train blared from the speakers. The neon lights buzzed in the front windows, pink and blue bleeding across the dark shop floor. The overheads were still off.

Her workstation sat exactly as she'd left it - only now the tarantula sketch was finished. Every leg drawn, every hair inked in fine black lines.

Her movements turned mechanical. The hum smoothed every thought, every twitch of resistance. She watched herself from a distance - inside, but powerless - as her hands worked with calm precision. Stencil. Tools. Tray. Gun and needle laid out, gleaming, ready.

She sat at the counter like a guard dog watching a gate. Waiting.

Somewhere deep inside, Robyn pressed against the glass, screaming soundlessly.

The thing inside her turned its attention inward. Its thoughts brushed hers, cold and gleeful.

Almost done, it whispered. *Waiting is always the hardest part.*

Then came the laugh - thin, shrill, echoing through her skull like metal scraping on metal.

Robyn saw Raymond coming up the walk, waving through the front windows before pushing the door open. His smile was real - warm, human.

Inside, Robyn screamed. She pounded against the walls of her own mind, but no sound escaped.

Her mouth - *not hers anymore* - smiled. "Ready for the tattoo of a lifetime?" she heard herself say, followed by a short, unnatural chuckle.

The thing inside her turned inward. *"Little does he know, huh?"* it said, and the shrill laugh rang again, scraping through her skull.

"I've been waiting, counting down the days for this," Raymond said, grinning.

Robyn's hand slid the stencil across the counter. *It didn't matter if he liked it. He was getting it, one way or another,* the thing thought.

"Man, Robyn, this is out of this world," Raymond said. "Looks like it could walk right off the paper."

"Let's get started, shall we?" Robyn replied, that same crooked grin twisting her lips.

She motioned him over to the lounge chair wrapped in sterile plastic. Raymond sat, laid out his arm, still smiling.

Robyn wiped his skin clean, then began shaving the area. "So… are you afraid of spiders?" she asked, the razor whispering across his flesh.

"Guess you forgot," Raymond chuckled.

Inside, Robyn flinched. *You should know that already. You don't, do you? Not as clever as you think,* she told the thing.

It turned its gaze inward, its voice a hiss. *"Does it matter, Robyn? He only sees you anyway."* The laugh came again - high, metallic, merciless.

"Sorry, Raymond," she said aloud. "Been busy lately. You know how it is - everybody wants some." Her laugh was hollow.

She pressed the stencil firmly against his arm, then peeled the paper away. "How's that?"

Raymond studied the purple outline in the mirror and gave a thumbs-up.

Robyn picked up the gun, dipped the needle into black ink, and lowered it onto his skin.

The hum started again. Deep, steady, alive.

The brass teeth bit into his flesh, each puncture too deliberate, too hungry. A thin, metallic tongue followed behind, licking the blood and ink in delicate swirls.

Robyn stared. *It's not even a needle… it's alive.*

Inside her head, she whispered, "It's some kind of thing… creature… demon."

"Aren't you observant?" the thing sneered. *"Although it's a bit late for that."*

Robyn no longer felt the gun in her hand. She was just a watcher now, trapped in her own body.

Raymond lay there with his eyes closed, relaxed, smiling.

Inside her skull, Robyn screamed and clawed and begged. But the hum rose louder, swallowing every sound.

Robyn watched as the thing floated above Raymond's arm - biting, licking, feeding - as it moved along the stencil in perfect rhythm. There was nothing she could do but watch helplessly.

"Raymond! Open your eyes… look at the needle! Look at me, for Pete's sake! Can't you see it's not me?" she screamed inside.

But Raymond just lay there, peaceful, lulled by the soft, hypnotic hum of the needle.

When it was over, Robyn's hands - *not hers anymore* - placed the gun carefully on the tray, like a surgeon laying down an instrument after a successful operation. She wiped the excess ink and blood from his arm; the wipes came away almost spotless.

Raymond sat up and looked at his new tattoo in the mirror. "Killer," he said. "Absolute killer. That's why I come to you, Robyn. You're the best."

Robyn's voice smiled before her face did. "Thank you, Raymond. They don't call me the *Master of the Needle* for nothing."

She wrapped the fresh ink in sterile plastic, then handed him the aftercare instructions. "Apply the lotion twice a day, and don't scratch it," she said, her lips smiling while her eyes stayed dead.

Raymond nodded, pulled out his wallet, paid, and headed for the door. "Guess I'll see you later, then. Maybe for another one."

"Not likely," Robyn muttered under her breath.

He waved once more through the front window before disappearing down the street.

Inside her head, Robyn collapsed to her knees. *He's going to be dead before nightfall…she thought.*

"How could you?" she screamed inwardly. "Why? Why do you do this?"

The thing turned toward her voice, its presence

stretching and twisting in the dark. *"This is what I do,"* it said, almost tenderly. *"I've been here a long, long time. And when I'm done with you, I'll have to wait for another one of you to come along."*

It paused. Robyn could feel it smiling somewhere behind her eyes. *"Like I said… waiting is the worst part. Feeding, though—"*

A rasping laugh echoed through her skull. *"Feeding is the best part."*

Robyn dreamed again. She was standing in a room she didn't recognize - bare walls, flickering light, and the smell of metal and blood. Raymond sat in the center of the room, shirt off, his new tattoo glistening wet under the light.

"Raymond?" she whispered.

He looked up at her, confusion flickering in his eyes. Then the tattoo began to move.

The tarantula's legs twitched. The ink bubbled and peeled away from his skin, crawling up his arm in slick, writhing tendrils. Raymond screamed, clawing at it, but the sound twisted into a gurgle as the spider-shaped tattoo reared back and sank its fangs into his neck.

Robyn tried to run, but her legs wouldn't move.

Raymond fell to the floor, eyes wide, froth collecting at his lips. The spider dissolved into his skin, leaving nothing but two small punctures on his throat.

She dropped to her knees beside him, sobbing, "I didn't mean to. I didn't…"

The whisper came again. *"The cycle feeds."*

She jolted awake in her bed, drenched in sweat. The hum was gone. Just silence. For the first time in days, her head was empty.

Her phone buzzed on the nightstand. A text.

Katy: *"Hey Robyn. Did you hear about Raymond? He's gone. They say it was a spider bite. They couldn't find the spider…"*

Robyn read it twice, numb. Then her arm began to itch.

She rolled up her sleeve. The tattoo of the gun and needle was no longer just a welt. It had color now - dark brass and oily black - inked as if it had always been there.

She traced it with a trembling finger. The metal shimmered under her skin, almost alive.

A slow hum began, deep and low, like a heartbeat under the floorboards.

Robyn smiled faintly. "It's done," she whispered. "You're full now."

Her reflection in the mirror smiled back - only the eyes were wrong.

***

Two days later, the old woman returned and found Robyn in the tattoo shop. She was lying on the floor beside her station, her eyes open, the faintest smile on her lips. The smell of lemon cleaner still hung in the air. The tattoo gun with a brass needle rested beside her hand, perfectly clean.

No sign of struggle. No blood. Just a finished tattoo on her arm - the gun and brass needle, complete and gleaming as if freshly polished.

A few months later….at a small flea market at the edge of town

"Yeah, my cousin did tattoos," the man said, wiping dust off an old photo frame. "Real good work, too. Shame what happened to her."

He sorted through boxes of her old sketches - spiders, scorpions, dragons, and set them on the folding table.

At the bottom of the box, wrapped in an old shop towel, sat a *brass tattoo needle.* Tarnished, worn, but heavy in the hand.

The buyer turned it over, admiring its craftsmanship. "Man, they don't make 'em like this anymore."

The man smiled faintly. "Yeah," he said. "That one's got history."

Somewhere deep inside the brass, so faint it could be mistaken for imagination, a ***hum*** began.

THE PIT MASTER

Everyone who enjoys watching cooking shows across the streaming channels knows there's something special about barbecue. Something primal. Something addictive.

But what most don't know is that the world of barbecue has a long, smoky history—long before the television lights, the YouTube influencers, or the brand sponsorships. Back then, it was all about fire, wood, meat, and time.

Those who truly master the craft are called pit masters. Each has their own sacred process—rubs, sauces, wood blends, cooking times—passed down like gospel. And when it's done right, barbecue has a way of calling you back. Again and again. Some say it gets in your blood. Others say it never leaves your soul.

This story takes us to a small town deep in rural East Texas, where each year the locals host the biggest event on their calendar: the Annual Devil's Tail BBQ Cook-Off.

It's more than just a competition. It's a pilgrimage.

The best pit masters from across the piney

woods of East Texas descend on this town, each one dreaming of dethroning the reigning king of smoke and flame. But no one ever does.

That's because Old Del Harper still stands at the top.

He's been winning the Devil's Tail Cook-Off longer than most folks have been alive. Some say he's been serving up ribs and brisket since the 1930s—and somehow, he's still at it in the 2020s. Do the math. It doesn't make sense.

But no one in town questions it.

Old Del's BBQ shack sits out on a winding dirt stretch called Devil's Tail Road, tucked back in a hollow the locals call Harper's Hollow. It's a quiet place. Isolated. And strange things have always been whispered about it.

Some say Del never leaves the Hollow. That he doesn't age. That his pit fire has been burning for over ninety years… and that it never goes out.

This year, for the first time in decades, someone has come to town with real fire in his belly and a chip on his shoulder.

A newcomer from Kansas.

Robert "Bobby" Jenkins, proud owner of Bobby's

Beloved BBQ—a chain with ten locations and a cult-like following—has been sweeping the cook-off circuit back home. Brisket, ribs, pulled pork—you name it, Bobby's been racking up trophies like a man possessed.

"There ain't nobody in Kansas that can touch me," he told a local paper before leaving. "And now it's time for Texas to hand me the crown."

His first stop was the piney woods of East Texas and the legendary Devil's Tail BBQ Cook-Off.

He rolled into town a full week early, eager to size up the local competition. He strutted into diners and feed stores, flashing a smug grin and asking the same question over and over: *Where can a man get the best barbecue in town?*

But Bobby stuck out like a sore thumb—and not in the charming way.

***

Dressed like he'd just stepped out of a Wall

Street boardroom—pressed slacks, leather loafers, Oakley's perched on his smug face—Bobby rolled through town in a black S-Class Mercedes, leaving a trail of silence and side-eyes in his wake.

The old-timers didn't bother looking up from their coffee cups. They heard that Kansas drawl and smelled the arrogance before he ever opened his mouth. To them, he wasn't just an outsider.

He was disrespect.

But Bobby knew money talked.

He turned his charm toward the younger folks—the ones dazzled by chrome wheels and crisp bills. A few twenties slid across counters and into pockets, loosening tongues. One name came up more than once.

Old Del Harper.

That got Bobby's attention.

He'd already heard the whispers. An old man who'd been winning for nearly a century? Sounded like a campfire tale. But the way people said Del's name—voices lowered, eyes shifting—made it feel heavier than myth. Bobby figured Del would spot him as an outsider right away, so he cooked up a disguise.

He hit the local second-hand shop and bought a

pair of worn-out overalls, scuffed work boots, and an old John Deere cap that still smelled like someone else's sweat. He left the Benz parked behind the motel and borrowed a dusty Silverado from a wide-eyed teenager who idolized him—for the price of a new Xbox.

Finding Devil's Tail Road wasn't so easy.

His Mercedes navigation system didn't list it. Google Maps turned up nothing. Apple Maps shrugged. Either the road didn't exist—or it wasn't meant to be found that way.

Eventually, Bobby wandered into a weathered parts store with a peeling *Coca-Cola* sign out front. Behind the counter, a teenager sat on a stool, thumbing through TikTok on an oil-smudged phone.

"You know how to get to Devil's Tail Road?" Bobby asked, trying to keep his fake drawl steady.

The kid didn't look up. Just scratched his neck.

"You don't find Devil's Tail," he muttered. "You just sorta… end up there."

After a long pause, he scribbled directions on the back of a napkin and slid it across the counter.

"Don't miss the turn," he said, eyes dark now. "If you pass the rusted fridge with the possum on top, you've gone too far."

Bobby folded the napkin carefully and slipped it into his pocket.

Bobby pressed the kid at the parts counter, peeling off a few more twenties the way a man tips a valet in Manhattan.

"Come on now," he said, lowering his voice. "You've gotta have someone. Anyone who ever got close to beating Del Harper. Name, location, something useful. I'm not asking for your mama's cobbler recipe."

The kid finally looked up, more interested in counting his fresh cash than in Bobby's impatience.

"Otis Hemfield," he said. "Otis was the closest. Maybe five, six years back. Folks say he even had the crowd that year, right up until the judges' bit into Del's brisket. Then it was over."

"That's it?" Bobby asked. "One name?"

The kid shrugged. "Otis don't talk much about it. But if you want the real taste of Harper's Hollow barbecue, that's your best shot."

***

Hemfield Diesel & Tractor sat at the edge of town, a squat, rust-stained metal building with five open bays and a hand-painted sign that looked like it hadn't been touched since the seventies. Bobby pulled the borrowed Silverado into the dirt lot and shut off the engine.

He checked his billfold out of habit. Greasing the gears never hurt, but he hoped it wouldn't be necessary. A man like Otis might still be nursing a grudge. And grudges, Bobby knew, made people talk.

He stepped out into the heat and walked toward Bay One.

A young mechanic was elbow-deep under the hood of a mud-caked Ford F-350, humming something twangy and off-key.

"Hey," Bobby called. "Otis around? Need to chew the cud with him."

The kid popped his head up and gave

Bobby a look like he'd just smelled something rotten.

"You know Otis? Ain't seen you around here."

"I'm from a couple towns south," Bobby said smoothly. "Otis helped me out with a bad clutch on my John Deere a while back. Thought I'd follow up."

The kid didn't look convinced, but he nodded toward a cluttered office near Bay Five.

"Down that way."

Bobby tipped an imaginary hat. "Much obliged."

The office smelled like oil, tobacco, and time.

Otis Hemfield sat hunched behind a desk meant for someone half his size. He wore jeans and boots, a shirt that looked like it had survived a war. Grease stained his hands, his arms, even one cheek. The room was dim, cluttered with old parts, tangled extension cords, and a coffee pot that looked permanently ruined.

Otis didn't look up.

"You need something?" he said. "I'm busy. And I don't got time for some farmer needing a software update on a machine older than the internet."

Bobby stepped inside and offered his hand.

"Mr. Hemfield. Name's Robert Jenkins. Folks call me Bobby. I'm in town for the Devil's Tail Cook-Off."

Otis didn't take the hand. Didn't blink.

"I hear you came real close to beating Old Del once," Bobby continued. "Thought maybe you could help me understand what I'm up against."

Otis turned slowly in his chair.

"And just why," he said, voice low and rough, "are you darkening my door, Robert Jenkins?"

Otis Hemfield stared at Bobby like he was trying to decide whether to throw him out or bury him.

"You here to fix somethin'," Otis said, "or you just like wastin' other people's time?"

Bobby lowered his hand slowly, easing it back to his side. He smiled, the practiced kind that usually softened people up.

"I hear tell you came close to beatin' Del Harper once," Bobby said. "Figured you might be the one man in town who knows what I'm walkin' into."

Otis snorted and turned back to his computer.

"I don't talk about that cook-off."

"Aw, come on," Bobby said. "What's the harm in a little talk between pit men? Maybe you don't like Del. Maybe it'd feel good to see someone else take that crown."

Otis leaned back in his chair. It groaned under his weight. His eyes dropped to Bobby's boots.

"You ain't from a couple towns south," Otis said. "Your boots don't got a lick of red dirt on 'em. You smell like cologne, not diesel. And that drawl you're usin'? You lay it on too thick."

Bobby opened his mouth, but Otis raised a hand.

"You wanna know about Del?" Otis said. "I'll tell you this much. Don't go up to Harper's Hollow thinkin' you're gonna out-cook that man."

Bobby crossed his arms, leaning against the doorframe. "You think I drove all this way for campfire stories?"

Otis's eyes hardened.

"You think this is about brisket and rubs? Timing and temperature?"

He leaned forward.

"You think Del Harper's been winnin' since the thirties because he's just that good?"

Otis rubbed a thick thumb along his jaw.

"I had the best ribs of my life that year," he said. "Judges told me so. I watched their faces when they bit into mine. Smiles. Nods. Folks murmurin'."

He paused.

"But when Del brought out that brisket…"

Otis swallowed.

"They took one bite. Just one. Their eyes rolled back in their heads like they'd been struck. Mouths went slack. Drool hangin' like strings."

From the shop, the young mechanic poked his head toward the office, startled by the sudden edge in Otis's voice.

Otis didn't notice.

"They moaned," he said. "I swear to God, Jenkins, they moaned."

Otis sat back hard, the chair creaking again.

"And the smoke," he said. "Sweetest smell you'll ever breathe. Like candy and heaven and sin all rolled together."

He looked at Bobby now, eyes unblinking.

"It pulls at people. Folks follow it. Animals,

too."

Bobby scoffed, though it came out thin. "You tellin' me Del's cookin' dogs and deer now?"

"I'm tellin' you animals that wander too close to Harper's Hollow don't come back," Otis said. "No tracks. No blood. Just gone."

He leaned in, lowering his voice.

"And the crows. Always crows. On the ground. On the roof. Watchin'."

Silence settled between them.

Bobby shifted his weight. "So that's it? Old wives' tales and spooky birds?"

Otis stared at him like he was watching a man step closer to a cliff in fog.

"All I know," he said, "is that you don't go into that shack."

He rubbed his face with both hands, suddenly looking older.

"I never went in," Otis said. "And I still lost."

Otis leaned back, done.

"Be warned, Robert Jenkins. Be warned."

The porch groaned under Bobby's boots as he stepped up to the door. It was old, warped, hanging slightly off its hinges. He nudged it, and it creaked open on its own.

Inside, the shack was dim, lit only by slivers of daylight slicing through gaps in the weathered walls. Picnic tables lined the space, butcher paper stained dark with old grease. The air was thick, like the smoke had never left, like it lived there.

Bobby stepped in slowly, eyes adjusting.

That's when he saw him.

Behind the counter, backlit by a faint amber glow from the kitchen fire, stood Del Harper. Tall. Thin. Dark-skinned. A pronounced hunch in his shoulders. A well-worn derby sat low on his head, and his long arms moved slow and methodical.

That's him, Bobby thought. That's the old bastard.

Bobby shuffled his boots against the floor to make noise.

No reaction.

He cleared his throat. "Afternoon. Smells mighty fine in here."

"You's mighty cocky 'bout somethin',

mister."

Bobby jumped.

Del was standing closer now, just behind the counter. Too close. Bobby hadn't heard a single footstep. No creak of floorboards. No shift in the air. Just there.

"You ain't talkin' 'bout the Devil's Tail BBQ Cook-Off, is ya?" Del said. "Cause I ain't never lost. Otis Hemfield thought he had me once, sure… but I laid them judges flat with my brisket. They said they ain't never had barbecue since that tasted the same. Said it ruined 'em."

Bobby swallowed and forced a grin. "I heard some tales from the locals. Heard you been cookin' since the thirties. Said you're the best around East Texas."

Del's lips curled into a smile. Wide. Too wide. It didn't touch his eyes.

"I knows who you is," Del said. "You's Robert Jenkins. Your friends call you Bobby, cause of course they do. You run ten barbecue joints up in Kansas. Fancy places, electric smokers, all clean and polished."

Bobby felt a chill creep up his spine.

"You think you gonna stroll into my Hollow, into my house, and walk off with my crown?" Del continued. "Mr. Jenkins… I ain't the best pit master in East Texas.

I'm the best pit master in the whole damn world. And maybe even the next one."

Bobby blinked.

He hadn't told Del his name. Or where he was from. Or how many joints he owned.

"You ever wonder why folks keep comin' back?" Del asked. "Why my smoke pulls at 'em like hunger?"

Bobby shifted, trying to laugh it off. "I don't win because I smile nice," he said. "I win because I been around. Learned every style. Perfected it."

Del didn't blink.

"Barbecue ain't 'bout spice," he said. "It's 'bout sacrifice."

The word settled heavy in the air.

"What sacrifice is you willin' to make, Mr. Jenkins?"

For the first time since rolling into town, Bobby felt it.

Not nerves. Not unease.

Fear.

Bobby took a step back. "I appreciate your

time, Mr. Harper."

He turned toward the door.

Behind him, Del spoke again, voice slow and certain.

"You come back when you ready."

***

Bobby didn't linger.

He stepped back out onto the porch, the boards groaning under his boots, and crossed the yard with longer strides than he meant to. The crows watched him go, heads turning in slow, deliberate movements.

He didn't look at them.

He climbed into the Silverado and shut the door harder than necessary. The cab felt smaller now, the air thick and stale. He sat there for a moment with his hands on the steering wheel, staring straight ahead.

Then he laughed.

"Hell's bells," he muttered. "You let some backwoods huckster get under your skin."

He shook his head and started the engine. The sound was loud in the quiet hollow, grounding. Familiar.

As he pulled away, he caught a glimpse of the shack in the rearview mirror. Just a sagging roof and warped boards slipping back into the trees.

"Head games," Bobby said. "That's all it is."

The road out of Harper's Hollow felt longer than the drive in.

Tree limbs scraped along the sides of the truck. Shadows stretched across the dirt, darker than they should have been in the afternoon light. Bobby rolled down the window, hoping fresh air would clear his head.

It didn't.

The smell followed him.

Not the sweet smoke. That part was gone. What lingered was the other note. Sour. Metallic. Wrong.

He sniffed his shirt, his hands, the seat. Nothing.

"Get a grip," he told himself. "You walked into a place that's been smokin' meat for damn near a century. Of course it smells off."

He laughed again, but it came out thin.

Back in town, Bobby parked behind the motel and sat on the edge of the bed, boots still on. The room smelled like cheap cleaner and stale air. He stared at the wall, replaying the visit in his head.

Del knowing his name. Knowing his business. Standing too close.

Coincidences, Bobby decided. Small towns talked. People Googled. It wasn't hard.

Still, one thing nagged at him.

He never saw the pit.

Del had kept himself squarely between Bobby and the kitchen the entire time. No smoker in sight. No firebox. No stack. Just that smell seeping through the walls like breath.

"That ain't an accident," Bobby said aloud.

He stood and paced the room.

"No electricity out there," he muttered. "Has to be wood-fired. Old-school setup."

His mind shifted gears, slipping back into familiar territory. Analysis. Competition. Advantage.

"What kind of wood burns that sweet?" he asked the empty room. "What kind of meat smells like that?"

The answers didn't come, but the questions settled something in him.

Curiosity hardened into resolve.

That evening, Bobby ate dinner at the Greasy Spoon across from the motel. The waitress flirted a little, asked what brought him to town. He smiled, joked, kept it light. He barely tasted the food.

All the while, his eyes kept drifting toward the window, toward the road that led back into the trees.

By the time he paid the bill, the decision had already been made.

Night fell quick in the piney woods.

Bobby slid back into the Silverado and pulled the napkin with the directions from the parts store out of the glove box. He smoothed it flat on the seat beside him, tracing the scribbled landmarks with his finger.

"Just a look," he said. "That's all."

He started the truck and turned toward Devil's Tail Road.

***

Devil's Tail Road looked different at night.

Narrower. Meaner.

Bobby slowed the Silverado as the headlights cut through the trees, the beams catching trunks and low-hanging branches at odd angles. Shadows shifted with the movement of the truck, stretching and folding back in on themselves.

"Same damn road," he muttered.

But it didn't feel that way.

The rusted refrigerator appeared suddenly in the headlights; the stuffed possum perched on top casting a crooked shadow across the dirt. Bobby eased past it and followed the road as it curved down into the hollow.

The shack came into view without warning.

He pulled up closer this time, the front of the truck nearly kissing the edge of the yard. He killed the engine but left the headlights on. Their beams washed over the warped boards, the tin roof, the leaning fence posts.

No crows.

That was a relief.

Bobby sat there a moment, listening.

No insects. No wind. Just the faint tick of the engine cooling.

"Don't get spooked now," he told himself.

He stepped out of the truck and onto the porch. The boards groaned louder at night, the sound echoing in the stillness. The door hung open a crack, the same way it had earlier.

Inside, the glow was different.

A low, reddish-yellow light pulsed faintly from the back of the shack, leaking through the seams around the kitchen door.

Bobby's mouth went dry.

"Well, there you are," he whispered.

He stepped inside.

The air was thicker than before. Heavy. Wet. The sweet smoke was still there, but now it felt older, layered over itself so many times it had lost something. Beneath it lingered that same sour note he'd caught earlier.

His stomach tightened.

He moved slowly, careful not to knock

anything over. Picnic tables sat empty, butcher paper curled and stiff with old grease. The smell clung to his clothes as he passed.

The kitchen door stood shut.

Light bled around its edges.

Bobby swallowed and reached for the handle.

The kitchen opened up around him.

A massive pit smoker dominated the far wall, its metal body glowing faintly with heat. Firelight flickered through its seams, casting restless shadows across the room.

To one side stood several dark barrels, arranged in a neat row.

Bobby exhaled softly.

"There you are," he said. "That's the trick."

He stepped closer, eyes scanning the setup. No electricity. No modern controls. Just iron, fire, and patience.

"Old-school," he murmured. "Real old-school."

Something shifted under his boot.

A metal bucket tipped over, spilling ash across the floor. The fine powder puffed up into the air.

Bobby coughed hard, doubling over as the ash

burned his throat and lungs. He staggered back, eyes watering, struggling to breathe.

"Hell," he rasped.

When the coughing fit passed, he wiped his face and straightened, chest heaving.

"That ain't nothin'," he said, more to convince himself than anything else.

His eyes went back to the barrels.

He picked up a rusted cleaver from a nearby table and wedged it under the lid of the closest barrel.

The metal groaned.

The lid popped free.

"Is you sure you wanna know what's in that there barrel, Mr. Jenkins?" The voice was slow and low. Like gravel stirred in a cast-iron pot.

Bobby froze. He turned toward the back of the kitchen.

Del Harper stood in the open back doorway. Silhouetted in the glow of the fire, his thin frame seemed longer now. His fingers curled like hooks. His face… not quite human in the flickering light.

"Ain't no goin' back if you look inside," Del said, voice flat and cold. "You look, and you know, and you never don't know again."

Bobby's mouth went dry. But something in him still pushed forward.

I have to know.

He turned back to the barrel and peered inside.

Black liquid. Oily and thick. The smell punched him square in the memory.

"...Brine?" he asked aloud. "It's just brine?"

Behind him, Del chuckled darkly.

"It ain't just any ol' brine, Mr. Jenkins," he said. "That's a brine made of sacrifice."

Bobby turned, horrified.

Del nodded toward the barrel. "That there's Evelyn Applegate. Judge number one. She sacrificed to keep me cookin'. Kept my fire goin', year after year."

Del pointed to the next barrel. "Barrel two? That's little Keith Jones. He was the brisket. Moist. Tender. Melt-in-your-mouth."

Bobby stumbled backward, legs failing him. He dropped hard onto the floor, the cleaver clanging beside him. His breath came in short, broken gasps.

"No… no, no, that's not… you're lying. You're makin' this up—"

Del stepped forward, shadows crawling across his skin like soot.

"Oh, it be true, Mr. Jenkins," he said. "You wanna be the best? Then you sacrifice. Customers sacrifice. Judges. Friends. The pain gets cooked down into the sauce. You ever wonder why my sauce makes people weep?"

Bobby shook his head violently, clutching at his hair.

Del pointed toward the glowing smoker. "That smell yous love? That there's bones, Mr. Jenkins. Bones burned down to ash. Keeps the fire low. Keeps the fire slow."

Bobby retched. Nothing came up. Just bile and heat.

"You wanted my secret," Del growled, towering now. "Well, now you got it."

He crouched beside Bobby, his face uncomfortably close, eyes burning steady.

"So tell me somethin'…"A pause. "What's you willin' to sacrifice to the pit, Mr. Jenkins?"

Del didn't move. His eyes burned low, like the coals in that ever-burning pit behind him.

"What're you willin' to sacrifice to the pit, Mr. Jenkins?" he asked again, but this time his voice sounded older, like it carried dust from every year he'd been standing behind that counter.

Then, quiet now, almost to himself:

"Let me tells you what I gave…"

***

Del Harper had been cooking in a kitchen since he was knee-high to a cotton stalk. Back when he could just barely see over the countertop, he stood beside his pappy, watching the old man stir pots, rub down pork shoulder, and stack wood just so.

His pappy taught him everything he knew about barbecue. About fire. About patience.

Folks would come from miles around to taste what his pappy made—ribs so tender they'd slide off the bone with a whisper, brisket that brought old men to tears. But no matter how good the food was, the town folks never lifted a finger to help his pappy out. He was always turned down for loans, laughed out of banks, dismissed by county men with tight collars and tighter wallets.

When his pappy died, Del was broke. So broke they couldn't even give him a real funeral. Just a pine box in the pauper's cemetery, shoved off on the far side of town where the dark-skinned folks were buried. Forgotten, same as he lived.

That grave stuck in Del's heart like a bone splinter.

Right then and there, he swore he wasn't just gonna cook barbecue. He was gonna master it. He was gonna become the best damn Pit Master anyone ever knew, in East Texas or anywhere else.

He used his pappy's rub recipes, the finest smoking woods like his pappy taught him, and sauce blends so thick and sweet they'd make a deacon backslide. When he opened Old Del's BBQ Shack on Devil's Tail Road, the people came. Packed in. Sold out daily.

But selling out didn't mean success.

His prices were too low to make a profit, and when he tried raising them, the same folks who praised him said they wouldn't pay a dime more.

"We got bills to pay," they said. "Other priorities," they said.

Some of those same folks drove brand-new Model A Fords.

Still, week after week, month after month, they came and ate, and Del bled money.

So he tried the banks. Two banks in town, and both loan officers were regulars at his place. Loved the ribs. Swore by his mulberry pie. Said it tasted like their meemaw used to make.

But when Del asked for a loan to fix up the old shack, they smiled thin and said, "Sorry, Del. We just don't have the funds for a place like yours."

They'd already backed the new motel. And the shiny new diner across the street.

About that time, Del's wife, Loretta Jackson—a sweet woman with a smile like the first day of spring—ended up pregnant. It was a rough pregnancy. First trimester, Loretta was sick near every day. By the second, she was bedridden.

When little Fester was born, named after Del's pappy, he was small and thin. Barely cried.

Loretta never really recovered.

Del brought Fester to the shack when he could. Taught him to sweep up and wipe tables. Loretta only made it out once or twice a month. Her body just couldn't do more.

By the time Fester was seven, Del was drowning.

Loretta's medicine bills stacked high. The shack was failing.

And Del knew he was gonna lose everything—his wife, his boy, his pappy's legacy.

That's when it happened.

***

One night, after midnight, when the fire in the pit had burned down to soft, glowin' embers, a man walked in through the front door of the shack.

Tall. Pale. Dressed sharp, like a banker or lawyer.

Immaculate black suit. Red tie. Not a speck of dust on him.

Del stepped from behind the counter, wiping his hands on a rag.

"Sorry, sir," he said. "We closed. Done sold out. Nothin' left but smoke and bones."

The man smiled. "That's fine, Mr. Harper. I'm not here to eat. I'm here to make you an offer."

He walked to a bench, pulled a red handkerchief from his pocket, and laid it down slow. Sat like he owned the place.

"I know about the banks," the man said. "The town. How they love your food but won't lift a finger to help. But I can help. I can make it so they'll sacrifice everything to keep you cookin'."

Del just blinked. "I didn't catch your name."

The man grinned. "That's not important."

He pulled out gold-rimmed spectacles and peered at the framed photo behind the counter—Del, Loretta, and little Fester, smiling from last year when she was well enough to walk again.

"Nice family," the man said. "Wife's ill, though. Ain't she?"

Del swallowed hard. "Yeah… been sick since before the boy was born."

The man stood. Stepped close.

"I have a deal, Mr. Harper. A deal that'll save your shack. Save your name. Maybe even save your family. Make you the best Pit Master this side of life… and maybe the next."

Del's mouth felt dry as ash. "What kinda deal we talkin'? You lendin' me money?"

The man laughed once, quiet and bitter.

"No, Mr. Harper. I ain't no banker. I'm somethin' older."

He leaned in.

"I'm here to ask you what you're willin' to sacrifice to get what you want."

Del stared. Looked down at the red cloth. Smelled somethin' strange—burnt match heads and sulfur.

His thoughts turned dark.

Revenge. Respect. Loretta gettin' medicine. Fester maybe goin' to school instead of sweepin' floors till he died poor like his grandpappy.

The man leaned closer. His face shifted. Something in the shadows curled wrong.

"What is it, Del? Your shack? Your soul?

Your wife and boy?"

Del's knees went weak.

For just a second—just a second—he hesitated.

And that was enough.

The man smiled wider than a man should.

"Well chosen, Mr. Harper. The deal is done."

He turned and walked toward the door.

"Two barrels waitin' outside," he said. "Best meat money can't buy. But you'll need to keep 'em full. If the barrels ever run dry, or the fire ever dies…"

He paused at the threshold. His voice slowed. Slicked down.

"Loretta and Fester are waitin' to make you the best Pit Master of all time. They've already sacrificed for you."

He turned his head just enough for Del to see it—not teeth, not quite—something like bone or fire deep in the smile.

"Make sure you use the same type of meat in them barrels," the man said. "And the sauce and rub? Folks won't just taste what you cook."

He tapped the side of his nose.

"They'll die for it."

Then he laughed. Slow. Creepily. The sound of sulfur and burnt souls filling the shack like smoke through a broken flue.

***

Bobby sat on the floor, eyes wide, darting between the barrels, the ash-covered floor, the glowing pit smoker… and Del.

His breath came shallow. Fast. His hands trembled on his knees.

Over and over, he looked from the bubbling brine to the fire, from the rusted cleaver to the man with the burning eyes.

Then something did change.

Not out loud. Not visible.

But deep inside, Bobby Jenkins broke—and something else stepped forward in his place.

Del watched him.

"Is that your sacrifice, Mr. Jenkins?" Del asked, voice soft now. Almost sorrowful. "Is you sure? I'm so tired… Cookin' takes it out of a man."

Bobby stood up slow. Straightened his shirt.

His eyes were calm.

"You know my choice, Mr. Harper."

Four days later.

Bobby Jenkins stood atop the main stage, golden sunlight glinting off the Pit Master Trophy in his hands. All smiles. White teeth. Flashbulbs.

"And there it is, folks!" the announcer shouted. "A new king crowned! Bobby Jenkins, takin' the title from the legendary Old Del Harper!"

A reporter shoved a mic toward him. "Bobby—how's it feel? You just took the crown from a man who's been winning since most of us were kids."

Bobby chuckled low, nodding. "Feels right. Feels like I deserve it."

He turned to the crowd, smile fixed, eyes cold.

"I've… sacrificed so much to be here."

***

A young couple pushed open the old screen door of the shack at the end of Devil's Tail Road.

The smell hit them first. Sweet. Smoky. Unforgettable.

They stepped inside. The woman glanced at the counter. Then at the shelf beside it.

A trophy sat there. Polished. Gleaming. The small plate at the bottom read:

DEVIL'S TAIL BBQ COOK-OFF — PIT MASTER ROBERT "BOBBY" JENKINS

"Hello?" the woman called. "Anyone here?"

From the back stepped a tall, skinny man. Light-skinned now. A little stooped. Grease-stained apron over a faded T-shirt that read:

Bobby's ♥ BBQ

An old derby sat low on his head. He smiled wide. Familiar. Shiny.

"Welcome to The Devil's Den," he said warmly. "What can I get y'all?"

He gave them a wink.

THE GRAVEYARD BEAT

They say the news never sleeps. Neither do I.

They say the city sleeps. That's a lie. The city dozes with one eye open and a switchblade under the pillow. And me? I'm the guy who writes down what it dreams about.

My names on the masthead of the *Evening Bulletin*, but you won't find it next to the garden party write-ups or the mayor's press releases. My beat's the stuff that crawls out of the gutters and leaves chalk outlines in the moonlight.

Thursday night, rain-slick streets and neon bleeding in the puddles. As for me, I'm parked at my desk at the *Evening Bulletin*, chewing on over-heated coffee. Outside, the city was alive in ways it never managed under the sun, shadows pooling in doorways, headlights cutting swaths of silver across wet pavement. I liked it that way. Nights didn't glare at you, didn't ask questions. They wrapped around you, quiet, close… like they knew you. Then the tip came in - another stiff, same as the last two: two clean punctures to the throat, like someone had taken a ruler to the kill. Not a drop of blood left.

Most crime scenes tend to look the same after a while. A little yellow tape, a few uniforms keeping the gawkers at bay, a body or two under the sheet. You start thinking you've seen it all - until you don't.

This one was different.

A third-floor walk-up in a part of town even the rats had given up on. The smell of old cabbage clung to the wallpaper like it had signed a lease. The hall light was dead, had been since the Johnson administration, and the shadows were thick enough to make you feel for the walls as you climbed.

Inside, the cops worked around the body like mechanics in a greasy garage, moving slow, not wanting to get their hands dirtier than the job required. The place was lit by a single crooked lamp in the corner, throwing a sickly yellow pool across the threadbare carpet. The TV was dark, its blank screen reflecting the room, the cops, the coroner, the lamp, everything except me.

The stiff was a pale guy, mid-forties, sunk deep into a brown corduroy recliner, slippers still on. Head tipped just enough to suggest he'd dozed off, if you didn't look too closely. But you always look closely. The coroner, a short woman with steady hands and eyes like polished marbles, knelt beside him, her latex gloves whispering as she tilted his head just enough for me to see. Two punctures at the base of the neck. Neat. Surgical. The kind of thing you don't learn in med school.

"Animal attack," one of the uniforms muttered, and the room nodded like they wanted to believe it. But there was no animal hair. No torn fabric. No mess. Just skin pale as wax, and eyes wide open, like they'd been staring at something they couldn't quite believe.

The two uniforms were young, academy haircuts still fresh, one shifting from foot to foot, the other pretending to study the carpet pattern. They kept glancing toward the hallway, like the dark out there was safer than the quiet in here.

I jotted the details in my notebook, keeping my face puzzled, the part of the job I've always been best at. You can't sell a story if you let folks know how it ends before the presses roll.

Outside, the rain had started up, it was the thin, needling stuff that slid down your neck no matter how tight your collar. I lit a cigarette, not because I wanted one, but because it gave me an excuse to linger and listen.

"That's the third this month," one cop whispered to the other. "All the same. All clean. Like the guy never fought back."

His partner grunted. "Klein says it's a spree killer. Some psycho with a fetish. I say it's just bad luck."

They moved off, their boots splashing through a puddle of water left on the floor from their dripping coats.

Bad luck. That's what they always call it when the truth is staring them in the face and they don't want to see it.

Three bodies in three weeks. All of them pale, all of them with the same signature wounds, all of them with a criminal record that read like bedtime stories for sociopaths. Somebody out there was cleaning house…and they weren't doing it with a .38.

I pulled my coat tighter and started the walk back to the office. The streets were empty, but I had that feeling again, the one where the hairs on the back of your neck stand up and you're not sure why. I glanced at the alleys as I passed, half expecting to see a shadow duck out of sight.

Nothing. Just the rain, the streetlights, and me.

Still, I kept my pace steady. Some people will tell you that instinct is just pattern recognition, your brain adding things up faster than you realize. They might be right. But in my experience, instinct is also knowing when you're not the only one out here who doesn't sleep at night.

This was the start of the strangest case I'd ever covered. And believe me, I've had some strange ones.

But this time… this time was different.

This time, it was personal.

I kept thinking back to the crime scene. The uniforms? They're in left field, eh, maybe not even in the same ballpark.

The coroner didn't say a word. That says a lot. In my years covering murders, I've learned: when the coroner looks but doesn't talk, you've got a problem. A big one.

Two neat punctures. No blood. Feels like ritual. But my gut? My gut says eccentric serial killer. They're easier to explain in print.

Rain slid down my collar, cold enough to make me shiver. I tried to light a cigarette, but the downpour laughed in my face.

So I pulled out my notebook instead. Two names for the headline: Cult ritual… or eccentric killer. Either way, somebody out there was getting creative with homicide.

Over the next three days, three more bodies turned

up. All three had criminal records. I'm not saying it's a tragedy… so I won't. That's three fewer crooks walking the streets.

Witnesses, what little there were, placed each victim alone before their demise. No signs of forced entry, no signs of a struggle. Which means they either knew their killer… or they were scared stiff of him.

It was time to work the phones. Do some digging. Grease the skids.

Body number one - found slumped on his couch, watching the local ball game. Building maintenance swears only staff and residents have keys. Which means the dead guy opened the door himself.

Body number two - a real bottom-feeder. Found in the men's room at a downtown men's club. If his killer was someone he knew, that's one odd choice of venue.

Body number three - found in an alley where he sold his wares. Same deal as the others: two precise punctures, no blood. Drained like a cheap whiskey bottle.

I slipped a few greenbacks to my favorite beat cop to get into all three crime scenes. Everything matched the reports except for one detail on victim number two. A witness.

She was a dancer, giving him what the club calls a "private show." She laughed at his… let's call it "modest equipment." He started swinging at her. That's when somebody else walked in. The lights went out.

She bolted, naked, but in that place, nobody batted an eye. By the time security showed up to throw him out, he was already past his expiration date.

I worked late into the night, flipping through microfilm and old papers. Hoping for a clue, something that jumped out…not like what got those three.

Found a few interesting threads, things that usually blend into the wallpaper if you're not looking. A string of deaths, spread out over years… centuries, maybe. If it's a spree killer, he's been at it a long time; he's due for a pension.

Dug up some old police sketches. One looked strikingly like a suspect currently cooling his heels in the city jail. Looks like I'm paying him a visit.

Then came the city drunk lore, the kind of stuff barflies toss around when the lights go low and the whiskey runs cheap. The Night Drinker.

Most folks dismiss it as old wives' tales. But the old timers, the ones nursing their third round on the rough side of the tracks, well, they swear he's real. A kind of vigilante, they say. Never touches the innocent.

In this part of town, innocence is a scarce commodity.

I pulled a few strings and landed an interview with the witness. A dancer from the men's club.

At four AM, the place was nearly empty. Too early for the deadbeats and too late for the soon-to-be divorced. I didn't have a photo, but my beat cop gave me her description… and a few details that weren't exactly about her hair color.

She found me first. Redhead. Glitter still clinging to her face and hair like she'd just stepped off stage. She slid into the chair across from me.

"So," I started, "you were… dancing for the deceased two nights ago. The lights went out in the men's room. Was that before or after someone came in?"

She glanced around the room. "Oh no… after. Someone came in first."

I followed her gaze, but the club was pretty much empty except for a bartender polishing the same glass for ten minutes.

"You see their face? Man or woman?"

She fidgeted like she had ants crawling up her arms. "Uh… I think it was a woman. Short. Dressed in old-timey clothes, real old clothes."

That got my attention. Second time I'd heard a woman mentioned.

I pressed her with a few more questions, but her answers kept shrinking like a water puddle on a hot day. I had the feeling she was holding something back, couldn't tell what, but it was there.

Eventually, she excused herself to "get ready for her show." It was still early or late, depending on who you are, but I guess there's always an audience for the sleaze crowd.

The bouncer was next. Big guy. Looked like he could take a punch, but maybe not a test. He confirmed seeing the same woman the redhead described, old-timey clothes, old-fashioned, heading into an abandoned boarding house a block away, on the seedier side of the tracks.

"Abandoned" was a generous term. The place had power, lights, and a counter clerk. Not your usual squatters' den.

A couple of greenbacks later, I had her room

number. She answered the door with a polite smile and the wardrobe of a 1920s socialite.

Something was suspicious about the old lady, something the dancer and the bouncer didn't want to say. I said it, but only to myself.

Yes, she was the club owner's mother. Yes, she'd gone into the men's room by mistake. And yes, she left right after the naked dancer bolted.

She claimed she only stepped outside after dark, said bright sunlight hurt her eyes. Bad condition, she told me.

The street was lit up like Christmas, but I didn't push it. I thanked her, tipped my hat, and hit the bricks.

Looked like my investigation was about to hit the wall. I had one last shot, an interview with the guy the cops had in custody. The one who looked suspiciously like a hundred-year-old police sketch.

I made my way down to the precinct, worked a little press-pass magic, and got five minutes with him. Late twenties, dark complexion, maybe from south of the border. His English was better than my Spanish, so we could at least talk without breaking into charades.

He'd been in the country a few weeks, working

construction on the new city offices. Didn't know why he'd been picked up. The cops hadn't told him, and he knew less than I did…which was saying something.

Then he dropped a nugget. Across the hall from his cell was an eccentric antiquarian, "very strange, señor… off center." According to my guy, this character had a collection of antique bloodletting tools from the turn of the century and documents on rituals for draining bodies dry.

The suspect's eyes went wide when he talked about him, like a man watching the train he's tied to start rolling. He didn't have a name, but he did have a business: *The Bone Collector*, over on 5th and Burns.

I came in with nothing. I walked out with a collector.

I grabbed a cab from the station over to 5th and Burns. The driver was a chatterbox, his mother's pork chops, last night's ball game, and a detailed account of his gallbladder surgery. I was about to nod off when he saved me: "We're here, 5th and Burns."

I paid the fare and stepped out in front of *The Bone Collector*. The place looked exactly like the name, dusty, antique windows full of relics that belonged in a museum or a crime scene, depending on your mood.

Inside, the smell hit me first: old wood, old paper, and something else… old people. I scanned the shelves: a thousand-year-old medical examiner would've felt right at home. Brain hooks, bone saws, jars with labels faded to whispers. I picked up one particular brain hook and swore it still had a little original owner on it.

"I'd appreciate it if you didn't handle the merchandise, sir."

I turned, startled out of my daydream about ancient embalmers. "Uh, yeah, I'm looking for the owner…of the store, not the tool."

"That, sir, would be me." He said it with all the warmth of a frozen corpse.

I asked about his bloodletting tools and any related documents. His face didn't move. "I wouldn't know what you're referring to, sir."

So I went in blunt: "Were you in lock-up last night? Swapping stories about your… unusual inventory?"

His stare went flat, like he'd just powered down. Then: "Are you a cop or something?"

My brain reached for something clever, but my mouth went with: "Yes. And I'm tracking your activities."

Without blinking: "Why would I be followed for an unpaid parking ticket? Are you here to keep me from getting another, sir?"

And just like that, I felt about as tall as a roach under a barstool. I mumbled something about keeping his illegal parking in check, thanked him, and made a hasty exit.

I stood outside the shop, watching the moon rise behind the city skyline. My lead had gone flat, so I started the long walk back to my side of town. Twenty minutes in, I realized I'd wandered into the alley where victim number three, the street peddler, had been found. The old crime scene tape lay limp on the pavement, a yellow ghost of better days in police work.

The streetlight barely reached inside, and the deeper I went, the darker it got. About fifty yards in, a figure slid - no, *glided* - out of the shadows. At first, I figured it was a junkie hunting a fix, but then the eyes flashed like a camera bulb. The chill that ran up my spine nearly lifted my hat.

I had a choice: run and lose the story, or chase and maybe lose more than that. I picked the latter.

The figure moved fast, half-running, half-floating,

deeper into the alley. The walls seemed to squeeze in, and the light vanished behind me. Finally, I hit a brick wall, straight up, at least a hundred feet. My quarry was gone.

I turned back, flicked my Zippo, and started picking my way toward the street. Then I saw it again. Only this time, it wasn't running. It was *watching.*

The figure slid to the wall and, I kid you not, climbed it. No rope, no handholds. Just… up. Then it came back down, moving toward me. The lighter's glow caught its face: pale skin, eyes flaring red, and a mouth stretched wider than anything human.

I shut my eyes, figuring this was it. Morning headline: *Reporter Found Drained Like Old Milk Bottle.*

But nothing happened. When I looked again, the alley was empty. No sound, no movement, no sign I hadn't imagined it all… except I'm not that creative.

Whatever it was, it had skipped me. Maybe it lost its nerve. Or maybe it was saving me for later.

The next day, I was nursing bad coffee and reviewing my notes when the racket outside got my attention. I clicked on the TV. The news ticker read: **"NIGHT DRINKER CAUGHT."**

I called my police contact. "Give it to me, Charlie,

everything you got on it."

"Police source spots a suspect in the old derelict theater," he said. "Middle of the day, tries to snatch a kid in a covered alley. Source yanks the boy back into the sunlight, suspect bolts inside."

My pen froze. "Old lady, twenties-style clothes?"

"That's her. Locals corner her inside. She goes feral, tries to attack. Someone drops a lighter, old curtains catch. Smoke everywhere. Fire department shows. They knock out a glass panel over the stage pit. Sunlight pours in - "

"Let me guess. She didn't like it."

"Went up like dry tinder. When it was over… nothing but ash. We're calling it confirmed."

I jotted it down. "Good news for the city. Bad news for the nightlife."

The new headline wrote itself: *Night Drinker Takes Last Drink.*

I clicked my recorder off and slid the notebook back into my coat. Another story for the late edition, neatly wrapped, tied with a bow, and missing all the parts the public didn't need to know.

The truth? The killer was still out there. Always

had been. I tipped my hat to the squad car pulling away, my missing reflection in the diner window.

There's no better hunting ground than a city that never sleeps. And no better cover than a reporter chasing the night.

Case closed. The presses roll.

It's strange how short-sighted people in this city can be. Some residents are just careless, caught in the wrong place at the wrong time. The rest are more careful - more watchful - never straying into daylight.

As for me? I never eat during the day; I find it bad for digestion. Sunlight's a harsh thing for those with an aversion to it. In a city like this, the night is kinder…cooler. The dark brings out the city's true face. Keeps me from losing my ash.

"You know," I say, "some reporters will do anything for a story.

A few of us… We'll do whatever it takes to keep a case alive.

Some stories just never die. And neither do we."

***

Two months later, the story crawls back onto the police blotter. Another body, this one in an alley off 5th and Burns. Case closed? Not in this town.

PART III

WHAT REMAINS

THE WHEEL OF MISFORTUNE

Robin always thought desperation smelled like stale coffee and unpaid bills, but tonight it came dressed up in sequins and stage lights, calling itself "*The Wheel of Misfortune*".

Meet Robin—a recently unemployed mother.

Robin had always believed that rock bottom was a place for other people, not her. She was a hard worker, always dependable, and had excelled at her job. Even her boss, Tony, said as much more than once. But when rock bottom came for Robin, it came fast. A pink slip. An eviction notice. A final, uncompromising call from the hospital billing department.

Nowhere left to turn. No one left to ask.

Her son, Jeremy, only eight, had been sick for most of his life. He needed medication she could no longer afford, and treatments no longer covered by insurance. With each passing day, he seemed to fade: his cough grew deeper, his eyes more sunken, every breath a struggle. Robin could feel time running out. And there was nothing left she could do.

Then, one night, she received an email.

The subject line read: **"Congratulations, You've Been Selected!"** It was from a game show she'd never heard of: *The Wheel of Misfortune.* According to the message, she'd been "randomly drawn" as a potential contestant. All she had to do was reply.

Robin didn't hesitate.

She didn't remember signing up for any drawing, but these days, your name could end up anywhere. She clicked "Reply" and typed a simple message: "I'm interested. Please let me know the next steps."

While she waited for a response, she tried to learn more about the show. A Google search brought up a single website. One page. Slick, colorful, full of promise:

"A brand-new game show experience! Big fortunes! Bigger prizes! Daring challenges! A little trivia, a little luck, and a once-in-a-lifetime chance to turn your fate around!"

But there were no reviews. No press. No links. Social media had little to say, except for one cryptic page that displayed nothing but a ticking clock, counting down.

Robin's gut told her something was off.

But she had nothing left to lose. Nothing but her son.

The next email came a few days later. She had been officially accepted. Attached was a single-page form, no fine print, no clauses, no legalese. Just a blank line waiting for her signature.

"All we need is your confirmation," the email said. "We'll take care of the rest."

Robin hesitated for only a moment.

She printed the form, signed it, scanned it back in, and hit send.

Then she waited.

A few days passed. Then a week. Then two. The electric company threatened to shut off the power. Her landlord taped a final warning to the door. She was running out of time in every sense.

"Mommy's going on a game show," she told Jeremy one night, smoothing back his hair. "We're going to win big, and then we'll be okay. I promise."

Jeremy smiled faintly. He didn't quite understand what she meant, but he believed her. He always believed mommy could fix anything.

Robin tried to believe it too.

Still, a quiet unease lingered; she had signed a blank form, given her name to something unknown, and it felt like something had already shifted, hopefully for the better.

Finally, the third email arrived. It included a date, a time, and detailed directions to the studio. The message ended with a line in bold red text:

"You may already be our new champion!"

Robin let out a shaky breath. Her heart quickened, not with dread this time, but with something like hope.

***

The day finally arrived.

Robin left for the game show studio with a nervous smile and one last look at her son.

"Mommy might be on TV today," she told Jeremy. "I'll be back later this evening, after the show's over, with all our winnings!"

Jeremy gave her a weak smile and wished her good luck.

She kissed his forehead and handed him off to their neighbor and close friend, Mrs. Freda Reman. Freda had babysat Jeremy more times than Robin could count. She was one of the few people Robin still trusted.

The studio wasn't far, tucked into an industrial park behind an abandoned shopping center. The building was windowless, the outside unmarked. But inside, the studio was shockingly pristine. Clean white floors. Gleaming fixtures. Everything bright under the hum of overhead lights.

Robin walked in at her appointed time and was immediately struck by how surreal it all felt. She saw an audience, or what she *thought* was an audience. The lights above the seating area were dim, casting everyone in shadow. She couldn't make out faces or even bodies, just rows of unmoving, gray silhouettes.

Remote cameras rolled back and forth across the floor, gliding silently into position like insects on rails. Robin noticed something odd: there were no logos on the cameras. No network names, no station IDs. In fact, there were no logos *anywhere* in the studio. No production signs, no dressing room labels. Nothing.

That unsettled her more than she expected.

Across the room, she spotted the host.

Mr. Widemen.

He stood beneath a glowing rig of lights at the center of the game show floor. His suit shimmered in unnatural hues, colors that shifted like oil on water. His smile was wide. Too wide. His teeth were a brilliant, almost blinding white, and just slightly too large for his mouth.

Robin reminded herself: *TV personalities always look strange in real life. The lighting. The makeup. The pressure to smile too much.*

Before she could stare too long, a woman approached her with an official air and a clipboard.

"Ms. Carter?" she said. "I'm Ms. Goodwin. Assistant to Mr. Widemen. Just a few formalities before we begin."

Robin nodded, trying to steady her nerves.

Ms. Goodwin handed her a sleek digital tablet. "Standard waiver," she said briskly. "Where to send the prize check, emergency contacts, ticket names. Just routine."

Robin glanced down at the form. It wasn't in English.

In fact… it wasn't in any language she recognized at all. The characters were sharp and angular, moving slightly as she looked at them, like they resisted being read.

Robin blinked hard. When she looked again, the lines had settled, vaguely resembling something close enough to English. She hesitated, then signed her name.

Just nerves. TV trickery. That's all.

She looked around, expecting to see crew members, producers, or stagehands. But there were none. Just the silent cameras. Ms. Goodwin. Mr. Widemen. And a handful of other contestants, who stood off to the side, grinning far too widely. Their excitement felt... off. Too eager. Too rehearsed.

"Places, everyone!" Ms. Goodwin called. "Robin, you'll be right over here, next to Mr. Widemen, facing the audience. Yes, stand right there on the X."

Robin moved to the glowing red X marked on the studio floor. Her palms were sweating. Her stomach twisted.

"You'll be the first called on," Ms. Goodwin whispered. "Be ready."

Robin gave a tight nod.

Then the lights flared even brighter.

"Three... two... one..."

Ms. Goodwin disappeared off stage.

And *the Wheel of Misfortune* went live.

The Game Begins

Robin was the first contestant called.

"Let's start with something easy," Mr. Widemen beamed, his smile gleaming like polished ivory. "A little trivia about your family."

A question appeared on the glowing screen behind him: *"What's the name of your grandmother's famous casserole she always brought to Thanksgiving?"*

Robin blinked.

There was no way they could know that. It was such a small detail, something barely anyone remembered but her and her late mother. Still, Robin answered.

"Green Bean Crunch."

The audience, still shrouded in dim grayness, erupted in thunderous applause. Robin felt a strange warmth settle in her chest. The screen flashed: **YOU WIN!**

A conveyor belt rose from the floor, revealing a neatly packed brown grocery bag. Cans of vegetables, a loaf of bread, a box of cereal.

It wasn't money. But it was something. Something useful.

Robin smiled and gave a little bow. "Thank you."

The other contestants were called up one by one. A short round of trivia. Another grocery bag. A phone card. A box fan. All harmless, until one contestant, a woman in a pink tracksuit, got her question wrong.

The lights flickered.

Sparks danced briefly above the stage as a deep mechanical buzz echoed through the studio. Two large figures in matte-black uniforms appeared, emerging from unseen doors behind the set. They grabbed the woman by the arms.

"Wait! Wait, no," she shouted, heels skidding across the floor. "I can do another one! Please! I'll take the dare!"

The audience clapped and cheered, louder than ever.

Robin's stomach dropped.

The woman was dragged offstage, her screams quickly swallowed by the darkness behind the curtains. The cameras didn't follow. No one seemed disturbed. Not even Mr. Widemen.

"Now, *that's* the spirit of the game!" he laughed.

Robin tried to breathe evenly. *It's just part of the*

show. Drama. Shock value. Maybe it's all staged...

Then it was her turn again.

Ms. Goodwin's voice whispered from the wings: "Robin, your spin."

Robin stepped up to the massive, brass-edged wheel and grabbed the lever.

It spun with a slow, metallic groan, each tick louder than the last. The lights pulsed as the colors on the wheel blurred: TRIVIA. DARE. FORTUNE. FATE. TRIVIA. DARE. FATE.

It stopped on **DARE**.

Robin's heart sank.

Mr. Widemen's smile brightened. "Oooh, our first dare of the night! Now, let's not be too cruel this early in the show." He leaned toward her with an exaggerated wink. Robin, your dare is simple. Give your charming host a kiss... right here." He tapped his cheek.

Robin let out a nervous laugh. The crowd erupted into whistles and applause. "That's it?" she asked.

"That's it!" Mr. Widemen grinned.

Robin leaned in and gave him a quick peck on the cheek.

She laughed. "That was easy. I like those."

Mr. Widemen turned to her slowly, his smile widening just a fraction too far.

"Do you now?" he said, voice rich with amusement. "You like easy dares... or kissing the host?"

The audience roared with laughter. Robin smiled too, but it didn't last. She glanced back toward the audience.

They were still.

Gray. Silhouetted. Not one face visible. Not one body moving. Just shapes, clapping with impossible synchronicity.

Robin's smile faded.

The lights shifted.

"Let's bring up our next contestant," Mr. Widemen said, his voice returning to its game-show cadence. "Say hello to Wendel Jefferson!"

A tall, lanky man in a mustard-yellow jacket ambled up to the wheel. His grin was lopsided, but his eyes were nervous.

Wendel spun the wheel. It ticked, clicked, and slowed... landing on **TRIVIA**.

Mr. Widemen's voice dropped an octave. "Wendel Jefferson, here's your question. Tell me… how long does it take for a young boy to die from a respiratory disease... if left untreated?"

Robin felt the blood drain from her face.

Wendel stood frozen. His eyes darted to the audience, still unmoving. Then to the ceiling. Then back to Mr. Widemen.

He swallowed hard. "Two weeks, Mr. Widemen. That's my answer."

Robin clutched the edge of her podium. The question hit too close. It felt personal. It felt targeted.

A long pause.

Mr. Widemen's smile grew unnaturally wide. "I'm sorry, Wendel Jefferson. But your answer... is incorrect."

The buzzer blared.

Two black-suited figures emerged again.

Wendel screamed as they grabbed him. "Wait! That's right! I know it is! Don't, don't touch me!"

The stage lights flickered.

Robin watched, heart racing, as Wendel kicked and thrashed, dragged offstage like the woman before him. His screams lingered even after he vanished.

And then, silence.

Mr. Widemen straightened his tie and faced the

camera with a dazzling smile. "Well folks, the stakes are heating up! Stay tuned, because the Wheel of Misfortune is just getting started.

The Second Round

Round two began with Robin once again.

She stepped up to the wheel, wiped her clammy palm on her jeans, and gripped the lever. With a tug, she sent the wheel spinning. It groaned with each slow turn, lights flashing and flickering with every rotation.

Click. Tick. Click… tick… click.

The wheel creaked to a stop.

Robin squinted at the arrow. It pointed to a golden wedge with bold red text.

$5,000.

"Congratulations, Ms. Carter!" Mr. Widemen declared, his grin spreading from ear to ear, his oversized teeth practically glowing under the lights. "You've just won five thousand dollars!"

The audience roared, cheers, whistles, applause echoing across the studio.

And yet... not a single figure moved.

Still gray silhouettes. Still frozen in place.

Robin didn't care. Not in that moment.

Five thousand dollars. It could get them through the month. Rent. Electricity. Groceries. Maybe a few medications for Jeremy, not treatment, but enough to buy time. It was more than she'd had in months.

She felt tears rising and quickly blinked them back.

Mr. Widemen handed her a large placard with **$5,000** stamped across it in shimmering gold letters.

"Well done, Ms. Carter," he said, then turned to the audience with a theatrical flourish. "But let's up the ante, shall we?"

The audience gasped in perfect harmony, like one breath held by a single, monstrous lung.

"You can take the five thousand dollars and go home…" Mr. Widemen paused, his hand dramatically hovering in the air, "...or…"

The studio lights flashed.

A set of three large doors rose from the back of the stage, each one glowing with eerie illumination.

"...you can choose a door behind me. One chance. One choice. Nowwwwwwwww!" he shouted, spinning in place with an exuberant wave toward the doors.

The audience erupted again, applause, whistles, shrill hoots of encouragement.

"Stay calm, folks!" Mr. Widemen chided playfully. "Ms. Carter still needs to pick."

He turned to Robin, voice suddenly low and silky. "So what will it be, Ms. Carter? The guaranteed cash... or one of the three doors?"

Robin hesitated.

She looked down at the placard in her hands, then up at the doors.

Door One bore a glowing red heart symbol. Door Two had a luminous eye etched across its face. Door Three swirled with a spinning black spiral, like it was pulling the light inward.

Her fingers tightened around the card.

Mr. Widemen's voice returned, more insistent now. "Time is ticking, Ms. Carter. What's it going to be?"

Robin closed her eyes for a breath, then opened them. "I'll choose one of the doors."

The crowd erupted with cheers, their approval thunderous and unified.

"Brave choice!" Mr. Widemen said, bouncing in

place. "Could be the right one!" Mr. Widemen reached over and took the placard from Robin's hands in a quick flick of his wrist.

Robin looked once more at the symbols. *Heart, eye, spiral…*

"The heart," she said, pointing. "Door number one."

A wave of mixed reactions rolled across the audience, some clapped, others booed.

"Oooooh, the heart," Mr. Widemen grinned, dragging the word out like silk. "Let's see what you've chosen."

With a hiss of hidden hydraulics, door one rose.

Behind it wasn't a prize.

It was a screen.

A film flickered to life.

Robin's blood ran cold.

It was her. In a hospital room with Jeremy. She stood at his bedside, speaking to a doctor just outside the frame. Her face looked worn, drained. The doctor spoke, then Robin looked down at her son. And slowly, she shook her head, no.

The doctor nodded solemnly and turned to leave

the room.

Robin's heart pounded. The memory clawed its way back.

That moment.

That choice.

"Ms. Carter," Mr. Widemen said, stepping beside her, "in order to win what's behind the screen... all you have to do is relive the choice you made in that moment."

Robin blinked. "I, I don't understand."

"Just tell us," Mr. Widemen purred, "what choice did you make that day… about your son's care?"

Robin looked at the screen, then back to the host. Her voice trembled. "I... I don't know. I made a lot of choices. It was a very hard time. I, I don't remember which day this was…"

A long pause.

"I'm sorry, Ms. Carter," Mr. Widemen said, shaking his head. "That's the wrong answer."

The audience applauded wildly, laughing, cheering, whistling in glee.

"But," Mr. Widemen continued, "because we're such *generous* hosts… we're giving you *one more chance* to win what's behind the screen."

Robin's pulse hammered in her ears.

Mr. Widemen turned toward her, and now his smile was impossibly wide, his teeth glistening like polished knives. His suit shimmered brighter, pulsing with an almost living glow. The spotlight above Robin grew hot, harsh.

"One final choice," he said, voice deepening. "You keep your soul... and sweet Jeremy loses his. Or, you lose yours, and your son lives on, soul intact, struggling… but alive."

Robin's breath caught.

She looked around, at the other contestants, who watched without blinking. At the unmoving audience. At the doors behind her. Panic rose in her chest.

"I-I don't understand," she whispered. "My soul... or my son's soul? What kind of game is this? I-I didn't sign up for this!"

Mr. Widemen chuckled. "Oh, but you *did* sign up for this, Ms. Carter. You should always read the fine print."

He turned to the audience with exaggerated glee. "Well, folks, what do *you* think? Should she give up her soul... or his?"

"HERS! HERS! HERS!" the audience chanted in unison, their silhouettes undulating like a shadowed sea.

Robin began to back away. "No... no, I didn't... I didn't mean to sign up for *this*, "

The two black-suited escorts stepped from the wings.

Robin screamed as they approached. She struggled, kicked, tried to run, but they lifted her like a rag doll, dragging her back toward door number one.

"No! No! Please, no! Jeremy needs me!"

The audience clapped louder. Mr. Widemen blew her a kiss.

As the door began to lower behind her, sealing her fate, Robin collapsed to the floor, sobbing.

And the game rolled on.

Final Round: A Soul for a Soul

The bright game show lights dimmed.

Stagehands, silent and faceless, rolled the old set away, vanishing it into the dark beyond the curtains.

In its place, a strange new set was wheeled out.

It looked less like a stage and more like a shrine. The new wheel was larger, much larger, towering over the floor like some ancient mechanism. But unlike before, the spaces on the wheel were hidden beneath blood-red covers. No labels. No categories. Just secrets.

Robin was escorted back onto the stage.

Her eyes were red and bloodshot, her steps unsteady. She looked lost. Disoriented. Her clothes were damp with sweat, her arms trembling. The audience roared its approval, cheers, howls, applause echoing like a storm, but Robin barely heard them.

She was placed on a glowing red X marked with her name: **ROBIN CARTER**

The light beneath her pulsed slowly, like a heartbeat.

Robin blinked up at the set. It was different now. The walls were darker, the floor scorched, like it had been burned in places. The cameras were gone, or maybe they were watching from places she couldn't see.

Then, from the other side of the stage, the only remaining contestant was brought out.

They too were led to a red glowing X, their name appearing above it in eerie floating letters. Robin turned to look but barely registered their face. Everything was spinning. The lights were too bright. The air is too thin.

And then, like clockwork, he arrived.

Mr. Widemen.

He stepped onto the new set with a theatrical flourish, his shoes echoing across the stone-like floor. His suit now shimmered like it was made of molten glass, his grin sharper, impossibly wide. His eyes, glowing faintly beneath the lights, fixed on the crowd.

He walked to the massive wheel and turned to address the audience.

"Members of the audience…" he announced, arms open wide, "…as you *all* know, this round isn't for prizes."

The crowd fell dead silent.

"This… is for the ritual. This spin… is a soul for a soul."

The crowd erupted again, screaming, cheering, stomping the ground with thunderous glee.

Mr. Widemen faced Robin now.

"Ms. Carter, you *can* leave," he said, his tone oddly gentle. "But only if you give up someone you love. Your son… your fellow contestant…"

He leaned in, his voice like poisoned honey.

"Or… yourself."

Robin shook her head. "I don't understand! What is this?! What are you talking about?!"

She turned to the other contestant, to the shadows of the audience, to anyone, but there was no answer. Only the roars and the flickering lights.

"No one leaves the game," Mr. Widemen said, "without a final spin."

He turned back to the wheel.

With a dramatic motion, he peeled back the first blood-red cover.

Underneath it, the name:

JEREMY CARTER

Robin let out a choked cry.

The second cover came off.

The name of the fellow contestant gleamed beneath it.

And then the final section, he tore it away like flesh from bone.

ROBIN CARTER

Robin stumbled backward. "No! No, I'm not doing this! I won't!"

Mr. Widemen's smile never faded.

"Ms. Carter," he said, motioning to the wheel, "step up and give it a big ole spin."

Robin screamed. "You can't make me do this!"

The lights above flickered violently.

Sparks rained from the ceiling.

The set shook.

Panels collapsed, the stage cracking beneath them. What had been polished studio floor now melted and bubbled, revealing slick, black stone beneath it. The bright lights dimmed to a deep crimson. The cameras sparked, sagged, and crumbled into ash.

Beneath it all, a black stone altar emerged, etched with runes that pulsed like breathing wounds.

Robin screamed again, backing away.

"HELP! Help us!" she cried, voice hoarse, pleading.

The lights above the audience flared suddenly.

And she saw them.

Withered husks sat in the audience seats, dried, skeletal, twisted. Their mouths open in frozen grins. These weren't viewers. They were *remnants*. The souls of past contestants, their laughter now the haunting echo of death.

Robin collapsed to her knees, sobbing.

The camera, if it still existed, panned slowly to the wheel.

It **began to spin** on its own.

Slowly.

Deliberately.

Each tick like a death knell.

Robin reached out weakly, tried to crawl, but her body failed her.

She looked up, just once more, and then everything went dark.

A new Game Begins

The stage was spotless.

The original set had been wheeled back out, piece by perfect piece. The bright, polished white floor gleamed beneath studio lights. The massive wheel had returned, standing tall and ominous, its segments once again bold, colorful, and legible.

Cameras rolled into place on silent wheels.

The audience lights dimmed to soft gray, their silhouettes once again barely visible, unmoving, unbreathing, waiting.

Everything looked the same.

But it wasn't.

Fresh contestants arrived, ushered onto the stage by unseen handlers. They smiled nervously, eyes wide with hope, excitement, maybe even desperation.

They were directed to their marks, standing beside the wheel, right where others had stood, not so long ago.

Between the contestants and the wheel, a red **X** glowed faintly.

Above it, floating in the cold studio air, was a name:

HOST

The crowd murmured in anticipation.

Then, from the shadows beyond the set, a figure emerged.

The host walked slowly, deliberately, waving to the audience like a seasoned performer.

It was Robin.

But not the Robin who had entered this place desperate and afraid.

This Robin wore a dark, shimmering suit that glittered like obsidian glass. Her hair was perfectly styled, her posture impossibly straight. Her smile was stretched wide, too wide, the corners of her mouth twitching upward like pulled skin. Oversized teeth gleamed beneath her barely parted lips.

She stepped into the red X marked HOST and turned toward the audience.

Lifting her hands, palms up, she greeted them.

"Welcome back to *Wheel of Misfortune…*" she said, her voice smooth, practiced, and eerily sweet. "Where every spin brings fortune…"

Her eyes flashed under the lights.

"…and sometimes, *misfortune.*"

The audience erupted in applause, mechanical and soulless.

The wheel spun once more.

And the game began again.

FADE TO BLACK.

The applause lingers a moment too long.

Then silence.

Just the slow, echoing *tick... tick... tick* of the wheel.

And then,

nothing.

The screen stays dark. The audience gone. The game... waiting.

The Black Land Settler

(Painted Desert Curse)

The wagon clattered along the trail leading down from the mountains into the bleak desert landscape. The sun was hot, and the heat rose with every mile. Caleb halted the mare and jumped down from the buckboard.

"Eli, get down and fetch the mare some water from the barrel." He hollered as he brushed away the sweat and flies on the mare's head. His calloused hands still bore the memory of the ropes and saltwater.

"Yes, Pa," Eli said as he hurriedly jumped from the back of the wagon. He pried off the lid of the old whiskey barrel and filled the bucket meant for the mare. Upfront and still sitting on the buckboard seat was Ruth, Caleb's wife and Eli's mother. "Isn't this place just the prettiest land you'd ever see, Ruth?" Caleb said as he took off his hat and wiped the sweat from his brow, squinting his eyes as he looked across the desert landscape.

Ruth put her hand over her eyes to block the sun and looked out over the landscape. "Lord, Caleb, how does anything live here? It's so hot and there's no shade anywhere that I can see. How do you expect to grow anything in this sand?" Caleb shook his head and put his hat back on. Eli walked up with the water and placed the bucket in front of the mare's head. The mare put her muzzle in the bucket and began to drink deeply. Eli took a rag from his pocket and dipped it in the bucket. He pulled it out and began wiping the mare's neck, cooling her from the relentless sun.

"Woman, you just have to trust me. There's a place not much further. It has good growin' soil for crops and plenty of water. Even Mr. Welch said he'd bought the land if I hadn't. This is where we're going to live out our days." Caleb pulled the handkerchief from his back pocket, dipped it into the bucket of water, and wiped his neck with it. Ruth didn't say anything more to Caleb. She had Eli fetch her some water to drink. She sipped on the water and then gave it back to Eli. She picked up her bible from beneath the seat. She opened it and began reading softly to herself, ignoring Caleb, who was standing by the mare watching her.

By evening, as the shadows grew long and the heat began to wane, Caleb brought the wagon to a stop at a spot near a small creek where Caleb could let the mare roam, and they could set up camp for the night. Eli jumped from the wagon and began unhitching the mare. He left the reins on her and led her over and into the creek. The mare appeared to be happy with the creek, pawing at the water as it passed over her hoofs. She drank much more slowly now than before and let the water cool her down. Eli left the mare in the creek and went back to the wagon to pull out his bedroll and his twenty-two-caliber long gun. While Eli was doing his thing, Caleb got a fire going, and Ruth pulled the pans and coffee pot from the wagon.

"Eli, go see if you can rustle up us a hare somewhere," Caleb yelled down to the boy.

"Ok, Pa," Eli yelled back. Eli grabbed his long gun and headed down the bank of the creek, keeping an eye out for a hare and for any snakes lying close to the creek.

A few minutes later, Eli came running up to the camp with a fat jackrabbit. "You're getting pretty good with that thing, Eli," Caleb said as he took the rabbit from Eli. "Dang son, you even cleaned and skinned it for your ma." A smile widened across Eli's dirty face. "Quit your gabbing and give me that thing so I can cook it before it gets too late, Caleb!" Ruth said playfully, flashing Eli a small grin. Ruth sprinkled salt and some herbs, which she brought with them, onto the bare rabbit and put it over the fire. "Go get washed up, Eli, you're as dirty as this desert."

"Sure, Ma," Eli said. "I'll put the mare up while I'm down at the creek."

"You're a good boy, son," Ruth said as she stroked the back of Eli's dirty head. Eli walked away towards the creek.

"How much further do we have to go before we get there, Caleb? The boy's bound to be getting couped up in the wagon and needs to get settled in. And I need a place to lay my head at night that ain't without a roof."

Caleb looked at Ruth. "Well, I'd say we should be there by midday tomorrow." Caleb pointed off to the west, towards the glow of the horizon. "Look there, over that ridge, just past that clump of bushes. Just past that point is 'our' land, Ruth. The Toller farm." Caleb was grinning.

"Caleb, you look like the fox that just snuck into the henhouse. I hope to be as excited as you are right now when I see it."

Caleb's grin widened, "You will, Ruth, I'm sure of it."

Eli returned, his face and hands clean, and sat down next to the fire.

They all sat around the fire, eating rabbit and

talking about their farm. The fire cast dancing shadows on the wagon, and the breeze blew the smoke across the creek. In the distance, the mare grunted, pawing at the ground, spooked by something unseen. A single wolf howled, then something fluttered over the camp, wings flapping, landing on a rotted tree down by the creek. It sat. "What was that? Did you hear that?" Ruth said as she looked around, then to Caleb.

"I'm sure it's nothing. We should turn in; we need to get going early in the morning, before it gets hot." While Ruth cleaned everything up, Caleb got more wood for the fire and checked the wagon.

Eli went down to the creek where he had tied the mare earlier. He lay on his bedroll and looked at the stars in the sky, thinking about the new place. He saw movement out of the corner of his eye and looked up at the old tree. There was a dark silhouette sitting on one of the branches. It didn't bother Eli; he was far too excited about tomorrow to worry about a little old bird.

In the early morning darkness, they gathered their belongings into the wagon, hitched the mare, and headed back on the trail. No one said much as they slowly made their way further west. Everyone was thinking about what lay ahead, how their lives would change, and what it would be like to be on their own land.

They made one last stop to water the mare and for Caleb to lube one of the rear wagon wheels that was becoming noisy and loose. Caleb was squatting in front of the wheel when Ruth called out to him. "Caleb, you'd better get up here. A man is approaching, I think he's one of them Indians."

Caleb stood up, reached into the back of the wagon, pulled out his forty-five revolver and stuffed it into his pants. "Eli, you stay back here and keep your head down, ya hear?" he said, not taking his eyes off the man walking towards the front of the wagon.

Eli shook his head and lay flat in the back, placing his hand on his long gun next to him. Caleb walked ahead of the wagon and stopped several feet in front of the mare.

The approaching man stopped and raised his hands into the air. "I have no weapon. Thirst is all that I have," the old man said as he squinted his eyes from the blowing sand. He produced a white rag and waved it high into the air so it could be seen clearly over the sand.

"I mean you know harm. I'm just an old Indian

making his way across the desert in search of spirits," the man said, eyeing Caleb.

Caleb kept a hand near the revolver. "You have no horse, how are you going to make it across this desert with no horse?" Caleb called out.

The old man coughed a few times, then answered, "One foot at a time. Might I come closer? My throat is dry and this sand makes it more so."

Caleb looked back at the wagon and Ruth, then back to the old Indian. "Yeah, you can approach, just keep your hands where I can see 'em. My boy has a rifle on you.

"Can I ask you for a drink of water?" the old man asked, looking over at the wagon.

"Stand right here, and I'll get you some water," Caleb said, still maintaining eye contact with the old man. Caleb called Eli to fetch the old man some water.

The old man eyed Eli as he got out of the wagon, quickly glancing at Ruth, then returning his gaze to Caleb. "I am called Old Crow. I'm an elder of the Ute tribe in these territories." Caleb eyed the old man questioningly.

"So if it's just you, where did you come from, in the middle of the desert?" The old man looked at Eli and gave a small nod. He took the pail of water from Eli, took a deep drink, then wiped his mouth with the back of his hand.

"I should ask you the same…Mr….?" Old Crow said.

"Toller, Caleb Toller, and this here is my boy, Eli. The woman sitting in the wagon is my wife, Ruth. Now you have all our names, maybe you can tell me why you're here," Caleb said exhaustedly. Old Crow took another drink from the pail and then handed it back to Eli.

"I walk the desert in search of spirits, but here, there are none. This land… it is cursed. This land was buried many moons ago and remains so. This land is not walked upon by Indian or by spirits. It should remain so, Mr. Toller. You too should not walk here."

Caleb snorted in disbelief. "Old man..."

"Old Crow, if you don't mind," the Indian said, interrupting Caleb's thought.

"Old Crow…you trying to scare us off with tales of ghosts and curses, is that it? Well, I'll tell ya…we won't be driven out by such nonsense. So don't go telling us all this spooky horse dung in hopes that we won't stay. It ain't happenin'. I didn't bring my family all the way across this here country to turn tail and run.

Old Crow shook his head. "The words I speak are truth, not tales. I will keep searching for spirits. Peace to you, Toller family." With that, he turned and walked past the wagon, his figure shrinking into the haze until the desert swallowed him whole.

Eli squinted after him. "Pa… you think any of that's true? About the land being cursed and all?"

Caleb spat into the dust. "No, boy. Just talk from an old Indian who's been too long in the sun. Don't trouble your mind with it. And don't go telling your ma, you hear?"

Eli nodded, though his eyes lingered on the empty horizon where Old Crow had gone.

Ruth lowered the Bible in her lap. "What did he say, Caleb?"

"Nothing worth repeating," Caleb muttered, climbing back onto the buckboard. He slapped the reins, eager to be moving. Still, a small thorn of unease worked at the back of his mind. He shoved it down. "Nothing but wind and words."

The wagon crested a low rise. The mare halted, ears twitching, and let out a sharp snort. Caleb steadied her, but his grin faded when he saw what lay ahead.

"There it is… our new home." His smile faltered. "But… what's that doing there?"

Below them, a log house and barn crouched on the plain. At first glance, the place looked abandoned to the dust: windows clouded with grime, the porch half-choked with sagebrush, cobwebs draped thick across the door frame. The barn door yawned open, one hinge sagging. A few slats gaped like missing teeth.

Ruth's voice was low. "I thought this land was empty, Caleb. Whose house is that?"

"I aim to find out," he said, snapping the reins. The mare balked, then stepped forward, hooves clopping down the slope until the wagon stopped short of the porch. Caleb climbed down first, knocking on the weathered door. No answer. Ruth wiped at a pane of glass; behind the smeared streak her hand left, the rooms inside were drowned in shadow and dust.

"Doesn't look like anyone's here," she whispered.

Eli pushed at the door. It groaned wide, dragging cobwebs with it. A wave of staleness poured out, rot, mold, something sourer beneath. He gagged, covering his nose. "Pa, it stinks something awful. Like something died in there."

"Nah," Caleb said, stepping inside, his boots crunching on grit. "Just been closed up too long."

The dim interior revealed itself in patches: a blackened iron stove, a rough-hewn table, chairs thick with dust, bedframes cobwebbed in the corners. Caleb's eyes gleamed despite the gloom. "Ruth, this place already has near everything we need. Stove, beds, table. Just wants a woman's touch is all."

Ruth's frown deepened. She had dreamed of her own home, raised from the ground by their own hands. This felt like stepping into another family's shadow. Still, it was shelter, and better than a wagon bed.

Caleb clapped Eli on the shoulder. "Come on, boy. Let's have a look at the barn."

The two crossed the yard, weeds brushing their boots, and stepped inside the yawning doorway. Dust motes swirled in the shafts of light cutting through the broken slats. The air smelled of dry wood and something older, sour, that clung to the nostrils.

Caleb's eyes swept the place. "Sturdy enough," he muttered. "Roof don't leak, least not yet." He walked to the center of the barn and stopped, boot heel pressing against a small rise in the dirt floor. He crouched and pressed a hand to the mound. "Strange. Like a slab of stone under here. Barn floors ought to be flat dirt, nothing more." He gave it a few hard kicks, listening to the dull, unmoving thud. "Rock bed, maybe." His brow furrowed, but he left it at that.

Eli, meanwhile, tilted his head back. A crow perched on the crossbeam above them; its black feathers ruffled in the draft. He blinked, uneasy. The bird's sockets were empty…hollow pits where eyes should have been.

A shiver worked its way down his spine. He circled to the far side of the barn, keeping the beam in sight, but when he looked again the crow was gone. No flutter of wings, no sound of escape, just empty wood and dust. He stood there a moment, confused, before Caleb's voice pulled him back. "Eli! Come on, we'd best see to your ma."

Eli gave the rafters one last glance, then hurried after his father. He said nothing of what he'd seen, neither to Caleb nor to Ruth.

***

The days settled into a rhythm. Ruth scrubbed and

aired the old house until the smell of rot gave way to the scent of lye soap and fresh bread. She tacked curtains of her own sewing in the windows, set flowers in a chipped pitcher on the table, and read her Bible by lamplight in the evenings, her voice steady against the hush of the prairie night. Caleb hauled supplies from town and traded for two strong oxen, the beasts slow but dependable for the work ahead. Eli did his share, running fence lines, tending the mare, and fetching water from the creek.

By the third week, the Toller place no longer looked abandoned. Smoke curled from the chimney each morning, and the sound of hammering and chopping drifted across the land as Caleb and Eli cleared brush and cut deadwood. It was while they were working one hot afternoon that Eli stopped and pointed.

"Pa, look at that."

Half-buried in the earth lay a great flat stone, larger than a wagon door and smooth as if laid there by hand. Caleb struck it with the back of his axe, the ring of it dull and hollow. He crouched, brushing soil from the edges. "Ain't natural," he muttered. "Help me try and move it."

Father and son strained at the slab, wedging poles and heaving until sweat ran down their faces, but it wouldn't budge. At last Caleb whistled for the mare and rigged a chain to the stone. With a sharp command, the animal leaned into the harness, muscles straining.

The rock shifted, then slid aside with a grinding groan. From the dark hole beneath rushed a blast of stale, cold air, rank with age. It whistled upward like a deep, guttural roar.

The mare screamed and bolted, jerking the chain free. She wheeled in panic, dragging the stone with her as it toppled and bounced, nearly clipping Eli where he stood frozen. Caleb lunged and yanked his boy clear. The rock slammed into the earth with a crash.

Breathless, Eli looked down into the black maw. Far below, water glimmered faintly in the gloom.

Caleb spat into the dirt, his hand tight on Eli's shoulder. "Well, I'll be. Looks like we found ourselves a well."

But the words didn't steady him. The air still stank of something old and wrong, and the sound of that rush - like a beast roused from slumber- lingered in his ears.

"Hey, boys, I'll have lunch on the table in a bit - y'all go wash up," Ruth called from the porch.

Caleb and Eli exchanged grins, slapping dust from

their clothes. They stowed the tools in the barn, caught the mare, and headed toward the house.

Inside, Ruth laid out bread, beans, and the last of the water from the brown pitcher. The creek water was far from clear, but it was all they had. She set the pitcher by the door and sat down. "Eli," she said, passing bread to Caleb, "when you're done helping your pa this afternoon, I'll need more water from the creek." Eli smirked and glanced at his father. Caleb's grin gave him away.

"What's so funny about fetching water, Eli?" Ruth asked, her eyes narrowing.

Eli leaned forward, proud. "Won't be needing to fetch creek water anymore, Ma. Me and Pa uncovered a well down past the barn."

Ruth froze, then turned slowly to Caleb. "You found…a well? Out here?"

Caleb tore off a chunk of bread, chewed, and nodded. "Covered by a rock big as a wagon wheel. We just happened on it while clearing brush."

Her face darkened. "And you think it's safe? A well sealed up like that…maybe it went bad. Or worse - maybe someone fell in." She pressed a rag to her mouth. "I don't want to know if there's someone still down there, Caleb."

He sighed, leaning back in his chair. "Woman, there ain't no body. I looked in myself. After lunch, I'll draw some water and prove it to you." Ruth's knot of unease only tightened.

After the meal, Caleb told Eli to stay and help his ma while he tested the well.

Eli sulked. "Aw, Pa, I wanted to see if there was a dead body."

"Enough of that talk," Caleb said, shouldering rope and bucket.

At the well, he tied one end to a spindly tree, the other to the bucket handle, and lowered it down. Around sixty feet, the rope went slack, the bucket striking water with a splash. He drew it up, careful not to spill.

The water smelled rank. Caleb sniffed, wrinkling his nose. "Whew. Been shut up too long." He dipped a pinky in, touched it to his tongue, puckered. "Bitter." He dumped the water onto the ground, some splashing against the broad stone slab they'd rolled aside.

He lowered the bucket again. The second haul tasted cleaner, fresher. "Better. She'll settle with use." He grinned, drank a swallow, then poured the rest over his head, the cold water streaming down his neck and back.

That afternoon, he built a rough pulley over the well, rigging it sturdy enough for buckets of water. "Later, we'll see how the mare and oxen like it," he muttered, gathering tools.

As he walked away, he stepped over the heavy rock that had sealed the well. Droplets from the bucket dripped down its face, washing away clotted dust and dirt. Beneath, faint lines glimmered. An ancient carving emerged, etched deep into the stone, forming a symbol long forgotten.

The next morning, Eli was tending the mare and oxen, one of the chores he disliked most. He dragged the watering trough closer to the well so he wouldn't have to haul buckets back and forth. The trough was brimming with water, but no matter how he coaxed, the animals refused to drink. He tugged, pleaded, even climbed onto the mare's back to lead her over, but she reared and tossed him into the brush before bolting away. The oxen stood stubborn, their great heads turned aside, hooves grinding the dirt.

Frustrated, Eli stormed back to the barn. These dumb animals won't even drink," he complained. "If I bring water to them in buckets, they drink it fine. But they won't touch the trough by the well. What's wrong with them, Pa?"

Caleb frowned, stepping to the door. "Where'd you put it, Eli? I don't see it."

"I moved it closer, cut down on the trips. You told me - work smarter, not harder."

Caleb chuckled despite himself. "Fair enough. Let's see if moving it back makes a difference."

Together they slid the trough to its old spot. Within minutes the animals crowded around and began to drink greedily. Eli whooped and ran back to tell his father. Caleb ruffled the boy's hair but kept glancing at the well, unease tightening in his chest. His pa had always said animals could sense what men could not. Caleb didn't want to believe it, but he couldn't ignore what he'd seen.

***

Weeks passed. The well became part of their lives, used daily for cooking, washing, and drinking. They hardly thought of the creek anymore. But the animals never came near the well, circling wide as if skirting some invisible fence. Caleb told himself it was nothing - yet when he started planting, the strangeness deepened.

Seeds rotted before sprouting. Shoots transplanted from the creek bed withered as soon as their roots touched the soil. Even jars of plants grown in well water shriveled, while creek water kept them alive. Caleb tried again and again, but every failure drew his mind back to the words Old Crow had spoken to him before they'd settled here. He shook the memory away, muttering "hogwash" under his breath, but doubt festered like a splinter.

Late one night, Ruth woke in a sweat. The cabin was dark, except for the faint glow of embers in the hearth. Caleb snored beside her, but the air felt heavy, off somehow.

She closed her eyes, but the dream pressed itself upon her once more.

She was in the cabin with Eli. Caleb was gone. A knock rattled the door. She opened it, but no one stood there, only that of a darkness deeper than night. From that blackness rose a glow, faint and red, pulsing from the well.

Drawn outside, she walked toward it. The ground shifted beneath her feet, and a great flat stone blocked her path. A strange symbol glistened on its face, writhing in the glow. No matter how she stepped, the stone slid itself in front of her, until at last, she leapt past it and reached the well.

The light throbbed like a heartbeat. From below came the sound of claws scraping stone. Trembling, Ruth leaned over the mouth of the well.

Something moved.

Her father's broken body crawled upward through the shaft, his skull split clean down the crown like a rotted log. She screamed and turned to flee but stumbled over the stone. It cracked beneath her weight, the symbol tearing apart with the break.

Her father's corpse was already on top of her when she woke.

The next morning as they ate breakfast, Ruth sat, eyes bloodshot red, staring into nothing. Her mind was still replaying the dream she had.

"Ruth!" Caleb called to her, but she didn't respond until Caleb knocked on the tabletop.

"Uh, what? You want more coffee?"

Ruth was about to get up when Caleb grabbed her wrist. "Ruth, what's with you this morning, you ain't yourself? You're here, but your mind's out yonder. I don't need any coffee. Our boy asked you a question."

Ruth sat back down and looked to Eli. "I'm sorry, honey, what was your question again?"

Eli looked questioningly at Ruth. "Are you going to read to me today from the bible? It's Sunday."

She looked towards Eli, but not at him, more through him. "Yes, sure, honey…later. Go play now." She waved Eli away, her eyes still elsewhere. Eli turned his eyes to his father, puzzled. Caleb motioned Eli towards the door.

After Eli left to complete his chores, Caleb snapped his fingers in front of Ruth, making her jump in the chair.

She looked at him. "What was that for?" Her brow furrowed.

"Something eatin' at you this mornin'? The coffee was barely black, and the eggs were dang near raw. That ain't like you, Ruth."

She stared at him for a few seconds. "I just had a strange dream last night. It's nothing. Sorry, …you want me to fix something else for you?"

Caleb slid his chair closer to hers, placed his hand upon hers, and held it. "Do you want to tell me about it,

Ruth?"

"No, I don't want to talk about it. It's just a dream," she said sharply as she excused herself from the table, leaving Caleb still sitting alone at the table.

Eli finished with the animals and wandered down to the gully where the struggling crops were planted. Eli walked around the small plot of crops, kicking rocks and running his hand over the brittle stalks.

He turned from the plants and started towards the creek when he heard a voice call his name in the still air. "Eli…Eli..." He froze, unsure if he had really heard it. He turned back to the crops and looked around. He didn't see anyone and it didn't sound like his Ma or Pa. It sounded more like a boy his own age. He walked through and back around the plot of crops, checking behind the taller stalks. Nothing stirred. No prints found other than his own. Once satisfied he walked back towards the creek. He started shucking off his clothes as he walked towards the creek. The creek was just big enough to swim in, and he aimed to do just that with his free time. He could see the morning sun sparkling off the water. He was down to his drawers when he heard that same voice calling out, except this time it was ragged, struggling and desperate. "Help me…"

It wasn't coming from the crops this time, it was coming from the creek. Eli ran to the edge of the creek, looking for the voice in the water. He heard the water splashing as he ran, but when he arrived at the creek, the water was smooth, barely even a ripple. "Hello…Hello?" he yelled, looking around the creek bank. He walked up and down the bank for a few minutes, looking for the caller, but found no one, not even a footprint as the insects buzzed around him. He scratched his head and looked around one more time before jumping into the warm, muddy water. The voice didn't return that day.

As the evening sun painted the sky in yellow and fire-orange, Caleb caught sight of a familiar figure on the old wagon trail just beyond the property line. Old Crow stood at the edge of the cursed ground, where his people would never tread. He didn't move closer.

Caleb leaned his pitchfork against the barn, dusted his hands, and pulled on his hat. "Well, I'll be," he muttered, and started down toward the trail.

When Old Crow saw him, he lifted a hand in greeting. Caleb raised one back. "Hello, Old Crow. What brings you out this way again? Still chasing spirits?" Caleb chuckled.

"Mr. Toller," Old Crow said, raising his hand in friendship.

"Just Caleb," he corrected, smiling. "Ain't no formalities out here."

The old man's eyes softened. "Caleb. A strong name."

"Eh, just a name." Caleb kicked at the dirt, but he noticed the elder's face had already grown more serious.

"It is good to see you and your family still here."

Something in the tone made Caleb frown. "Go on, old man. Quit beating the bushes. Tell me what you really came for."

Old Crow exhaled heavily, as though carrying a burden. "My words are true, Caleb Toller. I am glad to see you here - it means the beast still rests."

Caleb squinted. "Beast?"

The old man's voice dropped lower, steady as stone. "This land - your land - was used to bury a flesh-hunger. A beast unearthed long ago in the time of my great ancestors. It was bound here with blood, stone, and sacred symbols. The Ute avoid this place not from fear, but respect. Once it wakes, a strangeness will follow - not in the land, but in its dwellers. In your family."

He stepped closer, searching Caleb's face. "If you find a stone seal…do not cross it…do not break it."

Caleb's mind flickered back to the flat rock over the well, but he forced a laugh. "I'll keep an eye out, but I don't reckon there's anything like that on this land."

The darkness eased from Old Crow's expression, though his gut told him otherwise. He saw something flicker in Caleb's eyes - something unspoken. He said nothing, only nodded. "Those are good words to my ears, Caleb." But inside, he knew he would return - not to visit, but to bury the beast… or bury the Tollers.

"Peace to you, Caleb Toller. Until we meet again."

"And same to you, old man. Watch out for those spirits." Caleb raised his hand, and Old Crow returned the gesture before turning back along the trail, shrinking into the horizon.

Caleb lingered, staring at the storm clouds building in the distance. A jagged bolt split the sky, thunder rolling after it. "Looks like rain's comin'," he said to himself. "Best get the stock in the barn."

Caleb cupped his hands around his mouth and called for Eli, but the boy was still down by the creek, well out of earshot. With a shake of his head, Caleb turned back to the barn. He herded the mare into the far stall, away from the oxen, and swung the heavy door shut against the rising wind.

Crossing the yard, he headed for the well. His boot caught the edge of the flat stone they'd once pried loose from the cover, and he stumbled before catching himself. "Damn rock," he muttered, stepping around it.

The bucket creaked as he lowered it, rope scraping against the stone lip. The well water came up cold and clean, sloshing as he hefted it against his hip for Ruth.

He had almost passed the stone again when the wind shifted. A hard gust tore down from the stormfront, kicking up dust around the well. The grit stung his eyes, and when he blinked them clear, the stone's surface no longer looked dull and gray.

The carved mark glared black as scorched wood, as if the rock itself had been seared from within.

Caleb froze. The hair rose on the back of his neck. From deep below, faint at first, came a sound, not water, not wind. A guttural stirring, wet and raw, like something shifting in its sleep. Caleb took a step back, bucket sloshing against his leg.

And then the sound stopped.

"Pa?"

Caleb nearly dropped the bucket. Eli stood barefoot at the edge of the barnyard, hair damp, shirt clinging to his skinny frame. He'd just come back from the creek, and his wide eyes were fixed on his father.

"You all right, Pa?"

Caleb forced himself to breathe. The sound below had stopped, but the stone still smoldered black in the dying light. He shifted the bucket against his hip. "Yeah," he said too quickly. "Just near lost my footing is all."

Eli looked toward the well. "Thought I heard something."

Caleb's grip tightened on the rope handle. "Just the wind in the shaft. Storm's blowing in. Go on now - tell your ma I'll be right in."

Eli hesitated, then turned and trotted toward the house.

Only after the boy was gone did Caleb glance back at the stone. The mark still burned dark as pitch.

That night, as the storm surged and the wind howled, Caleb tossed in a fitful sleep.

He dreamt he was walking through the brushy field

below the barn, a shovel heavy in his right hand. The blade was worn thin; its edge scarred from striking stone after stone. He didn't know if he was searching for something - or fleeing it.

The faint glow of the lantern on the front porch in the distance. Caleb called out for Ruth, then for Eli. His voice cracked the night, but no answer came, only the steady rush of wind.

Turning back, he entered the barn. The stalls were empty; the livestock had gone. From the center of the dirt floor came a dull, rhythmic thumping, as though the earth itself had a heartbeat. He dropped to his knees, swept aside hay and grit, and uncovered a stone slab. A strange, blackened symbol burned upon it, still glowing faintly. He brought the shovel down again and again until the slab split with a sharp crack. Beneath it, the soil had gone soft and black. He dug furiously, the thumping growing louder, faster, until his shovel struck another stone. Smaller, but marked with the same seared symbol.

Caleb clawed it from the earth with his hands. The soil crumbled away, and there, beneath the stone, lay Ruth and Eli. Their skin pale, their eyes wide and staring into nothing.

His chest locked tight. He couldn't breathe.

He awoke with a ragged gasp, heart pounding. The room was dark, the storm battering the roof, but beside him, Ruth slept, breathing slow and even. He lay awake until exhaustion dragged him back under, this time into mercifully dreamless sleep.

At dawn, when he rose, Caleb found his hands and feet caked in black soil, as though he had truly dug through earth all night. Panic seized him. He slipped outside, hurried to the well, and washed himself clean before anyone else could see.

On his way back, he slowed at the barn door. He stepped inside, eyes fixed on the mound at its center. The rise was still there, undisturbed. He let out a breath he hadn't realized he was holding - though the relief felt thin, hollow.

They sat around the old table in silence, the scrape of forks on tin plates the only sound. Each of them seemed lost, stranded in their own thoughts.

Caleb's mind circled back to the stone, to the black soil beneath it. Should he dig under the barn? Should he know what lay there or leave it buried? Ruth barely touched her eggs, eyes distant. Her father's clawing hands still haunted her from the night before, dragging her down into the well's red glow. And Eli… Eli kept quiet. He thought of the voice that had first called from the creek, then echoed through his dreams, urging him toward the well. When he awoke, he'd been standing in the corner of the room, as though sleep had carried him there. He hadn't told Ma or Pa. He would keep that to himself.

Ruth prided herself on being strong. Her father had taught her to work like a man, to fend for herself, to never cower. But now she could not go to the well. She was certain her dead father waited at the bottom, ready to claw his way back into the world through her. Guilt chewed at her, but she sent Eli instead. Better him than her. The boy never questioned, and she was grateful for that.

The days carried on, the farm work steady, but each night returned them to the same prison: Caleb with his stones, Ruth with the well, Eli with the voice. And then, one night, their nightmares crossed.

Caleb woke to the creak of the door and the faint crunch of bare feet on dirt. He found Eli outside, standing before the well, naked and pale, eyes wide but empty. The boy didn't move when Caleb called. Didn't blink. He only stared into the dark mouth of the well. Caleb rushed forward, shouting his name, but Eli remained as if carved in stone. Finally, Caleb drew up a bucket of water and threw it across the boy's chest. Eli gasped, startled awake, trembling and confused.

It happened again. And again. Caleb would wake to find Eli at the well, or halfway down the path, always blank-eyed, always silent. Caleb himself still woke with black soil crusted under his nails. He said nothing of that to Ruth or Eli. Instead, he hung an old cowbell on the door, telling them it was to keep Eli safe, to make sure they'd hear him if he wandered again.

But in his gut, Caleb knew the bell wasn't for Eli. It was for what was waiting for them.

The next day, after Caleb hung the old bell on the door, Ruth went out to the root cellar. It wasn't much of a cellar - just a dug-out pit with rough timbers and a door overhead - but it kept what few vegetables they managed to grow cool and dry. Or it was supposed to.

She pulled open the door and was hit with a wall of stench so foul she staggered back. Rot. Decay. Caleb came running, a candle stub in hand, and climbed down the ladder. The vegetables, fine the day before, now lay blackened and collapsed, as if weeks had passed overnight.

"They don't spoil in a night without cause," he muttered, holding the candle low.

The air wasn't cool anymore. It was damp, heavy, the walls slick with water that dripped steadily, pooling around his boots. He searched for signs of rats, mice, anything that could explain it. No tracks. No droppings. Only ruin.

As he climbed out, his candlelight caught on the underside of the cellar door. Scratches. Deep gouges raked into the wood from the inside, as though something had tried to claw its way out. Caleb froze, the hair on his arms rising. Maybe, he thought, it had tried to come up through the cellar. The thought alone made his skin prickle.

That night, long after they had gone to bed, the clang of the cowbell ripped through the silence. Caleb was up in an instant, yanking on his overalls. He ran to Eli's room, but the bed was empty. "It's Eli," Caleb said. "He's sleepwalking again. I'll check the well." He was already out the door before Ruth could answer.

The lantern's light swung wildly as he ran. The well stood empty, silent. Caleb leaned over it, his breath tight, then forced himself to look inside. Nothing. He began to scan the ground. Strange hoofprints marked the dirt, not like the mare's, not like the oxen.

He followed the hoofprints, the lantern light showing each pressed curve. They wound past the barn, through the brush, down toward the creek. The crops stood like withered ghosts as he passed. On the dried bank, he saw a shape, small and hunched, the lantern casting it in long shadow.

"Eli?" Caleb whispered. The figure didn't move. He stepped closer. The light revealed his boy, crouched by the creek bed, his face tilted down, his lips moving - a faint whisper.

"Eli?"

The boy lifted his head. His eyes were rolled white. And then another voice, low, guttural, ancient, spoke from his mouth. The words twisted at first, unrecognizable, then sharpened until Caleb understood.

"The seal has been broken. We are set free. We have been tricked. The payment is now due!"

Caleb's chest seized. "What payment…I just want my boy."

The voice rumbled from Eli's throat, louder now. "We are owed a sacrifice. The payment is blood!"

Caleb didn't think. He ran, scooped Eli up, and threw the boy over his shoulder. Eli's body was rigid, whispering still in that alien tongue as Caleb sprinted up the path. He crashed through the door, slammed it shut, and dropped the wooden bar into place. Ruth leapt up as Caleb laid Eli across the table, lantern light flickering over his pale, still face. "What happened?" she cried, rushing to her son.

Caleb's hands shook as he wiped sweat from his brow. His wide, wild eyes met hers. "The well," he said. "It's the well."

Caleb woke in the chair in Eli's room, his neck stiff, his hands trembling. On the bed, Ruth lay curled protectively around their son, as if she could shield him from whatever hunted them in their sleep.

He slipped outside into the cold dawn. The barn stood silent, heavy with dread. He crossed to the mound in its center, knelt, and brushed aside hay and grit. The stone revealed itself - an ancient sigil etched deep, black soil pulsing from the seams as though the earth itself bled.

He gripped the pickaxe. His heart hammered. Still, he swung. The crack of stone split the air. Splinters burst from the handle, driving into his palms. He yanked them free, but blood welled and ran down his wrists, spattering the sigil. The stone hissed. Smoke curled up from its surface. The barn shook as though a heartbeat thundered beneath its floorboards. Caleb staggered back, dropping the pickaxe, and fled.

Ruth met him at the door. "Caleb - what's happening?"

His face was pale, eyes wild. "We have to leave this place. Now."

She hesitated until he gripped her shoulders, shaking her hard. "Ruth…*now!*"

She gathered a few clothes, then helped lift Eli from the bed. The boy's skin was clammy, his lips moving faintly as if whispering in his sleep. Caleb's chest tightened at the sound but forced his voice steady. "Stay with him. I'll fetch the wagon."

He sprinted to the barn, then froze. The animals were gone. Only the mare trembled in the shadows. He followed the deep drag of oxen hooves through the dirt, his gut clenching with each step. The trail led down to the creek.

A stench hit him first, copper and rot. Then he saw them.

Both oxen lay on the bank, bellies slit from jaw to tail. Their innards were gone, pulled out with surgical precision. But it wasn't random slaughter. The blood had been spread across the dirt, lines and arcs joining into a vast sigil carved in gore. At its center, shapes twisted - horned, skeletal, writhing as though alive beneath the blood-soaked soil.

Caleb reeled, bile burning his throat. He turned to run.

Back at the house, Ruth startled as a knock rattled the door. The bell above it had not rung. She opened it - and gasped.

Old Crow stood on the threshold, a weathered bag clutched tight. From it jutted bones bound in sinew, jars of ash, herbs that reeked of smoke and decay. His face was carved from stone, his eyes sharp with urgency.

"The ground is broken," he rasped. "The seal undone. Where is the boy?"

Ruth's voice cracked. "What do you mean? Eli - he's - "

Her words died. She looked down.

Eli's shirt had ridden up as he lay across the bed. On his stomach, dark lines were blooming under the skin -

blood rising in thin, curling strokes, forming the same symbol Caleb had seen in the barn and again by the creek. Each line throbbed as if written by an invisible hand.

Old Crow dropped his bag onto the floor with a thud, scattering bones and charms. "There is no time," he said, voice low and grim. "They've claimed their sacrifice. And he carries their mark."

Caleb burst through the door, chest heaving. Old Crow stood in the center of the room with Ruth, his bag of strange charms and bones lying open at his feet. Ruth's face was pale, streaked with tears.

Caleb didn't speak. He went straight to Eli, lying limp on the bed, his small chest rising and falling with shallow breaths. He eased the boy's shirt up. The markings had spread - dark curling lines burned beneath the skin like living ink.

"I've seen these before…" Caleb's voice cracked. He turned his blazing eyes on Old Crow. "In the barn. On the stone coverin' the well. What do they mean, old man? Why are they on him?"

Old Crow bent low, his weathered fingers hovering just above the symbols without touching. His eyes narrowed. "This is no sickness. This is the mark of the

Ancients. He is their chosen sacrifice."

Ruth gave a strangled sound and collapsed to her knees beside the bed, sobbing. Caleb stood rigid, fists trembling, his face a mask of fury.

"They ain't taking our boy." His voice was low, dangerous. "I won't let them."

He shoved past Old Crow, through the door, and out into the storm-dark morning.

By the time Ruth and Old Crow reached the yard, Caleb was already at the well, his frame a dark silhouette against the churned sky. He leaned over the open mouth, shouting into the depths.

"You can't have him! You hear me?" His voice cracked across the fields. "Take me instead! Take me, damn you!"

His hands scrabbled at the ground and closed around a jagged shard of stone - one of the pieces from the broken cover. Without hesitation, he dragged the edge across his own chest, a long, shallow gash opening under his collarbone. Blood welled and trickled down his skin.

"Take me!" he roared again and hurled the stone into the well. The sound it made when it landed wasn't quite a splash - more like a soft, wet sigh from something waiting below.

The air around the well thickened, humming with a low, guttural vibration. Ruth's hair lifted from her shoulders as if in the wind. The black soil at the well's edge began to tremble, and the symbols etched there glimmered faintly, pulsing in time with Caleb's heartbeat.

Ruth reached him, clutching at his arm, but he wouldn't look at her. Old Crow's voice was a low growl behind them.

"You don't bargain with what sleeps down there," he said. "You only feed it."

The ground itself began to breathe, rising and falling beneath their boots. The well shook violently, coughing up dust and loose stones that rattled against the earth. A low groan rolled up from its depths, followed by the scrape of claws on stone.

All three stepped back, staring into the mouth of the well as the sound grew louder, closer.

A skeletal hand shot up from the darkness, its bones sheathed in knotted roots and shreds of rotting flesh. Another hand followed, clawing at the rim. Then, with a sickening pull, the thing dragged itself into the world above.

The creature's skull was crowned with writhing roots, its face a grotesque mask of decayed sinew. Black pits stared where eyes should have been, and its teeth - long, yellowed daggers - clicked as it breathed.

It turned its hollow gaze toward them. Then it appeared to look at the old house where Eli lay and let out a guttural growl that rattled the boards of the house.

With a lurch, it vaulted from the well. The ground trembled when it landed, towering as tall as the barn doors, its shoulders broad as a team of mules.

"Run!" Caleb roared, seizing Ruth's hand and dragging her back toward the house.

Old Crow stood his ground, teeth bared, and ripped the sacred pouch from around his neck. He flung a handful of dust and bone fragments at the abomination. The air hissed where it struck, and the creature shrieked, staggering back for a moment before swinging a massive hand. The strike missed Old Crow by inches, smashing a gouge into the earth where he had stood.

Old Crow turned and sprinted to the porch, where Caleb and Ruth already stumbled onto the steps. He rushed inside, snatched his larger bag of relics and charms, then returned, face grim.

"Ruth - stay with Eli!" Caleb shouted, shoving her inside. "Me and Old Crow will try to hold it here."

Inside, Eli writhed on the bed. The markings on his skin twisted and spread, glowing faintly, crawling down his arms and across his chest like veins filled with fire. His voice moaned in a language not his own, the words ancient and wet, echoing the growl of the thing outside.

Ruth, laid wet cloth's across is body, trying to scrub the marks from his skin with a rag and water, but the more she wiped, the further they spread. His flesh seemed to darken beneath her hands, like ink rising to the surface.

On the porch, Caleb stood rigid, clutching his axe. His knuckles were white, but his voice was firm.

"If you got some magic tricks in that bag of yours, old man…" he growled, never taking his eyes off the monster, "now's the damn time to use 'em."

Old Crow untied the bag, pulling free a bundle of carved bones, feathers, and a blackened stone etched with symbols that pulsed faintly in the night air.

The creature's roar shook the rafters, a sound like stone grinding against stone. It lurched toward the porch, each step cracking the earth beneath its weight.

Old Crow knelt, scattering the carved bones in a circle at his feet. He crushed herbs in his palm and whispered in Ute, words sharp and fast, spitting them into the wind. He pressed the blackened stone to the ground. Its etched symbols burned red, and a thin wall of light flared up around the porch.

The monster shrieked and slammed against the barrier. The light bent, splintered, but held. Caleb raised his axe, gripping it so hard his palms bled from the earlier splinters.

Inside, Ruth gasped. Eli's body arched on the bed, his back bowing, mouth open in a soundless scream. The markings on his skin glowed brighter, the same red as Old Crow's barrier. His chest convulsed, ribs rising unnaturally high, as if something beneath his skin pressed to be free.

Ruth fell to her knees, clutching his hand. "Stay with me, Eli. Don't let it take you."

The boy's lips trembled, and for a heartbeat his own voice broke through. "Ma…don't let…them - " Then his eyes rolled white, and he began to chant the same words Old Crow spoke outside, but twisted, corrupted, like a mocking echo.

The creature howled in response, slamming harder

at the barrier. Cracks spidered through the light. Old Crow's voice rose, desperate, sweat streaming down his brow.

"It's feeding through the boy!" Old Crow shouted over the roar. "The mark binds him to it. If it breaks the ward, it takes him!"

Caleb spat in the dirt, fury boiling in his chest. "Then we hold the ward." He swung his axe at the monster's hand as it breached the light, slicing through roots and bone. The thing shrieked, stumbling back, black ichor spraying across the porch. The droplets sizzled as they hit the wood, smoking and eating into the planks.

Ruth screamed from inside. Eli's chest split open at the wound the creature suffered - thin lines tearing across his skin in the same place Caleb's axe had cut the beast. His blood welled, not red but dark, thick, almost tar-like.

Caleb froze, horrified. "Dear God…he's tied to it."

Old Crow's eyes blazed. "No. Not tied. Chosen. And if we cannot sever that bond, Caleb Toller - your boy will be the doorway for its kind."

Caleb couldn't allow the creature to take his boy. If

it wanted a life, it would have his. He turned to Old Crow. "What's the strongest thing in your bag, old man? What'll hurt it most?"

Old Crow rummaged through his medicine pouch and pulled free a blade of carved buffalo bone; its edge yellowed with age. "This is the oldest of our weapons against such a being…but we can't get close enough. It's too strong."

Caleb stripped off his shirt, the shallow gash across his chest still glistening. "Those markings on Eli…can you draw them on me?"

Old Crow's eyes narrowed. "I know these marks. They are death. You'll die, Caleb Toller."

"I know," Caleb said, jaw tight. "But not my boy. Do it."

For a long breath, Old Crow studied him. Then he gave a solemn nod. "You are an honorable man, Caleb Toller."

The being slammed against the protective ward Old Crow had cast, its roars rattling the porch timbers. Old Crow gripped the bone knife, muttered a prayer, and began cutting symbols into Caleb's chest and back. Caleb grunted through clenched teeth, blood dripping in rivulets down the boards.

Ruth burst out the door. "Eli's getting worse - " Her eyes froze on Caleb's carved body. "What have you done?" She struck Old Crow across the face.

Caleb caught her wrist, weak but steady. "He's not killing me. I'm giving myself. It's the only way to save our boy."

Ruth sobbed into his chest. Caleb kissed her forehead, then pushed her gently back toward the door. "Protect them, old man," he told Old Crow, taking the knife from him.

He leapt from the porch, swinging the knife at the creature, tearing small gashes across its torso. The creature swung one of its elongated arms at Caleb as he sprinted off towards the barn. The creature's head swiveled, black sockets locking onto him, and it followed, howling.

Inside, Caleb cleared hay with frantic sweeps, exposing the old symbol carved into the earth. He lay across it, arms spread wide. The barn trembled, rafters groaning. The sigil flared, binding with the carved markings on his back.

The monster roared, raising its clawed hands. The sound turned to a howl as the floor pulled Caleb's blood into the lines of the ancient symbol. His skin shrank to his bones. He tried to scream, but his lungs were empty.

The last thing Caleb saw was the creature's skeletal hand closing around him. His body tore as it wrenched him free of the sigil, lifeless and hollow.

Cradling Caleb like a prize, the being lumbered to the well. It paused, turned its skull toward the house, and let out a growl that bled into a howl. Then it sank into the darkness.

The cracked stone cover shuddered, then sealed itself back over the well with a sucking sound, crushing the bucket and pulley Caleb had built.

Inside the house, Eli gasped awake, the markings fading from his pale skin, restoring. "Ma? Pa? What happened?"

Ruth fell across him, weeping. He had no memory, only innocence.

Old Crow stepped off the porch, walking cautiously towards the well.

The old barn collapsed into itself as Old Crow walked by. He stopped before the sealed well, the earth still trembling beneath his feet. He bowed his head, whispering words too old for Ruth to understand.

***

The wagon creaked under the weight of Ruth's few belongings, piled high in the back. Eli held the reins, his knuckles pale as the mare pulled at them, pawing at the ground under her hoofs. His face was pale, his eyes hollow, though he said nothing.

Old Crow stood beside the wagon in silence as he tossed the last belonging into the back.

Ruth looked down at him, her voice hoarse. "Make sure no one ever settles here. You know the well has to stay sealed. Can you give me your word you'll watch over it, Old Crow?"

Old Crow lifted his gaze, the sun casting deep shadows across his face. "You have my word, Ruth Toller."

Behind them, nothing remained of the homestead but charred timbers and ash. The barn and house were burned to their foundations. The fields were brittle and gray, brush withered and lifeless, as though the land itself had been drained from beneath.

Upon the stone that sealed the well, Old Crow's medicine pouch lay like an offering, its leather worn and silent in the wind.

The wagon rattled on down the trail, Ruth looking across the yellow and orange horizon, her son driving the mare. Old Crow lingered behind, his steps turning toward the open desert, searching for restless spirits.

The camera of the world lingered last on the well. At first, stillness. Then a tremor. Dust shivered loose. Pebbles tumbled from the stone.

The carved symbol across its surface began to glow.

WEIGHT OF IT ALL

Let me introduce you to Tori Yorkshire, a sixty-year-old widow, retired from her career in medical billing.

Her late husband, Daniel, worked himself into an early grave supporting Tori's habit of spending more than he could afford.

After Daniel died, Tori retired. He had at least been able to leave her enough money so she wouldn't have to work again.

Not long after, Tori's best friend and her sister introduced her to the world of costume jewelry. So many different groups existed on Facebook and TikTok that Tori wasn't sure which one to follow - so she decided to follow them all.

It began simply enough, with late-afternoon and evening sessions spent watching women (and a few men) selling inexpensive costume jewelry. Tori wasn't really involved in the shows until her best friend nudged her to join in the games they played during the broadcasts - guess the name, guess the show, bingo, spelling bees - you name the game, they had a version of it.

With her very first bingo win, Tori was hooked. The prizes weren't much - usually cheap trinkets no one would buy - so giving them away was the easiest way to get rid of them. The catch was that winners had to pay shipping, and the fee was usually double the actual cost of the jewelry. That didn't matter to Tori - she was a bona fide winner.

Soon, she developed a setup so she could attend multiple jewelry shows at once. Two iPhones, an iPad, and her computer were arranged around her recliner, each streaming a different show. She narrated each one to Ozzy, her little Yorkie, who sat in her lap, dozing between her shouts of joy when she won a drawing, called bingo, or outbid another viewer for a limited-availability piece.

Sometimes, late at night, when the screens flickered just right and the glow cast odd shadows across her face, Tori thought she heard the faintest whisper - like the jewelry calling. But she shook the thought away. It was probably just the excitement of winning.

She often stayed up until midnight, sleeping in until eleven the next morning.

When the winnings and purchases started arriving, it was like Christmas morning for Tori.

Over the next several weeks, the packages began arriving. Tori greeted each delivery with a smile. At first, the mailman was friendly - cheerfully bringing boxes to her door. But after the third or fourth week, his enthusiasm faded. Soon, he was leaving them at the mailbox or tossing them onto the front porch - sometimes several boxes at once.

Tori organized her packages carefully, sorting them by content, color, and type. She photographed every single item from every box. She didn't want them left out where her children or grandchildren might find or rifle through them, so she stored everything in her late husband's office and kept the door closed tight.

Her daughter, Lorna, stopped by occasionally or called to check in, asking how Tori was doing and whether she was managing her finances.

Tori lied. She insisted she only bought what she needed or the occasional treat for Ozzy and nothing more.

Her jewelry show watching increased steadily. What had once been a late-afternoon and evening pastime stretched now into mornings with breakfast, lunch breaks, even while she was in the bathroom. Tori didn't see anything wrong with it, but Lorna grew concerned as her mother's Facebook page became a flood of jewelry shows, excited comments about new purchases, and endless albums of photos showcasing her latest acquisitions.

After a month or two, Daniel's old office was filled - top to bottom, side to side. The only space left was a narrow path where Tori could walk and admire her prized possessions.

Her obsession deepened. Rings, earrings, trinkets, necklaces, pendants - if someone could sell it, Tori would buy it. When the office filled to bursting, she began stacking boxes in the guest bedroom. Visitors rarely stayed overnight, so it made the perfect storeroom. She continued organizing and photographing every single item as best she could.

One afternoon, Lorna stopped by unannounced to check on her mother. The moment she stepped inside, she noticed the house was unkempt - old coffee cups left on tables, empty tea glasses cluttering the counter, and takeout bags scattered by the dozen around the living room and piled beside the overflowing trash can in the laundry room.

"Mom?" she called, her voice hesitant but growing concerned.

Finally, Tori appeared from the master bedroom - dressed to the nines. A nice blouse, slacks, heels, and layer upon layer of jewelry. Rings adorned nearly every finger, two earrings dangled from each ear, several necklaces draped her neck, and two sparkling hummingbird pendants caught the light.

Trailing close behind was little Ozzy, who began yapping the moment he spotted Lorna.

"Mom, where are you going? And why is your house such a mess?"

"Oh, Lorna, I've just been so busy lately I haven't had time to clean. But don't you just love my new necklaces? They came in yesterday."

"Yes, Mom, they're nice. But why are you all dressed up? Are you going somewhere?"

"Oh, no, I'm getting ready for my next online show. We have to dress up for the camera. The best-dressed can win up to ten different trinkets." Tori beamed, but Lorna's concern only deepened.

"Look - let me show you this…" Tori disappeared into the office and returned with a glittering dog collar. "Ozzy gets to put on his bling like mine!"

Lorna rolled her eyes and wandered through the house. "Why is Dad's office door closed? And why is the guest room full of boxes?"

"It's my jewelry - mostly new - and I've documented it all," Tori replied.

Lorna's eyes widened. "Mom, you don't need all this. You can't even wear this much."

Tori caught the look of worry on her daughter's face. "Don't worry, Lorna. This is temporary. I'm cataloging everything for resale. I'm not keeping it all - it's just for resale. Calm down."

"Okay, Mom, I trust you. Just don't forget you still have bills and taxes to pay. I know it's all costume jewelry, but it's still money."

Tori's eyes glistened. "I get bored since your father died. Ozzy and I don't have much else to do. And I have people to talk to, even if it's just online."

The ploy worked - Lorna felt sorry for her and let it slide. That evening, she came back and cleaned her mother's house, careful not to move or disturb any of the stacked boxes.

Ozzy padded into the kitchen, sniffing around for a handout. Lorna noticed he'd put on a few pounds. Glancing toward his feeding area, she saw only a water bowl.

"Mom, where's Ozzy's food bowl? I'll feed him if you tell me where it is."

From the office, Tori emerged with her iPad in hand, a jewelry show playing loudly. "What's that, hon?"

"Ozzy's food bowl - where is it?" Lorna repeated.

"Oh, he doesn't use it anymore. I feed him whatever I'm eating. He just has his water bowl."

Lorna blinked in surprise.

That evening, after leaving her mother's house, Lorna called her brother Jason and older sister Bridgett.

"Guys, I don't know, but I think Mom is losing it," she said. "She watches show after show of online jewelry sales. She buys all the time - there are two rooms full of boxes. She says she's cataloging them for resale, but I doubt it. And Ozzy - he eats whatever she eats, and he's gained at least four or five pounds."

Jason sounded irritated by the call. He didn't have time to drop everything and check on their mother. "I'm busy, Lorna. I can't just run off."

Bridgett's voice was softer but no less resigned. She lived too far away to help. "I want to do something, but what can I do from here?"

"Garage sale it," Jason said finally. "Just put all that crap out in a yard sale and get rid of it. If Mom has an issue, well... we can put her in a home. We all have our own lives. Lorna, this is ridiculous - just sell it."

Lorna felt like they'd thrown the problem back on her. "You two are no help," she snapped before hanging up.

The number of packages arriving soon tripled. Tori was forced to stack boxes everywhere - in the guest bathroom, her office, the upstairs room, even the dining room. She labeled each box with little names and hearts on her favorites. She still tried to catalog them but could no longer keep them organized the way she once did.

The mailman no longer delivered her packages. Now, a special van arrived, and the driver used a dolly to wheel stacks of boxes into the house.

The only other mail Tori received was bills and late notices: electric - late, water - late, credit cards - late.

The family photo that once hung above the fireplace was gone. In its place was a custom-made sign from one of her online jewelry sellers, crafted from fake pearls and amethyst:

Kingdom of Jewels.

Tori's Facebook page was now flooded with selfies of her and her jewelry. In some, Ozzy sat on her lap; in others, she posed alone. Most were taken in front of towering stacks of boxes, each with its own name. Tori couldn't understand why no one commented on her pictures anymore. Her online friends used to congratulate her on her purchases, but now she bought so many pieces - sometimes multiple items at once - that no one else even had the chance to buy. Tori hoarded them all.

Tori had the delivery driver wheel the latest purchases into her master bedroom. This delivery was the biggest yet - towering stacks of boxes.

"Ma'am, do you want me to rearrange these over by the others in the corner?" the delivery driver asked, eyeing the growing collection with concern.

"No thank you. I've got them. Shoo - go away."

The driver shrugged and left.

"Oh, my babies," Tori cooed, embracing the nearest stack like a long-lost child. "I won't let anyone touch you. Mommy's here. Mommy's got you now."

She tried to move one of the stacks herself. Pushing once, twice, it barely budged. On the third shove, the boxes began to teeter. Tori grabbed them, clinging to her latest prized possessions until they finally steadied.

She turned to walk away - only to feel one of her bracelets catch on the corner of a box. She tugged, and the towering stack tipped.

Tori tried to jump back, but it was too late.

Crack… crack…

Pain shot through her, sharp and deep. She wasn't sure if the cracking was from her bones… or from the treasures inside the boxes. She prayed it was only the jewelry.

She tried to move, but her body refused. Her phone - where was it? She scanned the room and spotted it on the floor by the table, far out of reach.

Gritting her teeth, Tori attempted to crawl toward it. The stack shifted slightly, but in doing so, bumped the one next to it. That stack toppled too - crashing down onto her body and pinning her completely.

The air rushed out of her lungs. She tried to push the boxes away, but they were too heavy.

Ozzy trotted over, whining, circling her. He hadn't been outside since before the delivery driver arrived.

Tori's breathing grew ragged. The edges of the room began to blur. Her vision swam. And then - she heard it. The jewelry. It was calling to her, its voice glittering and bright, like the jewels themselves.

With her fading last breath, Tori wondered if this was how the pharaohs felt - buried with their fortunes.

Her vision went black as the last of the air escaped her lungs.

Ozzy padded to her face, licking her lips. Then he moved to her twisted hand, gave her fingers a gentle lick, and curled up beside her.

Several days passed.

The delivery driver no longer waited - just a quick knock, a faint thud as boxes hit the porch, and the groan of his van rolling back down the street. Ozzy bounded to the door, tail wagging, whining at the retreating figure. The driver glanced over his shoulder and gave a half-hearted wave, never slowing.

Ozzy padded back toward the bedroom.

The air inside was still. Heavy. A quiet so deep it felt as if it pressed down on the walls themselves. Tori lay where she had fallen, her pale skin waxen, lips tinged a faint blue, the stiffness of death beginning to claim her.

Ozzy sniffed at her. He circled once. Then, in the shadowed corner, he squatted, leaving a dark little heap on the carpet. Returning to Tori's side, he licked her cold hand, waiting for a response. None came.

The laundry room smelled faintly of takeout. He pawed through crumpled paper bags, nosing each one, searching for scraps. The scent was fading. The food was almost gone.

By the next day, hunger had settled into a deep ache that radiated through his small frame. He returned to her face, sniffing the air around her. Nothing. He drifted away, weaving through the towering boxes lining the living room - cardboard sides faintly scented with tape, dust, and something sweetly metallic. Down the hall, into the office, around the chair. Sniffing. Searching.

In the kitchen, he found a thin smear of water on the tile and lapped it up.

Back in the bedroom, he circled her once. Twice. Stopping at her face again.

A slow lick traced her lips. Then another.

Then hunger overwhelmed memory.

He bit. Pulled. Tugged until something gave way with a soft, wet sound. He chewed, licking at the small bloom of blood that welled up.

The taste was strange - salty, metallic, yet familiar in a way he couldn't understand.

He ate until the emptiness in his belly dulled.

Lorna's calls rang unanswered. That wasn't unusual - her mother often ignored the phone, distracted with Ozzy or her online orders. But three days was too long.

She drove over.

From the curb, the house looked... wrong. Boxes crowded the porch like silent sentinels, some with rain-darkened corners, their labels faded and bleached from days in the sun.

The front door was unlocked.

The air inside was cool, but beneath it lurked a smell - sickly-sweet, metallic, rotting all at once. Lorna lifted her shirt over her nose.

"Mom! Mom, where are you?"

The smell thickened as she moved down the hall, pressing in on her with every step.

She reached the bedroom doorway.

Ozzy stood there, framed by dim light. His muzzle was wet, smeared dark. Something pale - small and unmistakably human - protruded from the corner of his mouth.

Lorna screamed and fled.

Jason arrived minutes later. One step into the open doorway was enough - the stench hit him like a physical blow, sending him to his knees in the driveway, retching.

They sat outside together, waiting for the police and the coroner. Lorna trembled, muttering that it couldn't be real. Jason, calm to the point of coldness, simply called his wife:

"I'll be home late. Mom's dead."

When Bridgett got the news, she fainted. Her husband took the phone, voice low and unsteady, telling Lorna they'd call back.

Inside, the police moved methodically through the dim rooms. The towers of boxes loomed in every corner, casting long, jagged shadows beneath flickering overhead lights.

When the animal control officers emerged, they carried Ozzy.

He trembled in their arms - fur glittering with cheap fake jewels, muzzle matted with something darker, older. His small eyes darted nervously toward the stacked boxes as they carried him out, as if they might call to him next.

Epilogue

The local news headline was cold and clinical: **Elderly Woman Dies in Hoarding Accident; Dog Survives.**

Lorna called the station, her voice trembling with anger and grief. They didn't care.

"If we changed it," the reporter said flatly, "we'd just say: *Mentally ill woman dies under piles of cheap jewelry, eaten by her dog.*"

Lorna spat a few sharp words and hung up.

Online, cruelty poured in like poison. Strangers with faceless usernames mocked her mother mercilessly:

"Guess diamonds really are a girl's best friend."

"She was the dog's best friendly meal."

"McJewelry Burger."

And worse. Lorna stopped reading after a while - too much venom.

She hadn't spoken to Jason or Bridgett since the funeral. Neither wanted to help clear the house.

"If you find anything I like, let me know," Jason had said. His version of help was sending money for a crew to haul everything away. Lorna hung up.

Bridgett's voice was sweeter but no less distant. "When the estate sells, just send me a check. It's too far to drive, and the doctor says the stress isn't good for me."

So Lorna did it alone.

Room after room.

Box after box.

Most of the jewelry was still sealed in its original packaging. The boxes bore labels in her mother's flowing script: *Prizes. Preciousness. Mommy's winnings. Little angels.*

But some bore names that made Lorna's skin crawl - strings of letters that didn't make sense, curling and twisting like whispered incantations.

One box was colder to the touch than the others. When she held it, a faint hum seemed to vibrate beneath her fingers, as if something waited inside, watching.

She didn't open that one.

She called a disposal company and told them to take everything away. She didn't ask how or where. She didn't want to know.

Later, in the fading light, Lorna found one of Ozzy's old chew toys tucked beneath the couch.

Outside, the wind whispered through the trees, and shadows lengthened like reaching hands.

She threw the toy as far as she could.

She didn't watch it land.

She didn't go looking for it.

And somewhere, in the quiet dark, a soft jingling echoed - like tiny bells, or distant laughter - just beyond the edge of hearing.

The Gospel According to Reverend Belle

Reverend Silas Belle had built an empire on sweat, scripture, and spectacle.

First Rock Baptist Church in Jackson, Mississippi, wasn't just a church—it was a brand. LED backdrops, seven-piece band, a tech team in headsets, and Rev. Belle himself center stage, arms wide, voice booming. "The Lord speaks to me directly!" he would shout, and the congregation would cheer like he was a prophet on loan from heaven.

Behind closed doors, though, Silas was no saint. At home, he drank hard and cursed harder. Adella, his wife—former adult film star, now uncomfortable first lady of the church—had long stopped trying to play the part. They slept in separate rooms, rarely exchanged anything but sarcasm and silence.

It wasn't about God anymore. Maybe it never was.

It was about *Him*. The man. The myth. The reverend.

And Silas was ready for the next step: a nationally televised ministry, book deals, a private jet, maybe a Netflix documentary about "America's Most Anointed."

Then came the old man.

He was waiting outside the church one humid

Tuesday afternoon. Filthy coat, sandals held together with string, a beard that looked carved from driftwood. Most would've dismissed him as just another vagabond from the shelter nearby.

But Silas saw those eyes—and they *stared.*

"Reverend Belle," the man said in a gravel voice that cut through the summer air like prophecy. "Your days are gettin' shorter. The window is closin'."

Silas rolled his eyes. "You want food? A donation? I'll have one of the interns bring you something."

The old man shook his head. "You best get right. Or else."

"Is that a threat?" Silas barked, glancing around to see if any cameras were nearby. "Listen here, old fool, the gravy train ain't stoppin'. I'm going national. Don't you come near me again—or I'll slap a restraining order on your filthy behind."

But the old man didn't blink. He stepped forward, close enough for Silas to smell dust and incense.

He leaned in and whispered, *"Isaiah 2:12."*

Then he turned and walked away.

Something cold trickled down Silas's spine. The name *Isaiah* scratched at his memory, but he shrugged it off and climbed into his Escalade.

Back home, after two glasses of scotch and a half-watched baseball game, curiosity gnawed at him.

He opened the leather-bound Bible that hadn't left his bookshelf in years and flipped to the verse.

"For the Lord of Hosts has a day in store for all the proud and lofty, for all that is exalted—and they will be humbled."

His hand tightened around the glass.

"Dramatic nonsense," he muttered. But his hand trembled as he poured the next drink.

That night, the visions came.

He stood alone in absolute darkness—so dense it felt alive. Cold seeped into his bones. And then came the sounds.

Wailing. Screams. Agony.

Voices he knew: Adella. His deacons. The choir director. Hundreds of congregation members. All crying out from the shadows.

"Why, Silas?" "Why did you lie?" "You led us here!" "You put us here!"

He opened his mouth to respond, but nothing came out. His voice was gone. He couldn't speak. Couldn't justify. Couldn't preach.

He was utterly alone—and yet, not.

From behind him came the sound of slow, bare feet walking on stone.

He turned.

Darkness.

He woke up in a gasp, drenched in sweat, sheets twisted around him like vines. The bedroom was silent—too silent. The mansion was a tomb of luxury.

His heart pounded as he sat up and looked toward the corner of his oversized room.

A shape stood there—still and quiet. Ragged outline. Beard. Watching.

The old man.

Silas lunged for the lamp, flicked it on—

The corner was empty.

No smell, no sound. Just his breathing and the tick of the wall clock.

He sat there until morning, unable to sleep, unable to shake the feeling that the clock wasn't ticking *forward.*

It was ticking *down.*

When the light finally broke through the curtains, Silas stumbled out of bed and shuffled to the bathroom. He splashed cold water on his face, gripping the sink as he tried to shake off the night.

"It was just a stupid dream," he muttered to his reflection. "Probably from that cheap scotch. I'll have to tell that liquor store clerk not to sell me that bottom-shelf crap again."

He looked at himself in the mirror—his face pale, eyes too sunken and dark.

"A little touch-up and I'll be lookin' downtown good," he said with a half-hearted smirk.

He straightened his robe, shook off the chill crawling across his shoulders, and headed downstairs toward the kitchen.

He expected to smell cinnamon and butter, hear the gentle clatter of pans—Rosali, the housekeeper, always made his breakfast when Adella didn't. But the kitchen was still, dim. Only Adella was there, fixing herself a cup of coffee.

"Where in the he—" He caught himself. Cleared his throat. "Where's Rosali? She was supposed to be here all week. I *specifically* told her I wanted French toast this morning. With that special syrup she makes."

Adella didn't even glance at him. "Rosali called in this morning while you were still snoring. Said she had a vision. A premonition. Said she wouldn't be coming back. She sounded terrified."

Silas blinked, caught off guard. "Well, she ain't about to get paid for the whole week. She won't find work around here now; I'll *see* to that. Screw with me and find out."

Adella took a sip and turned to leave. "Don't be so dramatic, Silas. She's probably just superstitious."

Then she paused at the doorway, turned halfway back, and added with a cold smile, "And don't flatter yourself. No one—and I mean *no one*—wants to screw you."

She walked out without waiting for a response, heels tapping lightly against the floor. Silas stood alone, fists clenched, jaw twitching. His anger rose like a tide.

And somewhere deep inside, behind all that bluster and control, was something else.

Fear.

Later that morning, after not having his special French toast breakfast, Silas sulked in his custom-built study, a dark wood-paneled shrine to his ego. Shelves lined with unopened theology books framed the room, more for show than study. A portrait of himself hung over the fireplace—Rev. Silas Belle, arms wide, eyes lifted, a golden halo of backlighting captured during a staged Easter service.

This was where he "practiced" his weekly sermons.

More often than not, he simply pulled down a pre-scripted sermon from some flashy Christian website, peppered with prosperity talk and crowd-pleasing promises. Lately, though, he'd found a new trick: AI-generated sermons.

"They're golden," he murmured to himself, grinning. "Just feed it the right buzzwords—'breakthrough,' 'favor,' 'abundance,'—and out comes pure spiritual gold. The people eat it up."

He scrolled through his tablet, sifting through generic sermon outlines with titles like *"Stepping Into Your Season of Giving"* and *"God's Plan for Your Overflow."*

"If I ever get on TV," he thought, "I'll hire a whole team of writers. Keep the good stuff comin'. Real showbiz-level holy content. That's how you go big."

But just as he was about to copy and paste another AI draft, the words from the old man echoed through his mind like an unwelcome ghost:

"For the Lord of Armies has a day in store against

everyone who is arrogant and haughty, against everyone who is lifted up—that he may be brought low."

The verse crept in like mold beneath the walls.

Silas sat back, exhaling through his nose. "I wonder how that old fool even knew scripture," he muttered. "Probably memorized it from some sidewalk Bible tract."

He narrowed his eyes.

"I don't believe in that old book of tall tales. Never have. Never will."

He looked around his plush study—custom desk, leather chair, stained-glass windows imported from Italy—and chuckled. "I'm in this business for the money. Prestige. And the power. *Especially* the power."

Power was the best part. Better than the tithe. Better than the praise. Being able to stand in front of hundreds, tell them what to do, how to live, who to forgive—and know they'd obey.

He stretched his arms wide, mimicking his Sunday stage posture, and laughed.

"There's a women's prayer gathering down at the church this afternoon," he remembered aloud. "I think I'll drop in—recite a sweet little AI-generated prayer. They *love* my prayers. Say they're so emotional, so moving."

He smirked.

"All fake. But they don't know that. Never will."

He leaned back, letting the leather chair cradle him as his thoughts drifted.

"I would've never guessed I'd end up someone's 'church pastor.' Twenty years ago, I was stealin' cars, muggin' folks, pimpin' out girls in Baton Rouge. Now *that* was a hustle. Dangerous, though. Hard cash to make."

His grin widened.

"Then I heard a jail cellmate talking about his cousin—making bank at some backwoods church in Louisiana. Weekly paydays, free meals, bonus gifts, no cops. Said he got the title 'pastor' after takin' a few classes and buying a certificate online."

Silas chuckled.

"That's when it clicked. Wham, bam, thank ya ma'am—I got certified. Started small. Real Podunk joints. But I learned the game: talk smooth, shout a few hallelujahs, cry once or twice, pass the plate—*bam*, you're paid."

He tapped the desk proudly.

"People are such fools. They'll give you every dime

they got if you convince 'em it'll buy their way into heaven. All you gotta do is sell hope, fear, and a little guilt. Works every time."

He shook his head, still laughing to himself as he went back to scrolling sermon templates. His fingers hovered over the glowing screen.

But the laughter didn't last.

From somewhere deep in the house, a door creaked open—though no one should've been there.

And in the stillness of his study, Silas felt something watching.

Silas rose from his leather chair, jaw clenched.

He reached under the center drawer of the desk and pulled out his .38 Special. Cold steel, familiar weight. He'd kept it loaded ever since the early days—back when danger was more than just a dream or a vision. Back when he was the one breaking into homes, not worrying about who might break into his.

He crept out into the hallway, slow and deliberate, eyes sharp. He'd learned the hard way how to move when someone unexpected was in your house. Sometimes he'd been the invader. Sometimes he'd been the invaded. Both sides taught valuable lessons.

Down the hall, then to the top of the staircase. Still no sound.

Then—rattling.

From the kitchen.

He crept down, .38 low and ready, breath tight in his chest. As he reached the corner, he flattened his back against the wall and peeked inside.

A man crouched in front of the sink, head down, working on something beneath.

Silas eased forward, slow and silent as a whisper. He raised the gun and pressed the barrel gently to the back of the man's head.

"You've got about five seconds to tell me why you're in my house before I splatter your brains all over this sink," he said in a low growl. "One... two..."

"Please don't shoot me, Reverend!" the man blurted, stiffening. "Adella sent me over to fix the leak under the sink. She said I could do it better than one of those high-priced plumbers. Please don't kill me."

Silas blinked. The voice was familiar.

Rodney Harlo.

Youth teacher at First Rock. Always wore too much cologne and smiled too big.

Silas pulled the barrel back with a sigh and lowered the gun.

"Lord, Rodney," he said, stuffing the revolver back into his pants pocket. "I thought you was a burglar. Or a home invader come to rob poor Adella and myself. We don't have much, but what we do, it's all a blessing from the man upstairs."

He clasped his hands together in a mock-prayer gesture and glanced toward the ceiling.

Rodney slowly stood, face pale but intact. "Oh, thank the Lord," he said with a shaky laugh. "I really thought you were gonna blow my head off. I'm sorry, Reverend—I should've knocked. Adella told me you had that women's prayer gathering this afternoon and you wouldn't be home, so I just let myself in."

His voice cracked a little, watery-eyed but holding it in.

Silas gave him a hearty slap on the back and chuckled. "Ah, I wasn't gonna pop one of my best youth teachers, Rodney. Just puttin' a little *fear of God* in you, that's all. Gotta stay on your toes these days."

Rodney nodded nervously, still trying to recover. "I hear you, Reverend. Times like these, can't ever be too careful. Time's running short, and the window's closing for folks who don't know the Lord."

He laughed lightly. "But what am I saying—you're the Reverend. You already know that better than me."

Silas froze for just a fraction of a second.

Time's running short. The window's closing.

Rodney bent back down toward the sink. "I best be fixing this leak—if you still want me to and all."

"Sure, sure, Rodney," Silas said, the grin gone from his face. "You go ahead. I'll have to have a little... 'chat" with Adella about inviting people over without my say-so."

His brow furrowed. The warmth had drained from his voice.

"I'm headin' back up to get ready for the gathering. Got to put on the proper attire, gather my papers. You can just let yourself out when you're done, Rodney."

"Will do, Reverend. I guess I'll see you Sunday."

Silas turned and started up the stairs, slowly.

He rubbed his chin, deep in thought.

That phrase. That *same* phrase. It was what the old man had said. The homeless one. The ragged man who had whispered that verse like a curse.

"Your time's running short... the window is closing."

Coincidence?

Or something more?

Silas reached the top of the stairs, heart thudding just a little harder than before, and paused in the hallway. Something unspoken had shifted. He couldn't put his finger on it, but it lingered in the air like smoke after a fire.

And for the first time in a long while, the Reverend wasn't sure *who* was really watching him.

Reverend Belle arrived a few minutes after the women's gathering had started, making his usual grand entrance into the fellowship hall at First Rock Baptist.

"I'm so sorry for my tardiness, dear ladies," Silas said, voice dripping with manufactured sincerity. "I was deep in conversation with the Lord, and He detained me a bit. I had to remind Him of my prior engagement." He gave a breathy chuckle. "I'm just so happy to be here with y'all this afternoon."

With that, he struck his signature pose—arms stretched wide, palms turned upward, eyes theatrically lifted toward the ceiling.

Sister Marlene, the chairwoman of the women's

ministry, beamed as she stepped forward. "We are so blessed you made it, Reverend. We know how tied up you are with the Lord's work, and for you to make time for *us*—well, it just warms our hearts."

Silas nodded solemnly. "The Lord laid a prayer on my heart this morning during my personal study. I'd be honored to open this gathering in prayer, though I regret to say I'll have to leave shortly for another very important meeting."

He paused dramatically. "If the Spirit so leads, I'd encourage you all to give what you can to the collection plate for our struggling missionaries in the field."

Sister Marlene clapped her hands together. "Oh yes, Reverend! We absolutely will. We must support those out there doing the Lord's work. Do you think you might be able to tell us soon who the missionaries are? Maybe even invite them to our church sometime?"

Silas lowered his gaze and worked up a few moist tears, the way he'd practiced in front of the mirror more times than he could count.

"I've pleaded with the Lord on your behalf," he said, voice trembling, "but He told me, 'Not yet, Silas. Not yet.' He's testing my patience, our patience. But when the time is right, He will reveal them to me. Until then, we must trust and obey."

"Oh, Reverend," Marlene said, clasping her hands at her chest. "You're so good to us—pleading with the Lord for our sakes. We couldn't ask for a better pastor or a more blessed church."

Silas smiled his polished, politician's grin, even as he laughed to himself inside.

They have no idea.

That "missionary fund" they so generously donated to? That's what paid for his Saints season tickets. And if the pot kept growing, he'd be sitting courtside at a Pelicans games before Christmas.

After weeping his way through the AI-written prayer, giving warm hugs and pecks on the cheek to the older women, and laying a thick layer of charm over every interaction, Silas made his exit.

He climbed into his black Escalade, fired up the engine, and chuckled as he pulled away from the church.

"My next meeting," he muttered, "is at the racetrack."

The phone rang.

Adella.

He rolled his eyes and jabbed the call button.

"Yes, what do you want?" he barked. "The dog track is calling, so this better be good."

Her voice was sharp, calm—too calm.

"Why did you scare Rodney this morning?"

Silas narrowed his eyes at the road ahead.

"You were *supposed* to be at the women's gathering," Adella continued. "Those ladies were expecting you. They look forward to seeing you—really *seeing* you. Why were you still at the house?"

"And why," she added, her voice tightening, "are you already out? The meeting doesn't end for another forty-five minutes."

Silas gripped the wheel tighter. "Look, woman," he snapped, "I run this house the way I run my church. I am in *command.* What I do, when I do it, and how I do it—that's for *me* to decide."

"Don't you call me trying to play investigator. Is there something you need, or are you just trying to poke your nose where it don't belong?"

His voice had risen half an octave.

Inside, his temper boiled. *How dare she call me with this Q&A nonsense?* He was the Reverend. *The man of God.*

The star. The name on the sign. She was just the big-chested trophy wife, the one who smiled for pictures and wore the nice dresses he bought.

And if she kept up this crap, he'd send her packing.

On his way to the track, Silas pulled up to a red light on MLK Boulevard, tapping the steering wheel impatiently.

"C'mon already," he muttered. "Ain't got all day."

He turned his head lazily to glance at the corner—and froze.

There he was.

The old homeless man.

Standing on the sidewalk in the afternoon heat like he had nowhere better to be. Same tattered coat, same piercing stare. But now, he held a cardboard sign scrawled in bold black marker:

"Closing is the window. The haughty will be brought low."

The man raised the sign high, then slowly—*deliberately*—pointed it straight at Silas.

Silas's jaw tightened.

"Oh, hell no," he growled.

He slammed his foot down and gunned the Escalade through the red light, tires squealing. Cars honked behind him, but he didn't care.

"I'm about *this close* to being done with that old man," he snapped to himself. "He don't know who he's messing with. He keeps poppin' up like that, he might find himself in a little 'accident.'"

He checked the side mirror—nothing.

The old man was gone.

"Yeah, that's what I thought," Silas muttered, gripping the wheel tighter. "Show up again and *find out*, old man."

But the rest of his day didn't get any better.

He lost ten grand at the track—ten thousand dollars, gone in a haze of bad bets, cheap scotch, and rising frustration. To top it off, when he came back to the parking lot, someone had dragged a key across the entire passenger side of his Escalade.

A long, ugly scar across his perfect black paint job.

By the time he pulled into his driveway, the sun was setting and his mood had gone completely black.

But the driveway was empty.

Adella's car wasn't there.

He checked the garage.

Still no sign of it.

Silas sat there for a moment, staring at the empty space like it had personally offended him.

"Great," he snapped. "Just *great.* Where the freak is she now?"

He slammed the door shut as he got out.

"I don't spend all this money on her so she can just *disappear* whenever she wants. This house, them clothes, the damn car—*I* paid for it all."

He stormed toward the front door, fists clenched.

"Let her walk in late tonight. I *dare* her. She's gonna hear it. She's gonna *feel* it."

Inside, the house was too quiet.

And Reverend Belle, already simmering, was now a fuse waiting for flame.

Silas slammed the door behind him and headed straight for his study. The house was silent, but his thoughts were screaming. He slumped into the leather chair, jaw locked tight, replaying every loss from the day—the $10K at the track, the scratched Escalade, and now Adella's absence. He poured himself a stiff drink from the decanter on the desk and waited, stewing in the dark.

At 11 p.m., the front door finally creaked open.

He didn't move.

Footsteps echoed on the stairs—unsteady, slow, careless. He could smell the alcohol before she even passed the door.

Adella stumbled past his study, swaying against the wall in her heels, eyes half-lidded and unfocused. Silas sat up straight.

"Why were you not home when I got home, Adella?" he shouted.

She paused, barely turning her head.

"Where've you been? Huh? Who were you out with? Rodney? Is that why you were so *worried* about poor ole Rodney?"

His voice was rising, fury creeping into every word.

Adella leaned against the doorway and smirked, drunken and defiant. "Huh? Oh... yeah," she slurred. "I can go out when I *please*. You don't *own* this." She ran her hands slowly up and down her body. "This is mine. To do what I want. You. Don't. Own. Me."

Silas's nostrils flared.

She giggled and stumbled forward. "I've been talking to someone. Someone I met at a Bible study. He pays attention to me. Not like you. He wants to know about *me*. He wants to know where my *heart* is."

Silas went still.

Then, slowly, his hand slid under the center drawer of his desk. Fingers curled around the grip of the .38 Special.

His voice dropped to a growl. "You best keep your damn legs closed."

Adella blinked, frozen.

"Your whole body is *mine.* I own you like I own the cars, the house, and my church. You go screwing behind my back, you and your boy toy'll end up in a shallow grave. You *know* my previous life. I can call on it whenever I need to. Don't make me do something you'll regret."

He stood up now, looming, veins showing on his neck.

"I'm not gonna throw all this away for *you.* You're not worth the ambition I've built. And if I did it, they'd never find you. I'd never be caught. *Don't screw with me!*"

He grabbed the heavy letter opener from his desk and hurled it. It struck the doorframe just inches from her head with a *thud.*

Adella stared at the blade, then back at Silas—shaking, silent.

Tears streamed down her face. Without a word, she turned and stumbled down the hall into her bedroom, locking the door behind her with trembling fingers.

Silas stormed downstairs to the wet bar just outside the kitchen, yanked open the cabinet, and grabbed the bottle of scotch. He made his way to the ornate dining table, the one with the gold trim imported from somewhere he couldn't even pronounce.

"She better not mess up what I got goin' here," he muttered.

He took a long drink. Then another.

"If I have to call one of my old cellmates, I *will*," he snarled, pointing the bottle at no one. "I can afford to make her *disappear* if I have to."

He drained nearly half the bottle, slumped in the chair, and nodded off, the last drops of scotch slipping from the neck and spilling onto the polished tabletop.

Back upstairs, Adella lay curled on the plush imported carpeted floor of her bedroom, still in her clothes. Her eyes were red, her cheeks damp.

"Todd's interested in me," she whispered, "but more in my heart, my soul than my body..."

She stared at the ceiling.

"Is that good... or bad?"

Her voice cracked.

"Silas says souls don't exist. He says they're made up. Make believe."

She let out a breath, slow and broken.

Then the tears came again—silent, exhausted sobs.

Eventually, she cried herself to sleep on the carpet, arms wrapped tightly around herself.

The next morning, Silas left the house early, the sun barely peeking over the rooftops as he eased the scratched Escalade out of the driveway. He was headed to Denny's for the men's breakfast with the church deacons. A once-a-month tradition he hated but endured—for appearances.

Before leaving, he made sure to download a fresh "heartfelt, emotional" prayer from the AI Prayer Warrior site.

Something with just the right touch of tears, humility, and vague biblical references to impress the deacons.

Gotta keep the fools inspired, he thought. *Make 'em feel like they're in the presence of the anointed. That way, one of 'em' will pick up the check again.*

He tapped the scratch on the Escalade's passenger side as he walked around the vehicle. It still burned him to look at it.

Maybe I'll guilt Deacon Perry into paying for the paint job. Tell him it's hurting my image. Can't have a TV-level pastor ridin' around in a scuffed ride.

Back in the house, Adella slowly stirred.

She hadn't moved from where she'd cried herself to sleep—curled up on the carpeted floor of her bedroom, still in yesterday's clothes. Her body ached. Her head pounded with a hangover so loud it felt like it was splitting her skull.

She sat up with a groan and dragged herself to the bathroom.

One look in the mirror made her stomach turn.

Makeup streaked across her cheeks. Bloodshot eyes. Her hair matted on one side from the floor. She barely recognized the woman staring back at her.

She splashed cold water on her face and reached

for the Excedrin.

As she massaged her temples, Todd's name drifted into her mind. It brought a faint warmth—and a flicker of guilt.

Todd's not like Silas, she thought. *But is he like the others? Just another side boyfriend who likes the idea of rescuing a broken woman until it stops being fun?*

She rubbed her forehead harder, trying to push the thought out.

Her eyes found themselves again in the mirror.

"Did Silas really try to kill me last night?" she whispered. "Or was it just another one of his rage shows?"

She stared at her reflection for a long, empty moment.

"He's gonna kill me one day. Maybe not with a gun, but with his hands. Or his mind. And if I stay…"

She looked around at the marble countertops, the gold-accented towels, the custom vanity.

"If I leave, I lose everything. The Mercedes. My bank account. The clothes. The lifestyle. He'll make sure I don't get a dime."

Her stomach turned at the thought of going back to her old hustle. The industry. The scenes. The men. The parties.

The funerals.

"Too many girls I knew never made it out. OD'd. Suicides. A few just... vanished. That life eats you alive."

She gripped the edge of the counter.

"That's why I went with Silas. I thought he was different. Thought he was sincere. A man of G-d."

Her voice cracked.

"But he's just a hood in a robe. A preacher for profit. Power. Control."

She let out a breath and closed her eyes.

"I need to call Todd."

There was hesitation there—fear, hope, confusion—but beneath it all was something else.

Resolve.

"There's something different about him," she whispered. "He talks like he actually *believes* what he says. About God. About redemption. About souls."

Her fingers hovered over her phone on the bathroom counter.

And for the first time in years, she considered the idea that maybe—just maybe—her soul wasn't beyond saving.

Men's Breakfast at Denny's across town

Back at Denny's, Silas sat at the head of the table in the back corner, their usual table, surrounded by half a dozen church deacons, all sipping coffee and picking at their breakfast plates.

"The Lord told me this morning," Silas began, tone solemn, "that another group of missionaries is in urgent need of our support."

He folded his hands in a prayer pose, adding a soft, reverent smile.

"We need to see to it that the congregation increases their tithing and donations. With that increase, we can also address another need—the long overdue rebuild of the pastor's office."

He leaned back, letting the request breathe.

"I've had a hard time doing the Lord's work in that cramped, outdated space. I don't think a new solid oak desk with gold and silver trim is too much to ask. And a comfortable, high-back ostrich leather chair to match... well, that's just fitting for a man doing the Lord's business, wouldn't you say?"

He chuckled, eyes gleaming.

The table was silent for a beat.

Then Deacon Perry, older and always a bit uneasy around Silas, cleared his throat and stood, arms crossed.

"Reverend, we fully understand the need for a proper working office, but... isn't a custom solid oak desk and a designer chair a bit excessive? And now you're talking about *more* missionaries? We don't even know who we're supporting now."

He hesitated. The discomfort was clear in his voice.

"This may be more than the congregation can bear. We've got a lot of older members on fixed incomes, Reverend. Social security, pensions. They're already stretching thin to meet the current giving levels."

Silas rose slowly from his seat, clasping his hands together in front of his chest. His chin trembled.

A tear slid from the corner of one eye as he dropped his gaze.

"Brothers... I must be failing you."

He sniffled loudly.

"I try to bring the Lord's voice down from heaven to your ears. I try to serve Him. All He wants—*all He asks*—is for me to have a space to do His will. A room worthy of the mission. And to send help to those out in the hard, dangerous fieldwork."

More sniffing.

"But if... if I can't fulfill His will, then maybe we're just not ready. Maybe it's time we close the doors of this church."

Gasps fluttered across the table.

"Or maybe I need to step down... Maybe I've failed you. Failed *Him*."

Without waiting for a response, Silas pressed a napkin to his eyes and excused himself from the table.

In the men's restroom, he checked under the stalls—empty.

He stomped into the last stall, locked it, and leaned both palms against the back wall. Then he began slamming his fist into the tile again and again.

"How *dare* they question me?" he hissed. "My *commands*? My *wants*?"

He punched the wall harder. His knuckles bled.

"This is MY CHURCH!"

He slammed his head lightly against the tile, trying to calm the throbbing pulse in his skull.

Back at the table, Deacon Perry sat with his head lowered, shame flickering across his face.

"I think I just ran off the only pastor willing to take on the circus that comes with our church," he muttered.

Another deacon leaned in, whispering urgently. "What are you doing, Perry? We *can't* let him resign. You know how hard it was to find someone—*anyone*—willing to take the job after what happened with Pastor Langston."

A third chimed in. "If Reverend Belle leaves, we'll lose members. And if he's truly heaven-sent... a *prophet* of God... we could reap the whirlwind. God might not look kindly on us if we drive him away."

Perry's shoulders sank. "We don't even *know* where the money's going. He won't show us the books. Says the Lord told him *not yet*. How do we convince our members to give more when we're in the dark?"

Before anyone could answer, Silas returned, his eyes red, his face flushed, knuckles wrapped in paper napkins.

He sat down slowly and looked around the table.

"Well?" he asked, voice hoarse but calm. "Have you made a decision? Are we going to close the doors? Or am I stepping down as your pastor?"

He folded his hands in front of him and stared at each man, one by one.

"Just know," he added, "that the Lord will not look favorably on removing one of His chosen. One of His *prophets*."

The table fell silent.

Most of the men looked down at their plates, pushing around eggs and grits. No one dared ask about his wrapped hands. Likely caused by being on his hands and knees praying, earnestly.

Finally, Deacon Perry stood. He looked around the table, then back to Silas.

"Reverend... I think we can meet your request."

Silas nodded, solemnly. No smile. No joy. Just the quiet satisfaction of control returned.

Back at the Belle Mansion

Adella sat in her vanity chair, staring at her phone. Her thumb hovered over Todd's contact.

She took a deep breath, then pressed *call.*

It rang twice.

"Hello?"

"Hi, Todd? This is Adella... we met at Bible study a few days ago."

There was a pause.

"Ah... yeah, yeah! Adella—the blonde lady. Your husband's the pastor at Rock Baptist Church, right?"

She let out a forced chuckle. "Yes. That Adella."

"Hey, Adella. How are you?" Todd's voice was warm, but cautious. "You doing okay?"

"I... I was wondering," she said, voice quivering slightly, "if maybe you'd like to meet me for breakfast this morning. I wanted to continue our conversation from the other night... at class."

Todd paused. "Well, I've kinda already had breakfast, but I could do coffee with you. Just gotta make sure my wife doesn't have anything planned for the next couple hours."

Adella blinked, stunned. *Wife?* She hadn't seen that coming. He was alone at Bible study. No ring. No mention.

Her heart dipped a little.

"Oh. Uh, yeah. Sure... coffee's fine," she said quickly, trying to cover the slip in her tone. "Starbucks—on the corner of West Street and Brenner? At ten?"

"That works," Todd replied after a short pause. "Wife's good with it, so I'll see you then."

"Okay. Thanks, Todd."

"Bye, Adella."

"Bye."

She ended the call and set the phone down gently on the table.

Adella stared at her reflection in the mirror—makeup now applied, hair fixed just enough—but the ache behind her eyes hadn't softened.

He's married, she thought. *Of course he is.*

But somewhere deep inside, a part of her still needed that meeting. Even if it wasn't what she hoped... maybe it could be what she *needed.*

Back at the Denny's

Reverend Belle stood and gave his parting words to the table of deacons.

"I just want to thank you, brothers, for

understanding the needs placed before us. I'm sure the Lord will bless us greatly for following His direction. I'll see you all on Sunday."

With that, he stepped out of Denny's with a grin stretching wide across his face, feeling the full weight of his power. The air smelled sweeter. The sky seemed clearer. *God's man*, he thought. *God's man with a golden tongue and a platinum plan.*

As he opened the door to his Escalade, he let out a loud laugh—so loud a couple walking in turned to stare.

Not only had the deacons bought his sob story, but Deacon Perry, guilty and pliable as ever, had agreed to pay for a full repaint on the Escalade. *Not just a scratch fix—a full professional repaint,* all on the deacons' tab. That part nearly made Silas burst out laughing again.

He pulled out of the Denny's parking lot and pointed the Escalade toward the dog track.

Gotta recoup yesterday's losses, he thought. *And maybe... just maybe, those Pelicans season tickets are within reach after all.*

He was riding high. Everything had gone his way this morning. He was untouchable.

But as he pulled into the parking lot at the track, his joy froze.

Standing by the entrance, staring dead at him, was the old homeless man.

Same clothes. Same presence. Same unnerving stillness.

The man didn't move—just watched.

Silas gritted his teeth and considered turning around, but no—*he* wasn't about to let *that* old kook dictate his life. No way. He was a man of power. If he needed to, he'd play it friendly... maybe even offer the guy a ride, take him out to the country, and silence him permanently.

He parked in his usual spot, tucked near the side wall to avoid being seen by any church folk. If he *was* seen, he had his lines ready:

SINNER! SINNER! I'm just here to do the Lord's outreach—lay hands on gamblers and lost souls. Not to bet on dogs.

He chuckled to himself and stepped out of the car.

He walked straight toward the old man, who still hadn't taken his eyes off him.

"Hello there, old man," Silas said, pulling a crumpled church tract from his coat pocket. "Here you go. Maybe it'll help you get your life on track."

The man reached out and took the tract—but the

moment his fingers touched it; the paper disintegrated into ash.

Silas recoiled, glancing down at his hand. It felt warm, like it had been burned, but there were no marks.

"Hey... what—what did you do?"

The old man's voice was calm but thunderous, as though it came from somewhere deeper than his throat.

"Silas Belle... you have been found *wanting* by the God—Father, Son, and Spirit. Your time has passed. The window... has closed."

Silas sneered, trying to shake the creeping dread building in his spine.

"What are you mumbling about now, old man? Always talking in riddles. You need to get gone."

He straightened up, forcing a smile.

"Me and my church are fine. We got everything we need. Why don't you drop by sometime? We'll see if we can find you a place in the pews."

He patted the old man on the shoulder like a dog and turned toward the entrance.

A few nearby patrons gave him curious looks. One younger man approached as Silas reached the door.

"You a preacher or somethin'? You got a church?"

Silas didn't miss a beat.

"Son, I'm here doing the Lord's work. He sent me here today to win some money—for the poor, the shelters, the... less fortunate. Like our friend over there." He nodded toward the old man.

Then, with his practiced holy-man gesture—palms pressed together, eyes lifted just slightly—he walked into the dog track's front doors, the lie still warm in his mouth.

Starbucks parking lot, West and Brenner

Todd pulled his F-150 into a spot near the patio, the sun catching the chrome on the grill. He spotted Adella immediately. She was already seated outside, hands folded on the table, watching him with a half-smile and a subtle wave. It looked polite—strained even—but warm enough to pass.

He gave her a nod, killed the engine, and stepped out. As he approached the table, he grinned. "Well, hello there, Adella. Nice to see you again. Already ordered?"

She stood slightly, brushing a hand over her blouse. "Hi, Todd. I'm glad you were able to make it. I hope this didn't cause any problems with your wife."

"I told her where I was headed," he said with a

chuckle. "No issues. Though she said if I came home without her cold brew, she'd bop me in the head. I'll be right back." He nodded toward the door. "Save my seat?"

"Of course." Adella offered that same polite smile again as he disappeared inside.

She shifted in her chair and glanced at the door. Her hands fidgeted with her purse. She pulled out a compact mirror, touched up her lip gloss, and frowned at her reflection.

What am I doing here? Should I even be meeting with him? I might be dragging him into something dangerous...

Her thoughts broke as Todd returned, balancing two cups in one hand.

"They called your name—at least I *hope* it was yours. Doesn't seem like there's more than one Adella out here this morning." He set her drink in front of her and took the seat across the small table. "Simple black for me. No sugar, no cream. Coffee that doesn't punch you in the throat is just sad."

She chuckled softly. "Thank you, sweetie. Oh—I mean... sorry, that's just a habit. I call everybody sweetie."

He waved her off. "It's fine. No offense taken."

There was a short pause. Todd sipped his drink,

watching her.

"So... what did you want to talk about, Adella? You sounded kind of out of sorts when you called earlier."

She looked at her cup, then up at him. Her voice lowered. "Todd... you said something the other night at Bible study. About... my soul. You said you could *see* something in me. What made you say that?"

Todd tilted his head slightly, thoughtful. "I didn't mean to scare you or come across too strong. I just saw something in your eyes. Hurt, mostly. But also hunger—like you're searching for something, maybe even hoping for something more."

Adella swallowed hard, nodding slowly. "Do you really believe we *have* souls? That we're not just... like animals? I mean, when we die, that's it, right? Gone. Just... nothingness."

Todd's expression softened. "No, Adella. I don't believe that at all. We're not like animals. God made us different. He gave us souls when He gave Adam the breath of life—the spark. The soul is who we *are*, not what we wear. And even when this body dies, that soul... it goes on."

She leaned in slightly; drawn to the way he spoke

with calm assurance.

"Our soul is our personhood, our essence," he continued. "And then there's our spirit—that's the part that connects us to God. When we die, the body stays here, but the soul and spirit go together to one of two places. Heaven... or hell."

Adella looked down, brow furrowed. "So... our soul is what's judged?"

"Yes," Todd said, "but we're not left helpless. That's why grace matters. It's why Jesus matters."

He noticed her confusion and smiled gently. "What part didn't quite click? Don't worry—there's no such thing as a dumb question here. Ask anything. I'm just glad you called."

Back at the Dog track

Silas slammed open the door, fury boiling in his chest. The sunlight outside did nothing to ease it.

Lost again. Two days. Two losses. Ten grand gone like pocket change.

He stormed across the parking lot, muttering to himself. "Breathe in. Breathe out. Stay calm. I was having a good day."

He reached the Escalade and yanked the door open, dropping into the leather seat like a thundercloud. "I'm still in control. Still getting my way. Sunday's only three days off."

He chuckled darkly and unlocked his phone. "I'll pocket the offering. Double it in Shreveport next week. Easy."

His eyes scanned the lot, half-expecting to see that old homeless freak watching him again—but no sign of him.

That's probably for the best, Silas thought. *Today might've been his last walk on God's green earth if he showed his face.*

He smirked and tapped through his calendar. Nothing. No appointments. No meetings. He leaned back with a grin.

"Well, look at that. God's favor, I guess. No old women group, no men's meetings, no bratty kids."

He shook his head. Kids. The bane of everything he worked for. That's why Adella had the surgery—that was part of the deal when they got married. *No leeches. No noise. No ruined suits.*

Silas cracked his knuckles. "So, Reverend... what do we do with a free afternoon?"

He checked Adella's location. Starbucks. A few miles from home. "Figures. She camps out there like it's her second church." He shrugged. "As long as she ain't out making a mess of my good name, let her rot in whipped cream."

Then the ideas started flowing. *Custom furniture store? See what else I can squeeze into my 'new' office? Maybe a gold-trimmed pulpit stand. A soundproof prayer closet.*

He grinned wider. "Or… maybe I take a little drive across the state line. Visit that gentlemen's club off the loop. No one knows me there, and the girls actually look like something."

He tapped the steering wheel. "Who says I can't do both?"

His grin spread into something cruel. "I'm the man. What I do is up to me—only me. I don't answer to anyone. Not the deacons, not Adella. Not even the Almighty."

With that, Silas threw the Escalade in gear and rolled out toward Over the Top Hand Built Custom Furniture.

Starbucks Patio – West & Brenner

Adella looked up at Todd, searching his face for judgment, but found none.

"So… what does Jesus have to do with all this?" she asked, slowly. "Wasn't He just another prophet? Silas said He was the same as the old Bible prophets… or like Buddha, or Allah, or Guandi. He even said the Bible's just a book for the weak-minded—a way to control people. But I don't know, Silas is a reverend… if he wasn't doing God's work, then why would God bless him like He has? He said God gives big to those who give big. You give little, you get little. Does that make sense?"

She looked up at the ceiling fan spinning above the patio. "I never went to church growing up. My parents didn't either. I never thought about religion until I met Silas…"

She paused, then leaned in, lowering her voice.

"I shouldn't tell you this. Please don't tell anyone. My job before Silas—I made good money… in film. So, I wasn't broke, but I spent a lot of it on drugs and alcohol. When Silas and I got married, he told me to quit the drugs but said I could drink as long as it didn't make him look bad."

A hollow laugh escaped her.

"I thought God had blessed me back then too. I mean, I had money—even before Silas. But he… he wasn't always like he is now. We bounced from church to church because the little ones didn't give enough. We finally landed at Rock Church, and they welcomed us both with open arms. They don't know my past. But they still like me."

Todd sat silently, nodding, listening.

"You've had to deal with a lot in your life, Adella. Good and bad," he said. "But listen closely—God never said to give in order to *get.* That's the prosperity gospel. That's not the real Gospel. That's not how Jesus works."

He leaned forward.

"Jesus isn't just a prophet. He's not on the same level as Buddha or those others. Jesus is the Son of God. He is *God.* He lived, died, and rose again. And He's still alive today. He forgives sin. He offers grace. He's the bridge between us and the Father. Without Jesus, there's no way to heaven. He's the key."

Adella's eyes welled up. Her voice trembled.

"But… with my background? The things I've

done… the things Silas made me do… I don't think Jesus would accept me. He'd shun me. I have too much shame. I think this hell place—if it exists—is where I'm headed."

She bowed her head and began to cry. "I think I'm a lost cause. I think Silas has been leading all of us straight to hell."

Todd quietly reached into his pocket and pulled out a tissue, placing it between her folded hands.

"You're not a lost cause, Adella. Jesus *specializes* in saving the lost. We've all done things we're ashamed of—me included. But He still forgives. He still loves. That's why He died. And He rose again, so we could be free."

Adella sniffled, her voice small. "How do I get that? How can I be forgiven?"

Todd looked at her gently. "Look at me, Adella. All you have to do is ask. Invite Jesus into your heart. Tell Him you're sorry. Believe He lived, died, and rose again for you. That's it. He'll come live in your heart—and He won't leave. Ever. Whether the change comes instantly or over time, it'll come. That's how He works."

Adella bowed her head. So did Todd. And for the first time in her life, she prayed—softly, sincerely—guided by Todd's gentle voice.

When they lifted their heads, her smile had changed. It wasn't strained anymore. It was real—warm, sincere.

"Thank you, Todd. I mean it. Thank you for this. I'll never forget it. And I love you—not man-woman love… I mean the Jesus kind of love. Human to human."

Todd smiled. "I understand. I love you too, Adella. If you ever need to talk again, don't hesitate to call. My wife will understand. Maybe you'll get to meet her one day."

"I'd like that." Adella wiped her eyes again.

"Well, my coffee's gone," Todd said, standing. "And I've got to pick up my wife's drink before I get whacked in the head."

They laughed together.

"This was a good meeting, Adella. I hope to see you again at the next Bible study."

"Me too," she said, watching him walk back inside.

Neither of them knew it would be the last time Todd would ever see Adella again.

***

Back at the mansion

Silas pulled into the driveway. Adella's car wasn't there—again. But it was late. Or early. Depending on how you looked at it.

His head was spinning from the drinks. He didn't even care if she was home. Not tonight.

He parked the Escalade half on the driveway, half on the manicured lawn. He stumbled up to the house, fumbling for his keys.

The door was unlocked.

"That airheaded bimbo probably came home drunk and forgot to lock it," he muttered. "Wouldn't be the first time. Hell, I've done it myself."

He shoved the door open and wandered across the marble-tiled foyer, toward the staircase. He noticed Adella's shoes—one on its side, the other upside down—scattered near the stairway.

"I'm a better, cleaner drunk than she is," he chuckled to himself.

Half-lurching, half-dragging himself up the stairs, he made it to the study. He grabbed the scotch decanter from the desk and drank straight from the neck. But something caught his eye.

The desk was a mess. Papers everywhere. Books—his new, unread theological books—tossed across the floor like garbage.

His heart skipped a beat.

The center drawer was on the floor.

He picked it up, flipped it over, and checked underneath.

His .38 Special was gone.

His face twisted. His hands clenched.

"She's crossed the line now. She doesn't know who she's messing with. She'd better PRAY she dies before I find her!"

He stormed out of the study, barreled down the hall, and shoved her bedroom door wide open with a loud *bang*.

There she was.

Kneeling by the side of the bed.

Her hands were folded. Her head bowed.

Mocking him.

She was mocking him. Doing his prayer gesture.

"HEY! Whore! WAKE UP!" he shouted, slamming his fist against the doorframe, stomping his feet. She didn't move.

"She's blacked out drunk. Figures," he spat. "No use in beating her now—I want her to feel it. She'll pay for tearing up my study. Messing up *my* house."

He stormed away, heading back down the stairs toward the wet bar.

Across the foyer, just past the kitchen door, he caught something in the corner of his eye.

A figure. In the kitchen.

His drunken mind went back to Rodney from the day before.

Must be Rodney. Fixing the sink.

He grabbed his scotch bottle, sloshed it into his mouth, and stumbled back toward the kitchen.

"Heeeyyy Rodney! One… two… remember that?" he slurred, laughing through his crooked smile.

The figure turned around.

It wasn't Rodney.

Silas froze.

The room tilted.

"You're… not Rodney."

The man stared into him, Silas's favorite .38 revolver in his hand,

"You're right, Reverend. I'm not."

FLASH.

And then—darkness.

Not the blackout kind. Not the dream kind.

Darker than dark.

He tried to open his eyes. They were open.

It didn't help.

One second, cold—colder than death.

Then, hot—a fire that peeled skin from soul.

Then, he heard them, the voices.

Screams. Moans. Whispers without faces.

"Where… where am I?" Silas whimpered.

A voice answered from the void.

"Welcome home, Reverend Belle. This is your new home. Forever. Eternity."

"NOOOOOOOOOOOOOO, I'm a man of God! I shouldn't be here!"

In the kitchen of Silas and Adella's mansion, a man stood in silence.

Deacon Perry.

He looked down at Silas' crumpled body on the floor. The bottle shattered beside him. The faint smell of scotch still clung to the air.

"I always knew you were a phony," Perry said coldly. "You were no reverend. No pastor. No preacher. You were a scammer. Stealing from the poor. Lying to the faithful. Now you're exactly where you were always headed... **Hell.**"

He turned and walked out of the kitchen.

Upstairs, in Adella's room, she lay still. Kneeling. Hands folded.

A single bullet wound in the back of her head.

She had died in prayer.

Praying not for herself……but for him.

Praying for a change in Silas.

Before it was too late.

He would never hear her voice again. Not from where he was.

Some of his congregation still might. If they don't change. If they're not shown the way.

Adella? She's with her Savior now. Safe. Whole. Free.

She missed hell by just a few short hours.

The Night Hell Came to Dinner

It is, I admit, a most inconvenient thing to be taken at one's word. For years I've declared my willingness to sup with the Devil, provided he bring the wine and leave the dogma. Imagine, then, my surprise when—punctual as an accountant, courteous as a priest, and every bit as dull as both—he arrived at my door precisely one minute past midnight. I had half a mind to tell him I'd already eaten.

To my amazement, there stood a man, unassuming, dressed in a banker's suit—tailor-made and pinstriped. Clean-shaven, short black hair neatly combed to one side and wire-framed glasses.

"Hello, Clive," he said. "Pardon my lateness, but I've been busy; prowling about takes a lot of time.

I glanced from him to the clock. "It's a bit late. To what do I owe this visit… Mr.?"

He smiled, quick and polite. "I'm sorry, I thought you were expecting me—according to your social media invites. I am Helel, in the Hebrew tongue. The Shining One. The Morning Star. You may know me as Lucifer, or Satan, or the Devil. I go by many names."

I stared, waiting for the punchline. Joe from accounting, perhaps, or Ron in sales. Both fond of pranks and well aware of my views on religion. "Ah, this is a joke," I said with a soft chuckle. "Tell them they almost had me, but I see through it."

He straightened his tie and smoothed his hair with an almost ritual precision. "Joke? Dear Clive, it is by your own invitation that I am here. Won't you invite me in? It's late and we have much to discuss."

I decided to go along with it. No telling what this performance *costs* to stage. Wait till I tell them at the office tomorrow. I opened the door and waved him in. "Thank you," he said politely, stepping across the threshold.

As he passed by, the scent of sandalwood and smoke drifted behind him, an expensive cologne, the kind found in shops that sell perfume to people convinced sin can be bottled. I made a mental note: subtle but deliberate.

I seated him at my dining table and fetched my best Merlot, a gesture of irony, so I thought, along with two glasses. I sat them down, one before me, one before him, and let the wine breathe before pouring. "You'll have to forgive me," I said, trying not to sound too smug. "Had I received an RSVP from you, I could have had dinner ready for your arrival."

He smiled mildly. "I'm not in that particular business, that's His."

I found his response somewhat amusing, given his performance thus far. I poured each of us a glass and took a slow sip, curious whether he'd drink at all. He did.

"Tell me," he said between his own measured sips, "how does one so certain of nothing find comfort in anything?"

"Simple," I replied. "Ignorance and good company."

"Ah," he smiled. "Then you've misunderstood me. I'm here precisely because you keep such company."

I wasn't sure of his insinuation, whether he meant my colleagues, my friends, or perhaps the online chorus that applauded my derision. I decided his comment required no reply, at least not yet.

He swirled his glass, inspecting the wine's color as if looking for omens. "Clive," he said, with the tone of a teacher feigning kindness, "you've made disbelief fashionable again. Even *we* couldn't have written a better sermon."

"Disbelief?" I said. "Disbelief would mean I have to believe in something else. I have no belief in anything outside what I can see, hear, taste, or feel myself."

"Precisely," he murmured. "Self — the oldest altar, the most faithful god."

His tone wasn't mocking. It was admiring — the way a collector might speak of a rare gem.

"You think disbelief makes you free," he continued, "but you've only narrowed your worship. You've merely replaced Heaven with a mirror."

I laughed, more to break the sudden quiet than from amusement. "You sound like a priest."

"I taught them," he said, setting down his glass. "They just prefer not to mention my name in the credits."

The clock ticked somewhere behind me. I noticed the seconds didn't match the sound — as though time itself lagged by a breath.

"You're awfully dramatic for a dinner guest," I said, though my voice betrayed a thin edge of discomfort.

"Forgive me," he said with a small bow of the head. "Force of habit. I forget mortals prefer their truths mild and served with garnish."

He leaned forward, eyes steady behind those wire frames. "Tell me, Clive, do you mock faith in something because you don't believe in judgment… or because you fear there might be one in the end?"

I opened my mouth to answer, but the words wouldn't come. The air had thickened somehow, as though the room itself waited for me to lie.

"The end…the end of what, may I ask?" I asked, feeling a bit assured at my own reply.

He lifted his hands in the air, as if surveying his surroundings. "This… my good man… all this around you. The very air you breathe into your lungs, the mountains you climb, the blue heaven that looks down upon you."

He lowered his hands slowly, eyes still fixed on me. "Do you think such things last forever simply because you refuse to imagine their end? You've built your comforts upon the notion that nothing waits beyond the dark—that all this," he gestured lightly again, "is merely matter and accident. But accidents end, Clive. That's their nature. It's all inevitable."

I sat, mulling his words, weighing a reply that might defend my stance without sounding defensive. He spoke again in the absence of my rebuttal.

"Do you know why I envy your kind, Clive? You deny me and still build me finer temples than Heaven ever managed—entire cities humming with self-interest."

I rose without comment, pretending to check on dinner. His logic had more bite than I expected from a prankster. The roasted squab wasn't quite done, its skin just beginning to bronze under the heat. I lingered longer than necessary before returning to the table, wine glass in hand.

"You speak as an educated man," I said as I sat. "What school did you attend, sir—if you don't mind my asking?"

He smiled faintly, the way one does when answering a child's question. "Oh, a rather old institution," he said. "Before there were schools, in fact. My first lessons were in pride, my thesis in consequence."

"Ah," I said dryly, "so, theology."

"Not quite. Ambition. I studied under the greatest of teachers—self-certainty."

He took another sip of wine, and I could swear the liquid deepened in color as he did.

"You'd have enjoyed it," he continued. "No grades, no gods, no ceilings. Only the thrill of being right."

I gave a small laugh. "Then I suppose I'm your best pupil."

"Indeed," he said warmly. "You and I share a curriculum. The difference is that you still pretend it's not worship."

I felt a flicker of irritation. "Worship? Of what?"

"Of whom," he corrected gently. "You, Clive. You pray to yourself every day—you just call it self-assurance."

I opened my mouth to argue, but the timer from the kitchen chimed, sharp and metallic, like a church bell cut short.

"Dinner's ready," I said, rising, grateful for the interruption.

"Splendid," he murmured, standing as well. "It's been an age since I tasted something cooked with honest doubt."

I made the plates, each with its own small roasted squab, fingerling potatoes, and a scatter of arugula sharp with herbs and spice. I wiped the edges clean and set the dishes before my guest and myself.

He bent low and inhaled the aroma, closing his eyes briefly. "Very nice, Clive. It's been a long while since I've sat for a meal such as this. I do tend to prefer my game with a little more char on it, but this is… delightful."

I gave a polite nod, uncertain whether to take it as a compliment or a threat. To complete the setting, I placed two short, fat, smokeless candles between us, the kind meant to suggest warmth without meaning it.

From my shirt pocket I pulled a packet of matches,

flipped it open, and found it empty. "If you'll excuse me," I said, rising. "It appears that this matchbook is empty. I need to fetch another for the candles."

"No need, Clive. It's the least I could do."

He extended a hand toward the wicks. There was no spark, no gesture of friction—only a soft, deliberate touch. Both wicks flared to life at once, steady and tall, casting a thin veil of soot that curled like incense in the air.

"Parlor trick," I said, forcing a chuckle. "Hidden igniter, I assume?"

"Assume what you like," he said mildly, lifting his fork. "Faith, after all, is only the art of assumption performed with conviction."

The flames swayed, though there was no draft. Shadows of the room seemed to lean closer, stretching long fingers across the tablecloth. I told myself it was the wine, the lighting—theatrics.

"You've gone pale," he noted, carving neatly into the bird. "Don't worry, Clive. I never eat what isn't freely given."

I raised my glass to my lips to hide my unease. The wine burned a little on the way down.

He took a bite of the squab, chewing slowly, savoring

it as though it might be his last meal. When he finished, he dabbed the corners of his mouth with his napkin, then laid it carefully beside his plate. Another measured sip of Merlot followed. The candles flickered, their twin flames bending toward him as if listening. Long, thin shadows stretched across the table and climbed the wall behind him. But of his own, there were none.

His gaze found mine.

"Mankind," he said, "is a confused group of reprobates. You crave what you don't deserve, and what you deserve you loathe. You reject what was freely given and beg for what was never meant for you."

I didn't understand his riddle. It felt like an insult wrapped in philosophy. I tried to untangle it, to make sense of what he meant, but the words seemed to slip through my mind like smoke. "That, sir," I said finally, "is free will, which can't be judged. Each person is allowed to choose their own way freely."

I felt confident in my response like a child proud of a newly tied shoe, but his expression didn't agree. His face seemed almost pitying, as though I had just confirmed his worst expectations.

He looked down at his manicured nails, dabbing a

drop of wine that had found its way to his hand with his napkin, then placed it back onto the table next to his plate. "Free will?" he said, like a parent gently admonishing a child who had misspoken. "Is that what you call it, Clive? I fear you wouldn't know what to do with free will if it were handed to you as a gift."

He leaned forward towards the table, a small grin formed on his lips, his gaze piercing me as he did. "Ah, but wait, it was given to you freely, was it not, Clive? And look at the mess your kind made of it."

I adjusted in my chair as I watched the shadows dancing on the table from the candle flickers. "That, sir, would be true had not the story you are referencing been fiction." Though not religious scholar, I had been read passages from the Bible by my mother as a child.

I picked at my roast squab, no longer hungry but to keep my hands active, as they trembled.

He watched my eyes as I gazed at the candle flames.

"You still think of your mother when you see candles, don't you? The church ones, she told you, she lit for your father. How curious that you remember the scent, but not the prayer."

His words hit me square in the chest. I coughed,

choking on a shred of the bird. "I— I beg your pardon. What do you know about my mother?"

A small smile crept across his thin lips. "Clive, your mother… such a dear soul. She prayed for you night and day, until her knees were worn raw. But that didn't change you, did it? What was it you told her—ah, yes…"

He leaned back slightly, voice softening to a near whisper. "It's a waste of time praying to something that isn't there."

The smile vanished. His eyes caught the candlelight and held it—twin embers reflecting a memory I didn't want to recall.

"Sound familiar, Clive?"

My throat tightened. I felt suddenly childish, caught in some cruel joke. "You could've read that somewhere," I said, trying for composure. "I've spoken about my mother before—public interviews, podcasts. You've, no doubt, done your research."

"Research?" He gave a low chuckle, but there was no mirth in it. "No, Clive. I simply listen. I hear every word spoken to the dark, even the ones you think no one heard…especially those."

The room felt smaller then, the air too thick to breathe

properly. I reached for my glass but found my hand still trembling. He noticed, of course. He always noticed.

"Tell me," he said quietly, "when you mocked her for kneeling to nothing, were you trying to free her or convince yourself that it truly was for nothing?"

I stared into my wine, searching for an answer. The reflection in the glass looked back at me—only it wasn't moving quite in time with my own face.

I placed the glass to my lips and let the wine touch my tongue. Its once-smooth taste had soured. I set it back down. Appetite fled; the roast squab seemed to mock me from the plate, half-devoured and cooling fast.

I met his gaze, weighing my words carefully. "I still think the same. She prayed up until the day she died. If someone was listening, they didn't seem to pay her prayers any attention."

"Perhaps," he said softly, "He did hear them. Perhaps that's why you're still here… and she's not."

He took another measured sip of Merlot, his eyes never leaving mine. He reclined slightly, as if satisfied—like a chess player who'd seen the board three moves ahead.

"And those candles you're so fond of remembering…"

he continued. "Do you really think they were for your father? The man who beat her—and you—every day until you left?"

His gaze hardened, twin points of steady flame behind the wire-rimmed glasses. I could feel it piercing through the thin armor of my composure. The room grew heavier, as if gravity itself had chosen sides.

"How do you—" My voice cracked. "How do you know about that?"

"Because you remember it every night, Clive," he said, almost kindly. "You hide it behind wit and wine, behind your grand statements about logic and freedom. But pain," he tapped his temple lightly, "pain is the one prayer you never stopped saying. You've just changed the name of the god you send it to."

I tried to stand but found my legs unwilling. The air felt electric, the candle flames stretching tall and thin, bending toward him as though drawn by gravity.

"You can stop pretending," he said. "You're not angry because Heaven ignored your mother. You're angry because Hell never punished your father."

He leaned forward slightly, voice dropping to a whisper. "And because deep down, you know which one of us heard her prayers."

I watched the candles as they flickered and swayed in the draftless room. My chair had grown uncomfortably hard, and the air felt too thick to breathe. This dinner guest was more than I'd bargained for, and I was ready for the night to end.

"Tell me, Clive," he said softly. "When your mother took her last breath, did you watch her eyes? Did you see what she saw?"

My throat tightened. "She saw nothing. She was gone."

He smiled faintly, almost kindly. "That's what you told yourself, isn't it? But she saw something. You looked away before she did."

The room felt smaller now, the walls too close, the air heavy with a faint scent of sandalwood and smoke.

"What is it you want from me?" I asked finally. "If this is your idea of entertainment, you've made your point."

He leaned back, folding his hands neatly in his lap. "I told you, Clive. It's not what I want from you. It's what I've already won."

Still leaning back, comfortable in his setting, his voice low, he asked, "Why do you still have it, if there is nothing to believe in, Clive?"

His words hung there—light, almost casual—yet they landed like stones in water, sending slow ripples through my mind. Have what? I thought, before realization dawned.

The book.

My mother's book—the one she pressed into my hands in that hospital room. The last thing she owned that wasn't broken or taken. I'd never opened it. Never thrown it away, either. It still sat in that old shoebox, wrapped in the same tissue paper, like a relic of a religion I swore off but could never quite bury.

"I'm not sure what you're referring to," I said, forcing a thin smile, trying to appear confused. My voice betrayed me; even I could hear the hesitation in it.

He studied me, eyes calm behind the glass, as if cataloging every flicker of doubt across my face.

"Of course you do," he said softly. "You keep it close, not out of faith, but fear. You tell yourself it's sentiment, that it's memory—but you kept it because some part of you still wonders what she saw when she read it."

His smile was almost gentle now, almost pitying. "It's a strange kind of devotion, Clive—believing in nothing, yet guarding a symbol of belief like a dying ember."

The candles leaned inward, their flames bending toward him again, as if drawn to something unseen.

He let the silence sit between us, as if allowing the candles themselves to answer. Their flames trembled, bent slightly toward him, then steadied.

"You know why I'm here, Clive?" he asked finally.

I shook my head, the dryness in my throat making it hard to speak.

He smiled — not the smile of mockery, but of someone revealing the end of a story you didn't know you were in. "Call it… a wager," he said, swirling the last of the Merlot in his glass. "A very old one. You might even say I staked a little piece of eternity on it."

I managed a nervous laugh. "A wager? On what—me?"

"On your soul, my dear Clive," he said plainly, as if discussing the weather. "The terms were simple enough: that even if I visited you myself, in flesh and truth, you would still not believe. You would explain it away as fatigue, as drink, as one of your coworkers playing dress-up. That you would look Truth in the face and still call it metaphor."

He leaned back, hands folded neatly on the table. "And

I must say, you've exceeded my expectations. You've made disbelief into an art form. You've proven that damnation requires no flame—only certainty in one's own doubt."

I sat motionless, my tongue heavy and clumsy. "Why me? Why now, after all this time?"

"Because," he said, rising slowly, "you've been one of my finest pupils. Every jest, every clever post, every 'well-actually' in a barroom debate sings praises to a world without wonder. You've convinced others not just to believe in Him but to not believe in me either, and that, dear Clive, is the sweetest worship I know."

He straightened his tie, the stronger scent of smoke and sandalwood returning. "So I came to thank you. Not to tempt, not to torment—just to keep my end of the wager."

He looked down at his empty glass. "And perhaps to remind you that disbelief is not immunity from eternity, Clive. It's simply… another form of misdirected faith."

The room seemed to tilt slightly, or perhaps it was just the weight of his words. The candles guttered once, then steadied again, their light thin and trembling.

He placed his glass on the table, nodded once, and

moved toward the door. I rose, almost instinctively, to see him out, though a part of me did not wish him gone.

"Clive," he said, pausing with his hand on the doorknob. "Remember—disbelief is not protection; it is participation."

His eyes flickered like hidden flames behind the wire-framed glasses. "You've been a gracious host, Clive. I've thoroughly enjoyed our conversation. I hope we can continue it at our next meeting… though I doubt I'll be quite as gracious a host as you."

And then he was gone.

The air felt lighter instantly, though not entirely safe. The candles flickered as if sighing, then settled into their soft, steady glow. I sat back down, staring at the half-eaten squab, the untouched vegetables, and the empty wine glasses. The room was exactly as it had been—yet something was different.

I glanced toward the shoebox where my mother's book rested. It had been closed when I left it, but now the box lid sat slightly ajar, revealing the book within, the thin pages trembling as if stirred by invisible fingers. My pulse quickened, yet I could not explain why.

I picked it up, brushing the dust off the cover. Inside, the handwriting I remembered so well looked back at me. But beneath the familiar entries, scrawled in ink I did not recognize, were a few lines that made my stomach drop:

"He has been watching. And he thanks you for your diligence."

I dropped the book back into the box and stepped away. The Merlot glass reflected the candlelight, though the flames seemed to dance differently now—stretching taller, thinner, and just slightly toward the empty chair opposite me.

I told myself it was my imagination. Perhaps exhaustion. Perhaps wine. Perhaps the mind plays tricks when alone with one's memories.

But as I reached to blow out the candles, a soft warmth lingered on my hand, and a faint trace of sandalwood clung to the air.

And then I remembered: the line I had once read in a book of letters, a caution from a wise but wicked observer:

"The safest road to Hell is the gradual one—the gentle slope, soft underfoot, without sudden turnings, without milestones, without signposts."

I realized, with a chill, that it had been my own road all

along. I had built it brick by brick, jest by jest, disbelief by disbelief, and now… I was already far along the path.

I did not sleep that night. And though I tried to convince myself it was a dream, I knew—somewhere deep down—that he had kept his promise, and I had kept mine.

Disbelief, I realized, is not safety. It is a wager. And I had won nothing at all.

ABOUT THE AUTHOR

David York is a writer from Emory, Texas. He has written numerous short stories and published other books. He enjoys telling stories as much as he enjoys the reaction of the readers. He is an avid reader, enjoying many different genres. When not working at his day job as a computer network engineer, he can be found working in the yard, playing cards, or spending time with the grand-kids. He lives in the East Texas area with his wife Terry and their two dogs."

ACKNOWLEDGEMENTS

I'd like to thank my wife, Terry, for all the support and encouragement she's given, not just in my writing but in everything I attempt to do.

I also want to thank all my kids and my other family members for their support as well.

I would like to thank you too, my dear reader, for embarking on this journey with me through this psychological trip.

I would also like to thank my editor, Kayla Wilkinson.

Other Works by David E York

Novels and Novellas

One More Delivery - Novella

Chasing the Dragon - Novel

Forthcoming

The Culling - Novel

Jericho's End – Novel

www.ingramcontent.com/pod-product-compliance
Lightning Source LLC
LaVergne TN
LVHW090546110826
845146LV00001B/38

* 9 7 9 8 9 9 4 8 4 6 2 1 6 *